THE RESTORATION TRILOGY BOOK ONE

White

DENISE WEIMER

White

THE RESTORATION TRILOGY: BOOK ONE

For Brenda—
Hope you enjoy the renovation romance with local history and mystery!

DENISE WEIMER

Denise Weimer
5/6/18

Canterbury House Publishing

www. canterburyhousepublishing. com
Sarasota, Florida

Canterbury House Publishing

www. canterburyhousepublishing. com

Copyright © 2016 Denise Weimer

All rights reserved under International and Pan-American Copyright Conventions.

First Edition: March 2016

Book Design by Tracy Arendt
Model and Costumer, Kat Nagar
Photographer, Dr. Vincent T. Peng

Library of Congress Cataloging-in-Publication Data

Names: Weimer, Denise, author.
Title: White / Denise Weimer.
Description: First edition. | Sarasota, Florida : Canterbury House
    Publishing, 2016. | Series: The restoration trilogy ; book 1 |
Description based on print version record and CIP data provided by publisher;
resource not viewed.
Identifiers: LCCN 2015050329 (print) | LCCN 2015046149 (ebook) | ISBN
    9780990841692 () | ISBN 9780990841685 (softcover : acid-free paper)
Subjects: LCSH: Historic buildings--Conservation and restoration--Fiction. |

Man-woman relationships--Fiction. | GSAFD: Love stories.
Classification: LCC PS3623.E4323 (print) | LCC PS3623.E4323 W48 2016 (ebook)

| DDC 813/.6--dc23

Author Note:
This is a work of fiction. Names, characters, places and incidents are either the product of the author's imagination or are used fictitiously, and any resemblance to actual persons living or dead, business establishments, events, or locales is entirely coincidental. Scripture is taken from the HOLY BIBLE, New King James Version.

For information about permission to reproduce selections from this book email to:
editor@canterburyhousepublishing.com
Enter Permission to Reproduce in the subject line.

CHAPTER ONE

The dream started the way Jennifer's actual visit to the house at 104 Main Street, Hermon, had begun, on a road that hurtled past green fields and dust-blown wildflowers into forever, ending in a community time had forgotten. The unused railroad tracks paralleling State Route 77 provided testament to both the town's rise and fall.

The house itself hunkered beneath four mighty magnolias right off the main road, but due to the depth of shade, one could pass the home without noticing. Surprising for the building's period of origin, the steep, faded red metal roof lidded only one story. The exclamation-like spindles crowning the cross gables and curlicue millwork tracing the porch proclaimed Gothic Revival influence, while a wide band board below the cornice hinted at Greek Revival. The curving cornices supporting the roof reflected Italianate style, making the place an architectural puzzle.

Jennifer walked a straight line over slippery magnolia leaves to the red front door framed by antebellum sidelight windows. In her dream, the trees disappeared as she passed them, but instead of expected sunlight flooding the yard, dark clouds rolled in. They moved fast, like an accelerated film clip. Taking shelter in a safe and distant past was a familiar and comforting concept, so when the rumble of thunder propelled her into the hall's embrace, she looked around with relief. Yet her satisfaction did not last, for to her shock and horror, the beveled gas wall sconces flickered and went out, the golden brown paint faded off the walls, exposing the plaster, and the plaster melted as if under a great heat. Time rolled back. In a sudden silence, the bones of the house stood naked while Jennifer stood frozen.

Then, a wind of tornadic force howled.

With no warning, wavy glass exploded inward, and Jennifer crouched down to shield herself. Sections of tin roof screeched, ripping away from wood beams. Lightning flashed, and lumber whirled upward into a gray cyclone. Soon nothing remained of the house she'd counted on for shelter, nothing but herself kneeling on the foundation, covering her head while the wind lashed her hair and the rain soaked her skin. Exposed to a mighty power she had no control over, she begged that unseen force to show mercy.

The dream jerked her awake. Sweating and shaking, Jennifer sat up in bed and pushed damp hair from her eyes as dawn filtered through the blinds into her apartment bedroom. She glanced over to make sure her roommate, Tilly, still slept.

Her mind went back to the day before, when she had toured the historic doctor's house and apothecary shop Michael Johnson wanted to hire her to restore. The timing of the job offer couldn't be better, with her graduation from the Master of Historic Preservation program at the University of Georgia coming in a couple of months. Yet this dream made her think something in her subconscious sensed danger, evil. What could it mean? If only she knew more before making her decision. All she felt certain of was that house held secrets, and maybe so did the man who owned it …

1904
Oglethorpe County, Georgia

I was born into a small world with a big name. Georgia Pearl, my daddy called me, partly on account of my skin color. I understood my first name had to do with the fact that he used to take me up on his knee and say, "Georgia Pearl, you're this century's Amanda America Dickson." I didn't know Amanda America's story then, but I knew she had been a mixed blood lady who had lived not far away in Georgia, too. I wasn't sure why she had the name of a country while I just had the name of a state. But then Daddy would bend his head close to me. I could smell Brilliantine pomade on his hair as he'd whisper in my ear, "And your daddy loves you just as much as hers loved her." So I didn't really care about the rest.

From my favorite place behind the counter in daddy's apothecary, I sat and watched him mix up medicines. A swinging gate prevented the public from stepping back to where the vials and bottles were stored. Mama wouldn't scold me as long as I stayed out of sight, and somehow Papa never got impatient with my hiding spot. He stepped around me like I wasn't there, although I knew he knew I was listening, because he would say out loud exactly what he was doing. He had strong hands, healing hands. Grinding with the mortar and pestle or weighing things on his scales while a customer waited, sleeves pushed up by garters, he said things like, "Now, trust me where this aspirin is concerned, Mrs. Clark. Acetylsalicylic acid may be newer on the market, but as often as you get your debilitatin' headaches, I believe it will work as well as acetanilide without any fears about its toxicity. I'm preparin' this pepsin for the upset stomach that accompanies the headaches." And she would answer like all the others, "Yes, doctor." There was respect in that "Yes, doctor." Because he was something special, I felt special, and that made me more than my skin.

Still, I knew my place in town. I stayed at the house and apothecary, although when certain visitors and customers appeared at either, I knew to make myself scarce. Mama chased me with a broom if I didn't. And she whacked hard.

Although our main income came from Papa's doctoring, his family owned land in the area let out to sharecroppers. When we could escape Mama's endless choring— cooking, hauling water from the well at the back of our yard, gardening, churning the butter by the woodstove, and running the cream separator on our back porch— and the ground got turned for watermelon planting, me and my brother and sisters hunted Indian artifacts. In the early summer we'd earn a bit of coin taking water to the field workers and shocking the wheat. Sometimes, the tenant farmers invited us to supper, where they served cornbread with molasses, fatback and stew made from some kind of wild animal and vegetables. They didn't eat as good as we did, and the walls of their cabins looked funny, lined with newspaper instead of plaster or wallpaper, but we liked that they treated us like important guests. Daddy's daddy had been a Confederate war hero until a shell exploded into the field hospital where he operated. He came back with a hole in his head. Everyone spoke of him with hushed respect, just like they did Papa, but I was glad he was dead and gone because a man with a hole in his head was frightening. I used to have nightmares about it.

We knew not to go into the Gillen's General Store where the men threw pennies in the floorboard cracks to see who would pay for the next round of "dopes." They called it dopes even though Papa said the good stuff had been taken out of the Co-Colas the year before "Miss Georgia Pearl" appeared in the world.

"Can't you take me inside?" I asked Papa after I heard Gillen's got the first elevator in the county installed.

But he said, "No, Georgia Pearl, we'll do our shoppin' together in Athens."

"Why?"

"Athens is farther away, and it's a big town, so there's less chance of creatin' a scene."

I didn't fully understand then, but it was worth it when Papa did take me to town. He never took Mama, or Cecil, or Minnie or Hazel, just me, his youngest, his Georgia Pearl. I assumed this was because he had only room for himself and one other passenger in his red Roadster. He only got it out of the barn for trips, far-away house calls or big emergencies.

"Is this a big emergency, Papa?" I'd ask.

With a twinkle in his eye, he'd say, "Yes, indeed, Georgia Pearl. Quite the biggest."

The emergency always included a trip to Costa's Ice Cream Parlor owned by the Green family, something I could brag about later when the boys sitting on the steps of Gillen's with their RCs picked on me. And they didn't dare say anything back, or Papa would come out of his apothecary and give them what-for.

Those trips with Papa were the best moments of my life. Most people drove wagons and rode horses in those days, but we zipped down the country road with the wind in our faces, eyes shielded by driving goggles. Mine were too big and Papa frequently adjusted them. He looked so handsome in his Fedora and suit.

We avoided certain parts of town, but I caught glimpses anyway. The poor black people living in unpainted shacks with shared outhouses and trash-piled lots in Lickskillet and Wood's Corner upset Papa. When I asked why he looked mad, he told me, "The city should offer all people proper sanitation services. It's wrong to discriminate. You know where the street cars run between Milledge and Prince?"

I nodded, remembering the clacking noise and electric lines.

"That area is home to a former postmaster, a lady who bakes fancy weddin' cakes for the wealthy, and government clerks. That's the future of your mama's people. One shouldn't be able to tell the homes of the colored people from the whites."

When we drove past the Morton Building at "Hot Corner," Papa pointed at it and said, "The first colored woman dentist in Georgia works in that building, and one of the founders of the Georgia State Medical Association of Colored Physicians, Dentists, and Druggists has an office and a drug store there, too."

Mama called Papa a very forward-thinking man for his time. But even she had her limits. While I waited on Papa to get the Roadster to take me to the opening piano concert at Morton Theatre, I heard her shouting at him.

Mama was a lady, mild-mannered in public, who I heard people call "Creole" although to me her coffee-and-cream skin didn't look much different from the colored tenant farmers. I have no idea where she came from or who her people were. No one would tell me. One day I heard some ladies talking, and they said it was a shame that Dr. Hamp had taken advantage of his power with Luella. That didn't make much sense to me, because I thought Mama was the one with the power. She told Papa when to wash up for supper, what she wanted for the household, and how he should take a hand to us when we needed it. She even laid out his clothes every morning.

Anyway, Mama's voice could get quite loud when she was riled. "You fillin' the head of that gal with foolish dreams, dangerous dreams. She oughta know her place in the world."

Why would Mama say that? My place. My place was beside my daddy, and that was in the white section of the black theatre, listening to that dreamy music from Ohio Conservatory. With Daddy by my side, all the world opened to me. Or at least all of Athens.

It wasn't for ten more years that I would learn my place.

Hermon, which could best be termed a community, lay half an hour from Jennifer Rushmore's hip university town of Athens and fifteen minutes from the tiny historic hamlet of Lexington. While driving there, she tapped her phone to make sure the blue dot on her map progressed properly, and Hermon had not been moved. Finally, the dot declared that she had arrived.

Standing outside her Civic in the yard of Michael Johnson's house, she wiped her sweaty palms on her jeans. A church steeple breaking above the treetops down the street brought back childhood memories of searching for something better than what her life offered, but never feeling good enough. Looking away, she surveyed the rest of the town: an antique store, post office, beauty shop, a convenience store advertising breakfast and lunch on a sign with missing letters, an old depot, a concrete block two-room city hall, an abandoned and gutted brick building of mysterious origin, and a couple of shoot-off streets flanked by a mix of nice historic and just plain run-down homes.

Part of her liked it, wanted to lose herself in it. Another part scrambled to hold onto the progress she'd made into the real world these past years in Athens.

Later, remembering the moment Michael Johnson stepped onto the porch of his Gothic Revival cottage, Jennifer wondered if the unsettling dream the night after her visit had more to do with the man than with the town's isolation or the historical mysteries of the house. He was not the type of person she liked to deal with: tan, athletic, tall and far too attractive. His unlined face and dark hair declared his youth, even though he probably had a good eight or ten years on her. The way Michael Johnson carried himself even in dusty khakis and an untucked flannel shirt told her he knew that he did not need fancy duds to convey a strong sense of presence. She hated men who were attractive and knew it.

But the architectural hodgepodge, the neglected disrepair of his house already piqued her interest. It begged for her expertise even if its owner only acknowledged her existence as a potential contractor. So she picked her way across the littered yard, her quick eye spying neglected landscaping contoured by broken bricks. Nose tickled by a pungent scent, she turned her head to appreciate a rear view of what seemed to be an old store sitting at the front of the property, separated from the house by a wall of overgrown boxwoods.

Once she'd made her way to the porch, she had to look at him. Jennifer put on a professional smile and stuck out her hand, leaning forward with a foot on the lowest brick step. "Jennifer Rushmore. A pleasure to meet you."

"Michael Johnson," he said, lunging downward to shake her hand. "Thank you for coming out so promptly." He studied her with a skeptical look.

12

"Yes, well, it's Saturday." Jennifer shrugged, refusing to give in to her discomfort by making excuses for her overall-clad figure when she intended to crawl around under his house. As for her gender and small size, she'd learned to project extra confidence in order to succeed as a historic preservationist.

"Right. You have classes during the week. And do I understand from Professor Shelley that you're graduating this May?" Michael gestured to the swing, the only furniture on the porch.

"That's right. Two more months. I have some papers and projects to finish up before then, but as I took classes every summer instead of going home, I've been able to take a light load this semester … which will allow me to help you here, should we decide that." Jennifer smiled.

Michael sat next to her. He smiled back, faint lines next to his blue eyes creasing. His polite but impersonal gaze made his proximity tolerable. "Which I assume is why your professor recommended you for this job."

Jennifer kept smiling without adding that it paid to be the teacher's pet. Assistant Professor Barbara Shelley had made it clear in the last year that she saw a young Barb in Jennifer and intended to do her best to help Jennifer realize her career potential. "You have the eye," she often said. Jennifer added, "She tried to explain to me how she and you came to talk, but I'm not sure I followed."

"Right. Through the property management company my grandmother employed for this place before she passed. She rented it out, you know, although for the past two or three years it sat vacant, which explains its current condition." Michael gave the yard a sweeping gesture with a long-fingered hand. "The man who owned the company during that time, Horace Greene, turned over the management to his son while he went on to real estate sales. He now specializes in historic properties. Horace made contact with the Master of Historic Preservation Department at UGA, and the department would send work crews to help with projects requiring restoration. So when I mentioned to him I needed someone to oversee the restoration of this property in a proper manner, he put me in touch with Dr. Shelley."

"I see." She examined the exterior of the house and nodded.

"She said you were considering a move to Savannah but would have some down time before that?"

"Oh, it's nothing for certain." Jennifer pushed her glasses back up on the bridge of her nose. "Dr. Shelley told me about a position at a preservation firm—my dream job, really—but it wouldn't start until January. They haven't even opened the window for applications yet, and of course I'd have to be selected." She chanced a glance at the man beside her. "She does have a friend who works there, though, who can put in a good word for me."

"But you'd consider this to fill the gap, and I think it will work out for both of us."

"Well, perhaps." As much as Jennifer counted on that proving true, the assumption in Michael's voice made her defenses rise.

"So I'll show you around, and you'll determine whether you could get things done by the end of the year, right?" He flashed her another perfunctory smile. She nodded with a straight face. There he did it again. Assuming. "I see you came to get dirty. That's good. I warn you, it's a mess in there."

Like a cat disgusted with humans, Jennifer blinked. "I'm not afraid of messes."

"No, I don't guess you could be in your job."

Before he could get up, Jennifer added in a firm tone, "I have a few things I'd like to be clear on before we tour the property, if you don't mind."

"No, of course not," he replied, but his dark brow inched down as he lowered back onto the swing. He hung his hands on his splayed knees. "Fire away."

She frowned. Just like a man to think they could hurry through something so detailed. He had called her, after all. She wouldn't let him rush her through the house and send her off without knowing half of what she needed to before she made such a big decision. To calm her nerves, Jennifer took her time getting out a notebook and pen. "So do I understand correctly, this is your ancestors' home and old store?" She poked the top of her pen toward the front of the yard.

The eyebrows went back up. "That's an apothecary."

Her mouth formed an 'O.'

"Apparently I come from a long line of doctors."

She scribbled in her pad. "An apothecary … very unique in the south. I'm sorry, I must have misunderstood. I thought Dr. Shelly said there was an old store on the property." Jennifer tried not to look too eager. The apothecary itself could earn the property a spot on the National Register. "Uh, you said 'apparently.' Are you not familiar with your family's history? Enough to date the buildings on the property and give me a historic overview?"

"I inherited this property from my grandmother, who died last year."

"Oh. I'm sorry to hear that. Did you spend much time here growing up?"

"No, neither she nor I lived here. In fact, I never laid eyes on the house until I drove up to see it after the reading of her will."

"I see. So are you restoring it for your family now?"

"I told Dr. Shelley I was unmarried, with no children." Beneath thick, dark lashes, Michael's blue eyes turned cold, and his expression closed.

Add aloofness to his list of shortcomings, Jennifer wanted to write on her pad, just to see if he noticed. "All I was told before this appointment, Mr. Johnson, was that a man in Oglethorpe County had inherited a historic family property with several structures in need of restoration, and that he wanted a professional to oversee the project. My professor did mention that she thought that you were a general contractor as well. I just have to ask, Mr. Johnson, what would make a single guy move from Atlanta into the boondocks and hire a historic preservationist? Most builders would be satisfied with just slapping on some new lumber and paint … that is, if you even intend to live here."

Either her direct approach or her double use of his last name made him stiffen even more. "To answer your questions, yes, I am a contractor, as is my father, who is staying with me in a camper we just moved into the back yard. My mother died early, Miss Rushmore, so my grandmother, Gloria, played a huge role in my life. We were very close. It was her final wish that I restore her mother's country home to its former grandeur, or some such notion. No, I don't know a lot about her people. Only that her mother moved to Atlanta from here in the 1920s or so, and that she was a WWII combat nurse who came from a long line of doctors. She always told me some of them were rather famous in their day."

"Really? That's fascinating." The impressive snippet of his history, and also the way he spoke of his grandmother, caused Jennifer to soften. She detected his own soft spot in a guarded exterior. "Look, I'm sorry if it seemed I was prying. It just helps to get a feel for the history surrounding any project, and I do need to know a building's intended use."

He nodded. "I intend to live in the house. And the reason I didn't just slap some paint and lumber on, as you say, was that Grandmother made clear she wanted things done right. We'll be here to do general labor, Miss Rushmore, and we can gather a small crew to help us, but we would give you authority to select experts for specific types of work."

"Of course, that sounds good." Jennifer tamped down excitement at the concept of overseeing her first job. "You'd want the house done first, then, I assume?"

"Yes, then the apothecary. And on the original land grant across and up the road, on Long Creek, is a log cabin. The property manager said he believes it was the first dwelling of the first Dunham doctor in Georgia."

"Dunham?" Eyebrows raised, Jennifer scribbled.

"The family name. English."

"Log cabin?"

Did she imagine it, or in the pause as Michael watched her, did he seem amused? "That would be your third project, should you accept this mission." He was amused. "Late 1700s. The Dunhams built a plantation there, and a son later came here to start a practice in town. I believe Horace said he'd heard the apothecary was built in the 1870s, as was part of the house."

"And the other part?"

An enigmatic look stole over Michael Johnson's features. "Why don't you come inside and tell me?"

He was testing her. So be it. She snapped her notebook closed, stuck the pen in the loop on her overall bib, stood and pulled out a handheld recorder. "Would you mind if I used this? To record anything you might choose to add as I make my own notes?"

"Sure thing." He stood holding the door open.

Upon sight of the long, golden-brown foyer, with thirteen-foot ceilings disappearing into shadows, she sighed with pleasure. One expected such an entrance hall in a Greek Revival mansion with a sweeping stairway, but not in a one-story country home. Original glass wall sconces and beveled fixtures hung by chains added charm and elegance.

"Surprising, isn't it? Not bad for a country house. As we go through you'll see some strange changes made by the last couple of tenants, but I think you'll find the bones are intact. And some of the changes were done well, including updating the wiring and heating and air systems."

"That's a huge bonus." Jennifer flicked on her digital recorder and spoke her observations, including her assessment of the architectural influences evident in the exterior design. A passing flicker inside her hoped she'd impressed the looming figure to her right, then she turned away from him, shutting that part of her like a damper in a fireplace, choosing to not care. She'd learned that self-protective technique as a hurt little girl. It still served her well today. "Trim work may have been done by a local carpenter, very unusual. No ceiling molding, but plaster cornices in evidence in entry hall. Latex gold paint." She added to Michael, "Not a bad color, by the way."

She wandered off, touching the door into a large front room. Jennifer loved analyzing historic details of buildings because the job employed logic, not messy emotions. "Four-panel doors suggest 1870s construction, but trim work which continues in front parlor looks several decades older. Could have been faux marbleized. Floors are six-inch wide heart pine with square head nails, needing sanding and sealing."

She forgot her host followed her as she admired triple-level baseboard trim unlike any she'd seen before and a bay window with black exterior shutters. In both front rooms, the six-over-six windows ran to the floor with beautiful, original wavy glass, the kind of windows one could imagine ladies in flowing party dresses stepping through out onto the porch, fanning, in search of a cool breeze after a round of dancing. Both rooms also boasted elaborate poplar mantels stained to look walnut. Jennifer's face lit up with appreciation for the fine interior details, causing Michael to study her and smile.

However, Jennifer noted to her recorder that the poorly repaired fireplaces lacked adequate brick work between the fire pits and wooden frames, making them nonfunctional. "Additionally, the bricks in the floors of the fire pits have burned down almost entirely to the sand." She jumped when Michael came up close behind her, stooping over to see. Jennifer straightened and told him, "These will need a lot of work. In addition to what I just said, see the missing mortar. I'll have to view the stacking in the attic and above the roof line, but I'd say a crew will be necessary to make the chimneys sound again. I assume you want to use the fireplaces if you can?"

He nodded. "If not, I was thinking gas?"

"I think there's hope for this one. We'll see about the others. How many fireplaces are there?"

"Six."

Jennifer drew back her shoulders. "Six?"

"Yes."

"So far these mantels, doors and windows support Horace's 1870s theory."

"Let's keep going."

"If you don't mind, I'd like to look into the later closet addition, since you know closets were taxed as separate rooms in the 1800s."

"I didn't know that, but I can tell plywood when I see it." Michael gestured toward the closet with a flourishing wave of both hands.

She ignored his sarcasm and peeked inside. No trace of old wallpaper. "In most homes of this period, at least one of the good rooms would have been papered," she told her host as he led her back into the foyer. "Parlor, best bedroom, or dining room. I'd say the room with the bay window would be the parlor, and this room would have been a dining room or a best bedroom."

"The dining room is farther back. I planned to make this room a bedroom, but the master is also back … here." He opened a door to a room behind the parlor, smaller, though with the same high ceilings. Upon sight of a built-out corner attic access with a post jutting into the room, Jennifer groaned in dismay. "I told you," Michael added.

"Why?" She hurried over and opened a door that gave her a view of very narrow, very twisted ascending steps. Everything in her pushed her into the edifice. She made herself shut the door and say, "We'll go up there once we've finished the house tour."

"Yes, ma'am."

Michael's expression looked dead serious, but his words made her double take. Once upon a time, this man had a sense of humor. What had made a gorgeous, intelligent young man retreat like a hermit to the ends of the earth? What made his grandmother's dying wish take precedence over everything else? To cover her confusion, she talked into her recorder about the terrible attic access. Then she asked, "Why is this the master?"

"Because the same people who added that enhancement also added a modern shower, a garden tub, and a walk-in closet through that door."

"Oh." Then, at that door, "Oh." Floor-to-ceiling mirrors flanked both walls of a deep-set and otherwise alluring corner garden tub. The sight made her shudder with almost as much horror as the attic access.

"Gaudy, right."

"Quite."

"You have my permission to remove those."

Jennifer looked at him and blushed scarlet. She shoved her glasses up and turned away. "The closet work is quite livable, though. You just need a rack and some shelves. And new carpet."

"Right, it's badly stained, but at least it's not shag, holding forty years of dirt and mildew. Behind this room, if we go back into the foyer and through this door at the back, is what will probably be my den, an old porch they enclosed. There's a sky light, and built-in shelving, and more filthy carpet. What?" He stopped.

Jennifer touched the window next to the door he had just gone through. "This was the back exterior of the house once."

"Yes."

"This window is nine-over-nine. And this door is two-panel."

"I know what that means, but I don't know what that means." Michael drew in his mouth and waited.

"It means older. Hand-blown glass had to be framed in smaller squares, you understand, so there were more of them. As machine-made glass became standard and strong, we see less panes of glass like in modern windows." Jennifer put a hand on the door behind her. "American Empire doors dated to the late 1830s through 1850s. Four-panel doors were popular before and again after that period. I believe the doors in the front three rooms were 1870s. I believe this door, and this window, to be approximately 1840s."

"And that excites you."

"It should excite *you*."

"OK." He lifted a shoulder. "If you say so."

He totally didn't care. What kind of luck gave a person who nailed two-by-fours for a living but didn't know a Corinthian column from a Doric a fascinating historic house, apothecary, log cabin and a long line of prestigious doctors, while she, who lived, breathed and sweated muntins and moldings, stood to not even inherit the tin trailer from hell in the South Georgia pines she hailed from? She huffed quietly behind him as he passed through the sun room, which would indeed be a nice modern den for a bachelor, past what remained of a portion of back porch, and turned right into a kitchen.

CHAPTER TWO

In the kitchen Jennifer stopped, not bothering to comment to her host. Instead, she dictated oral notes about the wide boards beneath her feet, narrow bead board ceiling painted white, a nice island, glass cabinets Michael told her came from the old general store, a gaping hole where a refrigerator should be, and a fireplace whose wide, plain, painted surround also screamed 1840s.

They stepped across a threshold onto narrow, diagonal, Minwaxed floors. The sudden change flagged a possible addition of an older kitchen from the rear of the lot. In this narrow hallway, a built-in butler's pantry captured her interest much more than the hole to her left which Michael intended to turn into a laundry room. They then arrived in the small, oddly shaped dining room, redeemed by elaborate white wainscoting and what appeared to be an original chandelier dangling from circular molding. Jennifer's fingers itched to strip away a section of the thick red paint on the upper part of the walls in search of wallpaper beneath. The built-in corner cupboard faced a window. Its later period, brightly stained glass told her that, while it now looked into the sunroom, it had once filtered sunlight.

Up the same hallway, the simplicity of an 1840s jewel of a fireplace in a small room to the left belied the surround's greater value.

"I'm thinking this will be my office," Michael said.

"Perfect. Just what I would do with it."

Their shared smile led to an uncomfortable moment before he led her to the small, full bath sandwiched between the office and the larger bedroom at the front of the house. Between every uneven threshold, the boards leaned slightly down from the center of the house. Despite herself, Jennifer already adored this architectural cornucopia.

"I would note a suspicion," she said, to Michael and the recorder, "that the dining room, office and what has been turned into a bathroom were the original structure, 1840s, while another building, perhaps an old kitchen from the same period, was brought up behind. Then, in the 1870s, the other rooms and front porch were added."

She paused. That announcement, which merited a preceding drum roll to any audience with an iota of education in historic architecture, should impress and please him. Michael just waited.

Jennifer sighed. "Shall we go see the attic?"

After retrieving flashlights from the closet, Michael led the way to the access door. He climbed up but waited on the small section of subflooring while Jennifer tiptoed along two-by-fours and clung to rafters. Mollified, she discovered two side-facing gables, weathered a good twenty years before enclosure in the current structure, which verified her theory of the 1840s section. But in view of Michael's lack of enthusiasm over the age of his ancestors' home, she decided that could wait for her full written report. She said once she crawled back to him, "You'll definitely need a fireplace crew. The mortar and bricks up here are in bad shape."

"OK. You have cobwebs on you," he reported before turning for the stairs.

"I'll just get more when we go under the house," Jennifer replied, but decided that in case any of the poisonous originators of the webs were attached, she'd give herself a good brushing off.

"Hopefully it's too early still for snakes."

Behind him, Jennifer's steps faltered. Snakes were the one thing that could separate her with great speed from a building in otherwise any condition of decay. As she followed Michael outside, she assessed the foliage. There was not much underbrush yet, only crocuses poking their tiny heads out of the remnants of brick-lined beds to the side of the yard, and beyond that, a riot of jonquils and daffodils near the woods. She might be safe.

Standing outside the crawl space at the side of the house, Michael paused. "Are you sure you don't want to see the apothecary before you get good and dirty?"

She didn't want him to think he'd scared her off with his talk of slithering things. "Let's do it."

To her surprise, he crawled in ahead of her and called it clear. But he didn't follow her when she wiggled off toward the 1840s section. No need to, she thought to herself, if he didn't care to hear her observations. As she'd suspected, stone piers supported the old part of the house, with brick pilings near the front. She followed him out, hesitating but accepting the hand he offered to draw her to her feet.

Only a streak of clay marred his handsome face and plaid shirt, while a glance down showed Jennifer that mud covered the entire front of her overalls. Her hair hung in her eyes. And from the rear of the property, a very clean man, average size but wiry, with graying dark hair and a broad smile, approached.

The new arrival extended his hand. "Hi, I'm James, Michael's father. You must be the preservation student."

"Uh, yes, Jennifer Rushmore. Sorry, I'm a little dirty." Jennifer shook his hand, then gave a few futile brushes at her clothing.

"That's OK. I have nothing but admiration for any girl who will crawl under a house. Finding any exciting mysteries under there? It sure is a fascinating old place."

She smiled. "Yes, it is. I've verified the back three rooms of the house are actually 1840s."

"Is that so?" James' tone and widened eyes indicated much greater interest than Michael had displayed.

"We were just about to go on to the apothecary," the younger man stated.

"Well, are you sure you don't want to wash up a little first? You can come to the camper. We don't have running water in the house yet. Some plumbing problems I have to fix," James told Jennifer with a quick glance.

She must look really bad. "I don't want to be any trouble."

"Oh, honey, you're not any trouble. Come on. I could use a cup of coffee about now, anyway." James turned her gently with a hand on her arm. "You can bring me up to speed."

She acquiesced. Even though he'd called her "honey" and touched her without her permission, both of which would have normally set her off, Jennifer didn't feel threatened or condescended to. Instead, James exuded a warmth that made her relax.

"You might want to take off your shoes, though," he suggested as he climbed up into the camper.

Jennifer sat on the hanging metal steps to remove her dirty old boots, set them aside, then followed him, with Michael leading up the rear. The portable home creaked and shifted under their weight.

James showed her through to the bathroom, which separated the living area from a bedroom with two twin beds. She washed her hands and her face as well as possible with damp tissues, then removed debris from her shoulder-length hair, which was mouse brown, straight and as unremarkable as her delicate features. Putting her glasses back on, Jennifer hastened to turn away from the mirror.

In the front of the camper, from where the scent of coffee wafted, James set out mugs that read "Johnson Construction." Michael squeezed his long frame into a booth and munched a cookie. The place was not too messy considering two grown men were cramped into such a small space. Jennifer sat on a geometrically patterned sofa and told James how she took her coffee. He asked her about her findings, and she filled him in. As she talked, Michael switched on a small TV and stared at a basketball game. Really? She frowned and focused on his father, trying to tune out the droning commentator.

"What other buildings are on the property? I see there are several."

"Oh, a smokehouse, a cabin that was probably either a slave cabin or a kitchen, an old shed built in the last fifty years, that falling down outhouse you saw right behind the house, and at the back of the property, a well. You'd think it would sit where the outhouse did and vice-versa."

"They knew how cholera spread even in the 1800s." Taking her mug from James, she smiled.

With her statement, Michael surprised her by nodding his head, even though he did not turn to acknowledge them.

"That makes sense. I'll have to take you back there to see it." James sat down in the booth facing her, looking past Michael. "You'd be amazed the type of work they did back then. The well is deep, perfectly circular, lined with the smoothest bricks."

"Wow. We could include it on the Register along with the apothecary and house. What about the smokehouse and cabin? What are your plans for those?"

"Michael and I thought we could fix them up, though of course we'd welcome your recommendations."

Jennifer nodded. "Definitely." She restrained the urge to remind him of the value of restoring such special structures to historic code. He and Michael had to have something to do to make them feel needed, after all.

24

"So tell us more about the National Register listing. You think you could get us on that?"

"I do. I'd start with a preliminary report called a HPIF, Historic Property Information Form. I'll need your help documenting floor plans and gathering maps, the history of the house and family, old photos and such. With the prominence of the doctors and the uniqueness of the apothecary shop, the property definitely has relevance."

Michael chimed in, asking over his shoulder, "Besides passing tourists stopping to read a sign, what would the benefits be?"

She pursed her lips. "It is considered a great honor to be listed on the National Register."

"Besides the great honor, what benefits?"

"Well, it's ideal if you apply, then wait for approval before you start work. That gives you the best chance to receive tax incentives."

"How long does the whole process take?" Michael asked, shifting his posture to look at her.

She had to be honest here, even in the face of his abysmal lack of enthusiasm. "It can take a year or more."

Michael laughed. "Miss Rushmore, can you really see the two of us crammed in here for over a year?"

She fixed him with a steady glare. "It is not necessary to call me that."

"All right, Jennifer, I'll be very clear that we want to start work immediately, preferably before you go to Savannah."

Despite his sarcastic tone, Jennifer nodded, choosing not to rise to the bait. "I see your point." They really did look like giants in a doll house. "Well, if you don't alter the historic appearance very much, especially from the outside, and if your restoration increases the property value by fifty to one hundred percent, you still might be eligible to freeze the county tax assessment for over eight years. Or you could receive a state income tax credit of a quarter of the expenses, capped at $100,000 for residences, or $300,000 for businesses or public use facilities. What do you intend to use the apothecary for?"

"We really haven't gotten that far in our planning," James admitted, sipping his coffee. "We just want to get her stabilized right now."

"Of course. So the house, then the apothecary, are what you want me to concentrate on, with no focus on the outbuildings."

"And the log cabin up the road on Long Creek. Michael told you about it?"

Jennifer nodded. "Yes. I assume you want that restored on site."

Michael said, "We want that moved here."

"If you move it, it will take it off the Register."

"We want it on this property, regardless."

Really, if the man would focus on the ballgame and let her converse with his much more sensible father, she'd make far quicker progress. She glanced at James, head tilted and eyes widened.

He responded to her silent frustration with further explanation. "There is nothing left at the old plantation site, really. The house burned a long time ago, leaving just the remains of some slave cabins and a bunch of brambles. The original cabin is only in decent condition because they were smart enough to replace the shake roof with metal and weatherboard the outside. I'm sure it held special meaning to them since it was the first home built on the property."

"I see." She sighed. "I might could prove relevance to this property to grandfather it in." She took a drink and gazed out the window to the rear of the fairly clear lot. The green glen beneath the grove of pecan trees would indeed receive a Colonial cabin well. "How much land do you have here?"

"Thirteen acres, and around twenty left at the original land grant up the road."

"It really is beautiful."

"That it is. How about I join you on your tour of the apothecary? But let me show you the well first. If you're ready?" asked James.

She nodded. As she laced up her boots outside, she asked, "Do you happen to have any old photos? They're necessary to a Register application, to document the original appearance of the house, apothecary and property."

"Oh, dear, I'm afraid we don't," James said, looking questioningly at Michael. "Although there might be some at the storage building in Lawrenceville, among Gloria's things. Her mother must have passed down some items to her. Donald might know."

"Donald?" Jennifer stood and followed the men out to see the well.

"Michael's grandfather. We put Donald's and Gloria's things in storage in Lawrenceville when he went into the VA home in Milledgeville."

"There might be something in the old shed," Michael suggested, nodding at said structure near the tree line.

"Among Miss Ettie's things, yes," James agreed. He explained to Jennifer, "Ettie Mae was a spinster of a branch of the family who lived here while Georgia Pearl was still alive but living in Atlanta."

"Georgia Pearl?" Jennifer sounded more and more like an echo. As they paused to admire the well, she thought she saw Michael send his father a slight frown. So he didn't appreciate her curiosity about the family. Since she generally maintained the same policy, she could understand that, but this was different, and he needed to know it. "I'm sorry it may seem like I'm prying. I just need to know about the history of the place and the people who lived here in order to write the Register report."

"We understand, and we'll help you all we can," James replied. "It's just that we don't know a lot about Michael's maternal grandmother's family tree. Horace, the old property manager, may be a good place to start. He knows everybody in the community. And we can look through the storage buildings. We can find you the documentation you need. It just may take a little while."

"That's fine, Mr. Johnson."

Realizing that restoring the buildings might prove the easy part of this project, she trailed him toward the apothecary, Michael behind her.

James proved a much better tour guide than Michael. In fact, she almost forgot the younger man was there. The apothecary sat very near the main road. The curlicue millwork on the porch of the quaint, three-room structure captivated her. A close examination revealed that some of it had originally been painted green to match the green shutters. And she gasped when they went inside. The dark green ceiling matched the trim on the compounding desk and curving shelves set into either wall. The insets on the desk glowed a dull, mustard yellow. Old plaster had fallen away from the walls in big sections to display tiny, intricate lathing. She and James yelled when they disturbed a mother bird making a nest in the front wall. She exclaimed as he opened drawers marked with various vial sizes to show her tiny bottles with the dried medicine still inside.

"And look at this," he said, holding up a torn, water-marked post-card. "'Oral Treatment of Arthritis with Oxo-cate B. Smith, Kline & French Co. $3.25/bottle. Philadelphia.'"

"This is fascinating. I've never seen anything like it." If the house had not already captured her, the apothecary sealed the deal.

The men showed her big jars, old canes, walking sticks and cro-quet rings they had discovered inside the shop. As they passed into the second room, Jennifer clasped her hands upon spying a reclining chair that must have been used for examinations.

"We believe this is where the doctors saw patients, while the rear room was used for storage or, at times, living quarters. You can see a fireplace once separated the back two rooms. I lean toward not recre-ating it, as it's been entirely removed with the floor rebuilt under it."

"I agree. I'd say we just close up this wall." Jennifer scribbled notes. It was too hard to talk into her recorder with James sharing as much as he did. She didn't mind, but the many surface distractions made it difficult to focus on restoration steps. She and James did dis-cuss the use of plaster rather than dry wall and the refinishing and repainting the shelving with oil-based paint.

"Wait until you see the back room," James said in an ominous tone.

"Why, what's the matter with it?"

She followed him through the door and stopped in dismay. "Oh." Rotted into a gaping hole, the floorboards in the middle of the room were stained with what appeared to be oil. James walked over and opened a barn-like door to reveal a ramp made of earth, stone and brick, leading into the tacked-on rear of the building.

"You're standing in Miss Ettie Mae's garage. Horace said back in the day they placed lumber over the ramp and the back room to support her red 1945 Caddy. She was very particular about it. When anyone was in her parking place at the general store, she'd beep her horn and wait for them to move."

Jennifer covered her face. "Oh, dear. That explains why she would completely destroy the back of the building. Well, all that will have to go."

"Yes, it will be quite a job."

"She sounds like quite a character. It's not like it's a far walk to what was the general store."

James chuckled and closed up the door. "Yes, indeed. Well, I'll let Michael show you the double-wide and see what you think about it."

"What?" Jennifer turned to the silent man behind her.

James grimaced and said, "Oops, I guess he didn't mention that yet."

Michael stirred. "It's next door, standing vacant since the old lady who lived there died. It might be available for us to rent from the owners as part of your package. It would save you driving back and forth. And if I understand right, you'll need a place to live after graduation anyway ..."

"That's true." Jennifer fell silent, contemplating with surprise, pleasure and a measure of suspense how much easier a local rental would make this project. Housing offered an unexpected boon, but what if she didn't like the place?

James let them out the front of the apothecary and locked it. "Well, it was surely a pleasure to meet you, Jennifer. I hope you can help us out. You can see we need a lot of it."

She shook his hand. "Yes, and I haven't even seen the log cabin yet."

Michael glanced across the falling shadows on the yard. "I'm afraid by the time I show you the mobile home, which you do need to see while you're here since the family lent me the key for today, you won't have enough light to evaluate the log cabin. I hate to ask you to come back another time."

"It's all right." She waved at James as he took off toward the house. "I need some time to absorb all you've shown me today, anyway."

"It's this way." Michael headed across the yard toward a line of Leyland cypress.

She followed, falling into her habitual planning mode and assuming her employer would want to know those plans. "What I'll do is prepare a report of all I'll recommend needs done, in order. Would you like me to include landscaping recommendations? I have my bachelor's in interior design, and of course the master's in historic preservation as of May, but I did take a class in landscape design as well."

"Sure." He didn't even look back at her.

Jennifer frowned and chewed her lower lip for a moment, then she said, "You didn't ask anything about my qualifications, where I did my internship last summer or my field studies in Charleston and Savannah. I brought a resume."

"I assumed if your professor recommended you, even though you are just graduating, she considered you qualified."

Assumed? Or didn't care? Jennifer wanted to say it but bit her tongue. They plunged into knee-high grass at the edge of the property.

"Sorry about this," Michael said. "Dad and I would keep it cleaned up for you."

"It's all right." She almost laughed that he worried about some grass when she looked like she'd been wrestling a wild hog.

"It won't look too bad when the place gets a little maintenance, that is, if you're not above living in a trailer."

Oh, he had no idea.

"Are you free tomorrow?"

Her steps faltered. Then she realized he was talking about the log cabin. "Yes."

They set a time as they stepped up onto the porch. Beneath their feet, the boards felt firm and dry despite peeling stain. Yellow forsythia bloomed on straggly branches on either side. Jennifer glanced at the property on the other side of the mobile home. An old beater and a pick-up on blocks further marred the dirt yard of a dilapidated 1920s bungalow. Too bad they couldn't share their excess of grass. Or renovation funding. There was even a plaid sofa on the porch. Her nose wrinkled like it sometimes did in moments of uncertainty or distrust.

Michael picked up on her reaction. "Kind of an eye sore, isn't it? Looks bad, but from what I hear the old man who lives there is harmless. He keeps to himself. Pretty much a hermit. We can plant you some more Leyland cypress on that side."

Jennifer nodded in agreement, and Michael unlocked the door. A musty smell wafted out. "It's furnished!" she exclaimed, peering in.

"Lightly. The pieces are dated but well-maintained. Nothing a wet vac won't cure."

"That's perfect, since I don't own much myself. I share a town-house apartment with three other girls."

She walked inside. Light and shadow danced merrily against the walls and over the plush carpet of an open living space. She peeked into the two bedrooms. She could move the bed in the master with attached bath into the spare room and bring her own bed in. The mauve countertops and ducks with matching, mauve ribbons march-ing along the wallpaper border dated the kitchen to the '80s. But she didn't mind. Since this was nothing like the trailer where she'd grown up, Jennifer could see herself here. She'd accept a time warp to any era, just as long as it wasn't back to her own past.

CHAPTER THREE

The morning after her visit to Hermon and her strange dream, Jennifer stood looking out the bay living room window of her apartment, drinking French vanilla-laced coffee. Though located off the Milledge Avenue exit of the Athens loop, university buses stopped at a corner shelter near the townhouse, then chugged by, belching diesel smoke, while sweating bicyclists wearing helmets and backpacks pedaled their way north toward town. Jennifer hardly noticed either today. In fact, so deep was her reverie that she did not hear her roommate, Tilly, come into the living room.

"Wow, he really must be a hunk," Tilly said with a wink.

That definitely got her attention. "I never said that. Why would you think so?"

"Oh, you did say that. In so many words. Then there's the cute blouse and pony tail."

"What?" Jennifer examined herself. Prepared to forge through woods and briars to the old plantation site, she knew to wear jeans and boots, and she'd thought her tailored, solid cotton shirt practical, despite its cheerful, spring peach color. She would hardly call it a *blouse*. "It's two years old," she mumbled.

"Whatever." Tilly swatted her pony tail in an arch.

"Come with me. You'll love it. You can even see the house and apothecary quick." Some company might help Jennifer's skittishness around Michael.

"No doing. I've got to finish that paper for non-profit management class. And it's got to be an 'A.'" Non-profit management was Tilly's area of interest. She wanted to run a museum one day, not work in the field. Although plain, the tall, dark-haired girl possessed a confident air Jennifer lacked, or at least had to work hard to generate. Her height and lanky, elegant bearing also silently demanded respect. She would make an organized and efficient boss. "But have fun."

She breezed out of the room.

Jennifer sighed. The idea of seeing Michael again made her nervous, because talking with him required so much effort. She was sure to be awkward. Their plan to meet at the house in Hermon meant that they had to ride in the car together. How far would that be?

Her phone vibrated with an incoming text, Barbara Shelley's response to Jennifer's glowing account of the house and apothecary. "Glad it went so well. Knew it would. So did you make up your mind?"

Yes. She texted back, "No, still need to see the log cabin on the original land grant today at noon and prepare my report. I have to see how he responds to that."

Giggles sounded on the stairs. Decked out for church in trendy, bold-printed, A-line dresses, roommates Shayann and Ellison, both art history undergrads, appeared in the living room. Jennifer didn't have time for religion, and apparently neither did Michael, which suited her fine since it meant he wouldn't be opposed to working on Sundays. Mom taking Jennifer and her older brother Rabon to VBS and Sunday school at the local Baptist church had been fine in the early days. They'd made crafts and drank Kool-Aid and sang songs about being in God's army. But later, all she'd learned about a loving Jesus had seemed not only pointless, but a cruel trick. Even though she'd yet to find anything to fill the void in her heart like the kindness in eyes of the Jesus pictured on her Sunday school wall promised to, Jennifer didn't want any part of a God who allowed children to suffer like she had. She got along fine with Shayann and Ellison as long as they didn't attempt to engage her in any discussions about God. They were just young and lucky. Eventually they'd learn about real life.

Another message came in. "Log cabins can be tricky. You haven't worked with a structure earlier than mid-1800s before. Sometimes they've deteriorated past saving, and that can be hard to tell the client. Want me to come? I'm free."

No. No, no, *no*. Barbara's presence took over any room or project, and having her there would make Jennifer look like a grade school tagalong. But how could she refuse the professor who'd done so much for her, who had in fact set up this entire arrangement? She typed, "If you want to."

"Good. Be there in an hour. Will bring my tools."

"Great."

Jennifer chewed her lip. Disgruntled, she went to brush her teeth. Barbara would insist on taking her Explorer, too, further eroding the capable and confident impression Jennifer wanted to portray to Michael. Studying her reflection, she thought she looked more approachable, yet still professional, with her hair pulled back. If only those wisps on the side stayed secured.

She told herself it was natural Dr. Shelley would want to see the property first-hand, especially after Jennifer had related how intriguing it was. She had worked herself into a gracious mood and waited on the front porch with a satchel and a jacket when her professor pulled into the short drive.

Barb waved and hit the unlock button. "Morning!"

"Good morning," Jennifer replied as she opened the door. "Want me to drive?"

"Nah, get in." Barb threw a stack of papers into the back seat. Her short, dark hair, light make-up, and lack of jewelry were typical, but the jeans and old Oxford shirt contrasted with the pants suits she wore to the classroom in Denmark Hall. "Just tell me where to go. I have a general idea," she said as they took off. "I'm so excited for you. This sounds like a marvelous opportunity. And the offer of the double-wide! How wonderful."

"Yes, that was lucky."

"But you better Lysol the whole place before you move in."

Wondering what Barb would say about the shabby single-wide where she'd spent her childhood, Jennifer turned a grimace into a grin. "Don't worry, I will. Thank you again, by the way."

Barbara smiled over at her. "You don't have to keep saying that. I'm happy to help hard-working students with potential. I know how much you want that job in Savannah. This will provide a big bonus on your application and give you income while you wait. You concerned he won't offer enough?"

"I don't know." Jennifer watched light green fields fly by the window, thinking her graduate school loans demanded payment, and fast, regardless of the amount Michael offered.

"My understanding from Mr. Greene was that money was not a problem on this project, as long as you don't go crazy. It was provided by the estate of the woman who died."

"Michael's grandmother. He did say she wanted it done right. I think I'm more worried he won't see the necessity of some of what I'm going to recommend."

"He doesn't have the eye," Professor Shelley stated and gave her a quick grin. "What do you think he'll balk at, particularly?"

Jennifer spent the ride out of town detailing her concerns. To her surprise, Barbara framed suggestions of historical recommendations in practical language a man like Michael might understand.

"He's not … dumb," Jennifer explained. "Not just an uneducated laborer. I think Michael and his father both know a lot. He just doesn't seem to appreciate the history."

"Always the biggest challenge preservationists face. That's why we have to learn to be salespeople, too. You can do this, Jennifer." Barbara thumped the steering wheel with her hand. "You just have to believe in yourself. Our program provided all the skills you need, and I'm here to mentor you along the way."

When they pulled into the driveway in Hermon, Michael sat in faded jeans and a t-shirt on the tailgate of a beat-up F150, hands on his knees. Barbara cut her eyes to Jennifer without comment, but her gaze said it all. Somehow, it acknowledged Michael's attractiveness without being impressed by it. Jennifer wished she could be so impervious. Maybe it came with age. Jennifer heard Barbara had been married once, but her marriage had ended a long time ago. She imagined the professor's absorption with her career squeezed out time for romance. Likely she'd end up the same way. Her chaotic childhood and mother's dependence on men had cured her of any romantic dreams of family and picket fence. Had Barbara sensed that, and that was the reason she tried so hard to set Jennifer on a path that still held meaning in life?

Now, Barbara strode toward the younger man with her hand extended. His look of surprise at her presence faded as she introduced herself. "I hope it's not an inconvenience for me to come along today," she said. "I couldn't resist the opportunity to help Jennifer assess a 1790s cabin."

"Of course not. Your expertise will be an asset." Despite his words, Michael studied her with the same guarded demeanor that he adopted with Jennifer.

Barbara paused as if taken aback by his language. Not the typical carpenter indeed.

"Well, Jennifer, have you recovered from the information dump yesterday?" he asked in her direction, then added to Barbara, "I'm afraid she looked rather dazed when she left."

Barb laughed, and her eye swept the property. She rubbed her hands together. "I don't blame her. You have a treasure trove of architecture and history here. It's a lot for any graduate to take on. But don't worry, Jennifer is my best student, and I'll be in the area for her to call on as needed."

Jennifer bristled. Barb always did an excellent job of covering herself with flattery while establishing her own authority. "I thought the field study in Savannah will take up a lot of your summer, though."

"Yes, well, we'll have you going good by then, and Savannah isn't far away." Her professor put her hands on her hips. "Let's get started then, shall we?"

"I thought we'd ride in my truck," Michael told them. "If you'd like to, you can see the house and apothecary when we return, Dr. Shelley."

"Unless it would be imposing today, I'd be bitterly disappointed to miss that."

"Not at all." Did Barbara notice the flat line of his mouth as Michael opened the passenger side door of his truck? She looked at him funny for a minute, in an out-of-character way Jennifer had never seen before. She glanced at Jennifer, then climbed in, settling on the middle seat with her tools at her feet. Jennifer sat by the door, surprised Barbara had not claimed that seat for herself. It was almost like the professor intentionally created a barrier between Jennifer and Michael. Well, Jennifer had hoped for a respite from conversation with Michael Johnson. She had it.

"So tell me about the ancestor who built this cabin," Barbara directed as Michael accelerated out of Hermon.

"He doesn't know much about his ancestors yet," Jennifer put in.

But Michael cut her a look. "I don't, but my father called Horace this morning. As you know, Dr. Shelley, he really is as much an amateur historian about this area as he is a real estate agent. He was able to tell us a little."

Barbara nodded. "Good. What did he say?"

Jennifer got out her notebook.

"According to an early Oglethorpe County history book, Levi Dunham came here in the late 1780s. His father was a tobacco farmer and a doctor in Virginia. Levi, a younger son, received a land grant for his service in the Revolutionary War."

Jennifer waited in the pause following his words, then asked, "Is that all?"

Looking past Barb, Michael widened his eyes and shrugged.

"OK, that's a lot more than you knew yesterday." She grinned as she finished her notes.

Michael pulled the truck off the main road, onto the faint impressions of tire tracks that led past a chained fence. He got out and unlocked the bolt, swinging the gate open. Jennifer sat forward as he returned to the wheel and eased them between high grass and overhanging branches that went scraping and thwacking past the truck. Barb grabbed the seat and Jennifer the hand rest as they lurched over ruts and roots. At last the trail opened into a small clearing at the base of a low hill.

"Oh, my gosh," Jennifer murmured. Her heart thudded painfully. The double chimney sentinels jutting out of a tangle of trees and bushes took her right back to the Lockwood Plantation in Stewart County, the safest place in the world for a little girl who had more to run from than to.

Michael stopped the engine at the edge of the thicket, and they got out. He pointed to heaps of weathered wood and brick scattered among the trees. "You can see the circle of cabins. According to Horace, this was once a thriving plantation and sanatorium built up by Levi's son, Silas. He became famous in these parts as a doctor trained in the allopathic school of medicine but who mainly used medicinal herbs from both Native and African American traditions."

Both women stared at Michael. If he was just parroting what the old property manager had said, he was doing a great job. He sounded like a text book. "Allopathic?" Jennifer echoed.

"Use of minerals, mercury, blood-letting, all the traditional treatments of the 1800s." Michael cleared his throat, frowned, and started walking forward. "Anyway, people would stay in the cabins until their health improved. Once the railroad came through, they came to this sanatorium from all over. Horace said Silas Dunham planted thirteen acres of herbs and rare plants."

Jennifer watched him, caught by the unusual pride in Michael's tone at this aspect of his family history.

"Fascinating," Barb murmured. She slung her tool satchel onto her back. "And Levi's cabin?"

"It continued to be used by members of the family for some time. It sits just behind the remains of the plantation. Horace said for a long time folks in these parts said it was haunted."

"Goodness gracious!" Barbara's strident tone sounded disgusted. "Why does every old house have to be haunted? Can't people appreciate history without ghosts rambling about? I suppose your 1800s house is haunted, too?"

"Of course not. Just old stories. I think this one had something to do with one of the women of the family. That's all he knew."

"Naturally, because it's always the women's fault," Barbara scoffed.

Jennifer experienced disappointment, then *déjà vu,* as they pushed past branches and the ruins of the plantation house. Only the chimneys and the steps remained. Why did it give her a similar feeling as the Lockwood place, an antebellum mansion which had still been somewhat sturdy though long abandoned by the 1990s? Maybe it was that air of desolation, that hint of another time that drove her to learn who had lived there and what their lives had been like. Both places also stirred the desire to stay, just to be alone with the birds and the wind and the past. She had to force herself not to sit down on the steps instead of following her professor and potential employer to the one standing structure.

The metal roof and weatherboarding of Levi's cabin had done their work, rendering it in remarkably good condition. Only in a few places did the torn-away outside covering expose the hand-hewn logs of the single pen structure beneath.

Barbara knelt and tugged out her tools. "Come here," she said to Jennifer. "First the foundation. What do you see?"

Jennifer pulled out her recorder. She noted aloud the overall cabin appearance, then said, "Stone chimney is beginning to sink, but stone piers are still evident." She clicked it off, turning a questioning gaze on her mentor. "Which is good, right?"

"Yes, the sill logs are just barely coming in contact with the ground, so deterioration is not too progressed. Look here." She gestured to a missing section of weatherboarding, past the vertical wood furring strips which had been nailed to the logs prior to application of the weatherboarding. "This is good. They whitewashed before enclosing. That helps seal hair line cracks in the daubing." She stood up and produced a tape measurer from her satchel, and the two began to measure the cabin.

"The heart pine cabin measures twenty-eight by eighteen, and displays standard V, or full dove-tail, corner notching," Jennifer recorded as Barbara probed the logs with a small ice pick. Barb's contagious excitement over the rare Georgia structure caused Jennifer not to mind that she led the investigation. The professor walked around the building, poking and tapping wherever log lay exposed.

Actually paying attention this time, Michael asked Barbara as she slipped the tip of the pick into one such fissure, "Are those long cracks running with the wood grain a problem?"

"Not necessarily. They just show seasoning of the wood, but they can admit moisture and fungus." She glanced at him. "Some weathering is to be expected, but too much can let rot in."

Mentally exploring that concept, Jennifer stared at the base of a nearby pine. That statement held true for people as well as logs, but only someone with her strange mind would think that way. She focused. "Is the floor inside safe?"

Michael waited while Barbara inspected a door sill, then pulled the door open. A scurrying sound accompanied the movement. "The mice think so, but I doubt it would hold our weight."

"I'm going in. Someone has to, and I'm the smallest." Jennifer stepped past him, inhaling the musty dampness smelling of age. The darkness shrouded almost everything within.

"Let me see if this shutter will open."

"I wouldn't advise that," said Barb's voice. "That window sill looks soft from years of rain. Here, hand her a flashlight."

Michael stepped into the doorway, extending the light. She took it and switched it on.

"Oh," she said.

"Your favorite word when you're excited."

Was he teasing her? For a fraction of a second she actually felt cute, like the popular high school girls with bouncy ponytails and pert expressions. Then she saw he wasn't smiling. He looked bored. How could he be bored? "This is your Revolutionary War great-great-something-grandfather's cabin," she stated.

"Your point is?"

"The point is, I'm more enthusiastic than you are. This is your family history. Aren't you a little bit excited?"

"It's great. Really." But he looked like he forced interest for the sake of politeness.

Looking away, Jennifer rolled her eyes. She never would understand normal people who lived locked into their present moment. Still, not moving for fear of falling through, she felt required to dictate into her machine in terms he would comprehend. "Cabin logs were only hewn on the inside, then lathed and plastered, probably at a date shortly after construction, to make it more comfortable. Hewn flooring used square-head nails. The single pen style is one-and-a-half stories accessible by steps which were also probably added later, in place of a ladder. No furniture is left in the cabin, but the chimney work is intact, with a stone hearth. The loft has a hole in the center."

Drawn by the sound of her voice, Barb appeared in the doorway. Michael moved out of the way so she could lean in. Her eyes glittered in the dim light, then met Jennifer's with an understanding and appreciation far more satisfying than Michael's manufactured approval. In that moment, she was glad the professor had come. She just hoped Barb wouldn't steal the project from her.

Michael stood on the porch with his arms crossed like a cigar store Indian, glaring at the chainsaw-wielding tree crew. Jennifer spied him from the open rear door of the apothecary shop and guessed the reason for his defensive posture. The restoration plan she e-mailed a week ago introduced their first point of contention: the removal of the two magnolias nearest the house. He clung to the privacy they

40

provided, but she remained firm. Letting roots, limbs, leaves and pods destroy a historic residence was just stupid.

The noise grated the neighborhood like a massive piece of sixty grit sandpaper at work. A surprising number of people walked or jogged along the main road, and today they stopped to gawk at the demise of the magnolia giants. A small lady with a swirl of white hair that reminded Jennifer of cotton candy on a stick came out of the beauty shop across the street and down the way, shading her eyes. Noticing that Michael appeared to have a cigar store twin on the porch of the old bungalow down the street, Jennifer muffled a chuckle.

A car pulled into the driveway, parking across from the exterminator's van. Painted disturbingly large, roaches and spiders created dashed tracks around the company logo on the side of the vehicle. Drawing back into the shop, Jennifer decided to let one of the Johnson men take care of the new arrivals, whomever they were. She didn't like meeting people, especially when she was trying to work.

She finished marking measurements on the floor plan of the apothecary, then put down her folder and uncapped the Nikon hanging around her neck. Training from her undergrad photography class had taught her to set the lens and aperture for various lighting and distances, which would prove helpful in the dim back rooms of the apothecary. In the front room, the two full-length windows let in a lot of sun. She went to work photographing the ceiling, windows, floors, shelves and counters and had just moved to the middle room when she heard voices. Oh, no.

"Jennifer?" James called.

In the face of his cheer, she swallowed her initial testy response. "Yes?"

"Here are some folks I'd like you to meet."

She put on a smile and walked forward. A grinning, rotund man in his mid-fifties and a faded beauty in designer jeans and a silk blouse stood beside James in the door. "This is Horace Greene and his wife, Amy."

"Oh, the property manager turned real estate agent turned historian." Jennifer smiled, hoping the man might prove a source of more information. She shook the beefy hand he extended.

"I guess that would be me." Horace beamed.

"And you and I, honey, have so much in common," the blonde woman at his side gushed. "We're both interior designers."

"*Really?*" Jennifer tried not to cringe at being designated an interior designer. Anyone with a two-year degree from any Podunk technical college, or no degree at all, could be an interior designer. In one month, she would hold a master's degree in historic preservation from Georgia's premier university. She had fought for every penny and scrap of information that represented, and a lot more. She reminded herself not to judge, part of the take-away remaining from church days. She preferred that loving aspect of God to the punitive father figure of the Old Testament. Maybe the sense that Amy embodied all her teenage fears of being stuck, and not their perceived differences, got her back up.

"Yes, and my specialty is old homes." The slim hand she waved appeared to descend under the weight of a large diamond.

"You don't say!"

"Amy owns Drapes and Drips in Lexington," Horace said as he placed a hand on his wife's hip, clearly proud.

James answered Jennifer's blank look. "She specializes in curtains, drapes and paint. She carries Sherwin Williams, so she'll be supplying us with samples when you're ready. And she runs her interior decorating services there, too."

"Oh, that's great! How clever." There might be more to the woman than she'd originally thought. After all, she ought to be the last person on earth to judge by appearances.

"Yes, Horace and Amy are staples here, real Oglethorpe natives. Horace was a football star back in his day."

Jennifer raised her eyebrows and studied his short, stocky build.

Making a shooing motion, Horace responded to James' praise and Jennifer's skepticism. "Nothin' like that, now."

James objected, "Now wait, the lady who runs the antique store over here was telling me you kicked the farthest field goal in school history."

"Well, yep, in '79, that was true." Horace tugged on his belt and grinned depreciatingly. "But by now I'm sure that's been bested by yards. But what I have real braggin' rights on is, I stole the homecoming queen." He placed an arm around Amy, who smirked and shook her head, her blue eyes slits.

"Oh, wow," Jennifer murmured. They didn't even notice the "yards" they'd lost with her there. Back at her own high school, no cheerleader or football player had known she was alive. Shoot, even the band members had turned up their horns at her. Only when she'd finally escaped to UGA had she found a small group of nerdy, artsy, quiet kids like herself—finally, gratifying company on her trips to the library and the coffee shop to provide occasional conversation. Which was quite enough for her. She pulled her attention back to the visitors. "I was just photographing the apothecary for the Register report. Is there something I can help y'all with?" She hoped the "y'all" would soften her impatience.

Apparently, it didn't. Horace blinked his bug eyes. "Oh. We don't want to disturb you."

"No, no. No disturbance," James hurried to assure him.

Jennifer made an effort. "Of course not. I just wondered ... did you want to talk about the paint today?"

Thank goodness, she'd covered herself. "Oh, no, honey, we don't have to do that," Amy said, patting her hand. "Although I can't wait to walk through the house and chat about what you want to do, I know you're not ready for that yet."

"But we can recommend some painters," Horace added.

"Oh, yes?"

"Earl and Stella James, live just over on Cherry Street. He can do inside and outside, both. Does a top-notch job, and has friends from church he calls on for help. Stella helps with the interior. I've got the name of a good roofing crew, too, did the house across the street."

Jennifer took out her notebook and jotted down the names and numbers. "That's very helpful, thanks," she said. "Anyone else come to mind?"

"Maybe 'stead of me just throwing names out there you should tell me what else you'll need a crew for, what you plan to do to the old place."

Jennifer nodded. "Yes, of course. Well, the plan I just put by Mr. Johnson here and Michael called for us to begin with the tree removal and metal roof replacement. The roof was our next step, so your suggestion is perfectly timed, as we'll need to hire help for that and to restore the fireplaces, all six of them."

Horace provided contacts from his cell phone, evaporating Jennifer's disapproval. She'd be wise to drink from the fount of local connections to which James had led her. The Greenes could be important community allies. "So then we have the exterior and interior painting. I will speak with the Jameses right away. Finally, the floors."

"Michael and I can handle that, no problem," James put in.

"Excellent."

"And we can also complete the work on the apothecary."

Jennifer turned to him with eyebrows raised. "Really?"

"You'll find we're good for more than just pounding nails." He grinned.

Hmm. She'd see how they did. If there were problems, they could always call in someone with more targeted experience later.

"So you're not going to go moving buildings around?" Horace asked.

"Only the log cabin that's on the other property, later this year. We thought we'd place it in the pecan grove. Other than that, it is best to keep the historic structures on their original foundations. It increases the historical value of the property as a whole, for consideration by the National Register."

Horace nodded and offered, "I know a man from Arnoldsville who's restored some log cabins. I'd be happy to put you in touch when you're ready."

Jennifer gave him a bright smile and said with warmth, "Thank you, Mr. Greene."

"Horace, please."

"Horace."

"So you're not going to do any demolition, move anything else, go digging up the property?"

She paused in confusion. Hadn't they already covered this topic? "Why would we dig up the property?"

"Oh, you know I'm a sucker for preserving everything possible, and I've got extra affection for this place since I managed it for Michael's grandmother for so long. Used to keeping an eye out, you know. Just wondered what you had planned for the other structures. Leaving them as is?"

"Michael and I will restore the smokehouse and cabin," James said. "We'll probably have to tear down the old outhouse. It's an eyesore and past saving."

Horace shifted his weight, fixing Jennifer with an accusatory eye. "Young lady, don't you have anything to say about that? I mean, it is a historic structure, right?"

She chuckled, unaccustomed to encountering someone who fretted as much about the future of an outhouse as she did. Did her obsessions with old buildings come across to most people as petty? "Well, yes. I'll have a look at it before we make a final decision. Of course, the more structures that remain on the property, the better. There's just so much to do, but I guess … nothing else we need help with." She turned her focus on Amy. "Except, of course, when I come see you about paint and drapes."

Amy's eyes, rimmed with coal-colored eyeliner and mascara, lit up. "I can't wait."

"And I'll need to do a lot of shopping for antiques." She couldn't keep the eagerness out of her tone. In Jennifer's estimation, antiquing on someone else's dime trumped winning a mall shopping spree. But then, since she hated malls, winning a cash prize might be a better comparison.

"Well, you can start right next door. Mary Ellen McWhorter may have a small shop, but she gets in some interestin' pieces from private dealers and auctions. If she doesn't have it or can't get it, she can send you to where it is. And let me just volunteer to tag along on any shopping trips." Amy stuck her hand up like an elementary school student. OK, maybe she'd grown in sweetness from her high school cheerleader days. Horace *had* said she was a cheerleader, right?

Jennifer smiled. "Thank you. I'll keep that in mind. I'll be looking for furniture for the house's earliest period."

"She pegged Michael right," James said, "that he would rather go for the simpler earlier look than something all fancy and Victorian."

"That sounds about right for a bachelor," Horace agreed.

Jennifer nodded. "It's usually best to portray a home's earliest period."

"Well, it sounds like it's gonna be a doozy. The entire town can't wait to see what the place turns out like." Horace elbowed James. "Honestly, it's a little strange, James, your son wanting to stay here so far out in the country, being young and single like he is. It would make more sense for him to fix the place up and turn a nice profit. I can help him do it."

James shook his head. "You're forgetting this is a family property, Horace. We have no intention of letting it go."

"Not even for the right price? You could retire comfortably in Atlanta."

"Heaven save me from such an end," James laughed. "I don't even think retire, comfortable and Atlanta all go in the same sentence."

"I take your meaning, but Michael … what's he gonna do out here? Not that we wouldn't be happy to have him. Just … I could see him really liking Athens instead."

Jennifer's forehead puckered. Greene made a better historic activist than pushy salesman.

"It's family property," James repeated. "And as for what he—we—would do, we were thinking of letting our manager in Atlanta run the construction crews there, while we built a small crew here. By the way, I'll be looking for some experienced workers to help us out, if you know anyone."

Horace struggled to get his meaty hand into his back pocket for his wallet. "Sure, sure! I got some ideas. I can ask around, too. OK, well, just in the back of your mind, remember if you ever want to sell or rent it out, me or my son Jeremy at Athens Area Property Management 'Move That Listing From History.'" Handing James a crisp business card, he pointed at the printed slogan and chuckled.

"Thanks," James said in a bemused tone, retreating from another dig of Horace's elbow.

"No pressure. Just a standin' offer. I know what a jewel it'll be and how many people might like to snatch up the opportunity for the quiet life in the country."

James smiled. "I can promise you, we're the people wanting that the most."

CHAPTER FOUR

Interesting that a 1980s double-wide marked Jennifer's first step backwards on the Hermon timeline. The month of April offered Jennifer a slate of days to prepare the home for her occupancy. Even though the family who owned it had cleared out most personal items of the matriarch who departed this world after her stay in a local nursing home—Jennifer had checked to make sure she hadn't given up the ghost in residence—the trailer yielded its own remnants of the past. An answering machine, clothes pins, odd pieces of Tupperware, Harlequin romances, a big sun hat, stationery, and a whole set of blue-flowered Corning ware, among other things. The owners instructed that she should use what she wanted and discard the rest. Grateful for the dishes and the sun hat, perfect for her landscape work, she piled the expendables in a couple of cardboard boxes.

As she worked that Saturday morning, her emotions ran the gamut from contentment to near panic. With all her heart, Jennifer anticipated a snug little place of her own, safe from any harm by others, a security her childhood home had denied. At the same time, it occurred to her that her cleaning efforts in the trailer, the front yard tree execution, and Ettie Mae's cast-offs and treasures waiting in the shed, all reflected on a deeper level the happenings in her own life. Even though she'd anticipated interest from her historic preservation friends, not a soul accepted her invitation to come out today. It was understandable, of course. Jennifer knew all too well how to make excuses for people, and right now, exams, romantic relationships, and summer plans for either internships, new jobs, or returning home to loving families captured the students' attention. All the friends she'd gathered in the past few years would soon disperse across the South, and no reunions were likely to occur, either. Fall class work and field studies would engross the returning students, whereas she'd be … here. It was a cleaning out. A stripping away. A testing to see what was real enough to last. Just when she'd finally gotten secure somewhere.

She sighed and, with an impatient gesture, brushed away a tear.

After sorting lots of blue towels atop the washer and dyer, she headed back to finish cleaning out the kitchen cabinets. Loneliness pressed its hounding nose into her hollow stomach. The chirp of birds constituted her day's sole accompaniment. What was she doing? This move plunked her square in the middle of nowhere. People would be around, yes, but no point in making friends. If things went as planned, after Christmas she'd leave for Savannah. Working in the year-round balmy climate, in the state's oldest city once ruled by pirates and cotton factors would be exciting, she tried to remind herself. But the prospect felt dim and far away. And uncertain. What if she didn't get the job? She couldn't live long or pay student loans once this employment in Hermon ended.

Anxiety escalated to near panic. She bent over the kitchen sink, trying to mash some calm into her stomach. Was coming to Hermon the right choice?

She could return to Westville, the recreated 1850s village where she'd worked through high school, and summers in undergrad. Even if they didn't have an opening for a director, she knew they'd take her in some position, maybe events coordinator, from where she could bide her time. They'd been very good to her there, paying her as much as they could on a limited budget to help her save for college fees not covered by her academic scholarship.

But then she saw in her mind's eye the single-wide under the pines, its siding stained and skirting half missing, and she knew even if she got her own place in Richland or Lumpkin, it would be too close. Everywhere she went she would bump into people from her childhood, and they would say, "Oh, you came back to Westville, did you?" and nod like they'd known all the time and money spent on college would be a waste. No, she would never go back to Stewart County. Or anywhere in South Georgia. She'd vowed to get out, and get out she had.

But to Hermon?

A knock on the door clenched her churning stomach. She stiffened. "Yes?"

The storm door creaked, and Michael stuck his head in. "Hi, sorry to disturb you. I saw your car, and I know you're busy, but Earl and Stella stopped by. I thought you might take a few minutes to come meet them and discuss the painting."

She turned around, hands behind her, leaning on the counter. "Oh. I thought they were coming first of the week."

"I did, too, but they said they had some free time and just stopped to meet us. Taking those trees out did something."

"Did what?"

Michael gestured with an open hand. "Like rolled a welcome mat out to the community. The folks in that historic house near the dairy farm came for a tour last week, and yesterday the woman from the beauty shop brought us a casserole. She said she knew us men all alone would appreciate it."

Jennifer stifled a chuckle. "Well, didn't you?"

He glared at her. "That isn't the point. People in Atlanta didn't just stop in without invitation or calling, at all hours."

"I bet your father is appreciating the warm welcome." She turned back to wash her hands with Dawn, then dried on her jeans.

"Yes. And they're great people."

"But you want to be left alone." Jennifer faced him.

He let out a breath and said nothing as she walked toward him. She stopped in front of him and allowed herself the momentary courage to look straight into his blue eyes. He was nothing like her. The world treated people like Michael with kindness. He should have no reason to be running or hiding. "Why?"

The eyes shuttered, and he looked away. "It doesn't matter why."

So be it. She pondered how to make it clear to him that his rebuff hadn't stung. Jennifer walked out the door. As they started down the steps, she said, "I get it. I'm kind of a loner myself. But I guess we're going to have to get used to a lot of people coming around, both working and satisfying their curiosity. We should remember they take community pride in the restoration of this property. You didn't know that your ancestors were famous in this county, but they were, and there it is."

As they walked across the yard, she realized her words also reminded her of the importance of her job. It gave her a place to go. Hermon was not Lumpkin because there were different people in it. She'd figure out the future as it came. For now, she just had to form professional and polite working relationships with these folks who Michael seemed equally threatened by, for whatever reason.

"Earl seems eager to get to work first of the week. I think he'll do a good job. He comes highly recommended."

"Did you ask him about his equipment?"

"I came to get you before we talked particulars."

She experienced a glow of satisfaction. "Thank you."

Stepping into the foyer, Jennifer saw a medium-skinned, middle-aged African American couple, both tall, standing with James as he pointed out a rough patch in the wall. The man wore dark jeans and an Oxford shirt, and his close-cropped hair, tinted with silver, emphasized his strong jaw line. Dressed in a flowing, floral over shirt with a deep pink shell, black slacks and heeled boots, the woman turned to Jennifer with the most gracious smile Jennifer had ever seen. In the moment, she tried to understand it. It was almost like she saw right through Jennifer but only recognized the good. And while her appearance and perfect posture would have passed muster in any country club in Athens, both were devoid of swagger.

"Jennifer, this is Earl and Stella James. Earl and Stella, our historic preservation grad and project overseer, Jennifer Rushmore. She coordinates all our work crews, supervises, approves, schedules, reports, you name it. Oh, and she crawls under houses. We're lucky to have her." James patted her back in a fatherly manner.

Jennifer blushed under his praise. Being valued still felt foreign, despite Professor Shelley's sponsorship. She shook hands with the guests. "Have you showed them the house, James?"

"We walked through the inside while Michael went to get you."

"And what do you think, Earl?"

"I think it sure need some work, Miss Rushmore." Earl scratched his head and looked around.

"Please, call me Jennifer."

"Like this here, Miss Jennifer, I have to do elastomeric treatment, put the material into the cracks and let the compound help it stick to smooth it out before painting."

Jennifer examined the area Earl's hand rubbed, more pleased that he recognized the need than bothered that he explained something with which everyone present was familiar. "Yes, I agree. And it's just Jennifer."

He nodded.

"Do you have scaffolding?"

"Sure do, and the hand poles to reach up in these high ceilings."

"And you help your husband, Stella?"

"That's right, I do. First step, we'll remove all the hardware and light fixtures. I'll come over and help scour them of old paint and dirt. Then I paint alongside Earl. I'm good at trim and finish work. But I'll let him do the outside." She winked at her husband with a sideways glance.

"Aw, she don't like to get her hair messed up," Earl teased.

Stella play swatted him.

"In all seriousness, that would be a waste of her skills." He touched the doorframe nearby. "This here will require a hand sander. Once you get all the old latex gunk off, Miss Jennifer, you'll start to see what the door *oughta* look like. It'll look real good."

Jennifer bit her lip at Earl's lapse, or stubborn civility, trying not to giggle. "How long do you think it'll take all together?"

He rubbed his jaw, producing a scratching sound and a thoughtful expression. "Lemme see the outside first, then I give you a good estimate."

"All right." Jennifer started toward the door, and the others followed.

As they gathered on the porch, discussing what needed done there, a figure rounded the corner of the apothecary. "Yoo-hoo!" A round, middle-aged woman with fair skin approached them, arms waving.

"Who's that?" Jennifer asked.

Stella smiled. "That's Mary Ellen McWhorter. She owns the antique store next door. Have you not met her yet?" She waved over the newcomer.

"I'm afraid not."

"Well, she won't be put off." Stella's husky voice reflected both resignation and affection. "Have you men met her?"

"Yes, we have," Michael muttered. "She toured the house the first week while we were still killing spiders and mice. She stepped right on a mouse trap."

"And squealed loud enough to scare any living creature off the property," James added.

Stella chuckled. "Well, it's you she's here for, then," she said to Jennifer. "She'll invite us for a Coke in her shop, just you watch. Do we have a minute, Earl? Can we go over while you look at the house with the men?"

"Sure, hon, I'll wait for you when we're done."

Jennifer bit her lip to hold in a groan. Why should she go chat with the ladies while the men discussed the job, when she was in charge of the whole project, as James had just bragged? Old Southern social and gender expectations got in the way when one had a job to do. Of course, had she sandwiched into a social strata with actual manners in Stewart County, she'd probably be well versed by now in acting sweet and gracious in the face of constant interruption. At Westville, she'd learned to put on a professional demeanor when she'd been too scared to open her mouth in public. This was the same thing. Besides, it *was* an antique store, after all. And she *was* a little thirsty.

Jennifer and Stella met Mary Ellen in the yard so she wouldn't get the notion to invite herself inside the house. Upon introduction, the rosy-cheeked woman wrapped Jennifer in a sudden embrace, pressing her wispy brown hair against Jennifer's cheek. Affection generated even more discomfort than approval. Feeling awkward and undeserving, Jennifer stepped back fast.

"I've been dying to meet you," Mary Ellen exclaimed, "ever since I heard you were coming. What an honor to have a *bona fide* expert among us. Imagine what we can all learn from you. I'm almost ashamed to have you come over to my humble shop, but you oughta feel free to pop in any time, put your feet up, and have a Coke with me." Oblivious to the fact that she echoed a commercial, she clasped her hands under her dimpled chin, looked from the elegant Stella to the frumpy Jennifer, then let out a delighted giggle. "Why, how about now?"

"We'd love to," Stella agreed, nudging Jennifer forward.

Admiring the pink dogwood and purple-blossomed cherry tree in the side yard, they opened the white wooden gate leading past the apothecary and what appeared to be an abandoned lot next to it.

"Who owns this lot?" Jennifer asked.

"Oh, that belongs to the Stevenson family," Stella told her. "Bryce Stevenson's almost eighty but still sits like a king on the town council. The family's been in Oglethorpe a long time."

"Did they once have a house here?" Jennifer eyed the trees and underbrush to their right, thinking she detected an overgrown dirt drive.

Mary Ellen snorted. "Sure they did. Old man Stevenson's daddy, Humphrey Stevenson, burned it plumb down in 1971."

"Kitchen fire?" Jennifer guessed.

"Nope. Around that time, Mr. Humphrey was terminal with cancer and was making up his will, but the kids squabbled so bad about who would get the house, which had been there since the early 1800s, that he decided none of them should have it. So he cleared around it and set fire to it. He even had whatever remained after the fire carted off. Now all that's left is that old field and second growth trees up front." Mary Ellen stopped walking and waited on their reaction.

Jennifer stared at her in shock. "Good heavens. How tragic!"

"It was a shameful loss of a beautiful old home," Stella agreed.

"And all those antiques, too," Mary Ellen added with indignation.

Inside, while Mary Ellen pulled bottles of Coke and Sprite out of her humming antique vending machine, Jennifer circulated with the dust motes through the crowded aisles. The shop's conglomeration of junk and value, tacky artsy and artisan, closed in around her. Plastic dolls clad in crocheted hoop skirts concealed rolls of toilet paper. Rhinestone pins winked from glass display cases next to Civil War daguerreotypes. '80s prom dresses poofed alongside Edwardian slips. But the sideboards, chairs, dressers and tables displaying all the clutter interested Jennifer most. Out-of-the-way antique stores often offered the bonus of cheap prices on good finds. She made mental notes for the future.

"This is very nice." Jennifer returned to where the women perched around the check-out register on a set of '50s bar stools. Mary Ellen pushed a basket of goodies toward her, and she selected a pack of peanuts. "Thank you, I'll have to pay you later. I left my purse up at the house."

Now that sounded strange, like she was some kind of local housewife. To complete the picture of the era the bar stools and comment evoked, she merely lacked bouffant hair, a sweater set, pearls and pumps.

Mary Ellen made a shooing gesture. "My treat. And my pleasure. I love to have company to pass the hours between customers." She chuckled loudly.

Jennifer grinned and swigged from the bottle. She'd forgotten how good Coke and peanuts were together. "Thank you, this is a nice break."

"How's it comin' up at the mobile home? You settlin' in?" Mary Ellen asked.

"Oh, no, not yet. Just cleaning. Next week I'll steam vac and Lysol the kitchen and bathroom. I won't move in until the first week of May."

"You need any help?" Stella crossed her booted ankles over the rung of the stool and managed to appear quite comfortable. When Jennifer started to shake her head, she asked, "Who wants to do all that all by themselves, especially when you're already workin' for the Johnsons *and* finishin' up classes? Two pair of hands make half the work." Stella's almond eyes twinkled at her.

"I'll come, too, if I'm free," Mary Ellen volunteered.

"Oh, no, really," Jennifer protested, but Stella retrieved a jeweled notepad from her large brown leather purse and jotted down her phone number. She ripped out the page and handed it to Jennifer.

"You just call me when you know you're coming."

"OK, thank you." Southern graciousness, she reminded herself. "You have some great pieces, Mary Ellen, and Amy Greene also mentioned you might be willing to help me find more when we're ready to furnish the house."

"Oh, my, yes, no 'might' about it. There's an auction runs monthly down at Union Point, where the railroad used to go south of here, you know. It's awesome. People come from all around." Mary Ellen lowered her husky voice and rested a soft hand on Jennifer's arm. "You wouldn't believe what comes out of these old family plantations in the country. Folks have to sell off as the old people pass, you know. Then there's a big flea market spring through fall in Greensboro where good finds sometimes turn up. And occasionally I drive to Augusta to an antiques warehouse. I can let you know when I'm going."

"I'd love that! Once we figure out how Michael wants to furnish the house, of course."

"Sure thing. We'll make a day of it. Say, you really should see Stella's place, too."

"Oh?" Jennifer raised her eyebrows at the stately black woman.

"She's been my best customer." Mary Ellen smirked. "She could put Amy Greene out of business if she turned her hand to interior decoratin'. Just don't tell Amy I said so."

"Oh, go on now." Stella waved her hand. "You know I got my time all taken up with them boys. But as for a visit, Jennifer, I'd love to have you any time!"

"Maybe I can take a break for that one day. You have children?" Jennifer asked.

"I sure do: Gabe, seventeen, and Jamal, fifteen."

"Both of them the pride of the OC basketball team," Mary Ellen said.

"That's great. Do you think they might be interested in helping with yard work this summer? Or do they have jobs already?"

"You mean at the Dunham place? Sure, I think they'd love that. Gabe works part-time up at the Chicken Express, but they'd both have time and are always lookin' for an extra buck."

"Yeah, they don't get enough of those when they're killin' and fryin' the chickens. Get it, 'buck, buck,' like 'bawk, bawk'?" Mary Ellen cried with an emphatic slap of her hand on the counter, causing both women to laugh.

"That would be wonderful! I'll do most of the landscaping myself, anyway, just need some strong backs and willing attitudes."

"Gabe and Jamal are good boys," Mary Ellen told her in all seriousness. "Respectful, reliable, and hard-working. They've done lawn maintenance for lots of the neighbors before, including me."

Jennifer nodded. She remembered to ask, "How about you, Mary Ellen? Do you have children?"

"I've got one daughter, but she's grown with two kids of her own."

"Oh, grandchildren! Do they live close by?"

"Sure do. Up in Crawford. I get to see them all the time. Sometimes I have to play grandma and watch them, so I just close up the store then." Mary Ellen sought her purse and whipped out a photograph for Jennifer to admire. "And you? Is there someone special in your life? You must be, what, twenty-four, twenty-five?"

"Twenty-four." Jennifer smiled. "And no. I dated a couple guys in college, but it was nothing serious."

"Well, I hate to tell you, young lady, but you probably won't find Mr. Right hiding under a bush in Hermon," Mary Ellen announced with another one of her belly laughs.

"What you mean? She's got the perfect candidate right over there at the big house," Stella said.

Mary Ellen leaned forward. "Who, Michael Johnson?"

"Of course Michael Johnson. You ever see such a good-lookin' man? Besides my Earl, of course."

Jennifer turned siren red. "That would hardly be professional," she murmured. "Besides, I'm sure I'm not his type."

"Now, how you figure that, honey?" Stella leaned in close to peer into Jennifer's face, like she was trying to see past the glasses and the hair.

"Really? I mean, look at me. I'm just not the sort of girl he'd notice." Unable to meet Stella's eyes, Jennifer brushed lint off her pants.

Stella patted Jennifer's knee. "Now don't you go sellin' yourself short. You're smart, pretty, talented and, best of all, right here. There are very few distractions around."

Jennifer shook her head. She couldn't remember the last time she'd been called pretty since being out of pony tails. People at the Baptist Church in Lumpkin had said she was a pretty little girl and they hoped she'd come back. Maybe the graphic art student who'd taken her to a couple of poetry readings at The Globe had complimented her, but that had probably been the effect of one too many beers. When, on the second date, he'd put his arm around her and started breathing in her ear about going back to his place, she'd wiggled away immediately … and permanently. Stella meant well, but Jennifer figured she was the type of kind, loving person who considered everyone beautiful in their own way. Her one correct observation was that being in the middle of nowhere provided Jennifer's sole asset in getting a guy's attention.

Mary Ellen relieved Jennifer's awkward moment by taking up the thread of conversation, a fine line of thought tracing between her thin brows. "You know, the only thing is, we don't know much about him, do we? I mean, we know who his people were, but all we know about him is, he came here from Atlanta and is restoring the property because his grandma left him money to do it."

"We know he and his father work in construction," Jennifer offered.

The shop owner refused to be satisfied. "Yeah, but he don't seem much like a construction worker, if you take my meanin', does he? Such fine manners and speech. He don't even sound Southern. Do you really think he intends to keep livin' here once he's done with the place?"

"He says so."

Mary Ellen rucked up her lips and tilted her head to one side. "Bet you fifty dollars he up and sells and goes back to Atlanta."

"He won't do that," Stella said, surprising Jennifer with her firm tone. It was almost like she knew something no one else did. Maybe she had the second sight some African American people were supposed to have. "He has a lot to learn. I dare say this project is going to change you both." She pinned Jennifer with her incisive dark gaze. "You won't be the same when you're done. And stay open, because you might both just be surprised about where you belong and who you belong *with*."

Several days later, Jennifer and Stella collected the light fixtures and hardware as Earl took them off the walls, doors and ceilings, placing them on the kitchen counters before immersion in a sink bath of soap and water. A can of paint thinner sat nearby.

"Stella?" Wearing rubber gloves, Jennifer lowered a sconce into the warm, sudsy water.

"Hmm?"

"I had to go by the tax assessor's office in Lexington this morning. I could print the U.S. Geological Survey map for the Register report from their online store, but I had to get some help for the local city and tax maps. The man in the assessor's office told me something crazy."

"Ha. He tell us all something crazy. Then he holds out his hand. It's his job."

Jennifer couldn't stifle a smile. "Right. Well, this was about the history of the place. I thought you might could verify."

"I sure will if I can."

"According to him, Silas Dunham, Levi's son who developed the plantation on Long Creek, became the first millionaire in Georgia."

"Seems to me I did hear that somewhere."

"Really?" Jennifer turned to her. "He said people talked about how Silas had trunks of gold in his bedroom, and when he needed to make a payment, or give his children some money, he just went and got it out. He also said when there was a run on the Bank of Athens, Silas Dunham bailed them out. He sent a whole wagonload of gold up to town."

"Is that so?" Stella laughed.

"The thing is, he mentioned as I paid for my maps, that people still think—"

"Stella?" Earl's voice wheezed from the foyer.

"Oh, my. 'Scuze me just one minute, honey. Comin', Earl!"

"I got this big fixture loose and need a hand."

"Well, don't fall off the ladder. I'm on my way!"

As Stella rushed into the next room, Jennifer chuckled and used a nonabrasive scouring pad on the sconce to rub away years of grime and careless paint drips.

She'd actually looked forward to coming today. The end of the school year swept everyone at the university along like a spring zephyr, but here, time somehow coalesced. Her stress over classes eased, and the company of Earl and Stella brought comfort in a way she'd never known before. She'd never seen a couple who'd been married that long treat each other with such obvious affection. And in their company, she didn't feel like she had to act especially grown up, wise or professional. She could just be herself. Most amazing of all, she didn't feel the need to guard herself. She'd learned most people pretended a desire to be real friends just long enough to take what they could from you, then disappeared. She could never see Stella or Earl being that cruel.

Stella huffed into the kitchen with her arms stretched around a beautiful, late 1800s, elongated globe.

"Oh, do you need help with that?"

"No, I got it, sweet girl."

"Here, let me clear a spot. We don't want it to roll off, so I should probably go ahead and clean it. Then we can put it on a towel in the laundry room."

"Laundry room to-be, yes." Stella eased her burden into the sink.

"Yes, Michael has a lot of kitchen and laundry renovations ahead. Maybe he can get to them once we finish all this." Jennifer smiled and started washing the etched glass like she imagined she'd bathe a baby.

"You were saying?" Stella prompted.

"Oh, yes, the tax clerk told me that some folks in these parts believed Silas hid or buried his gold somewhere, that it was never deposited into any bank."

Stella shook her head. "Folks always do like a good story. If one about a ghost isn't to be had, there's usually one about buried treasure. I'd say most likely he used it up on his children. I know that's what happens in *my* house."

"Probably so. Well, he said we shouldn't be alarmed if we ever see people with metal detectors here or on Long Creek ... not so much here now as the house is occupied, though, surely."

"I wouldn't think so."

"So you never heard about buried gold?"

"I don't believe a word of it, Miss Jennifer." Stella shook her head, covered with a red scarf for cleaning.

"And there are no ghost stories, either? Horace told Michael about a haunting related to the cabin, the one on the other property, Levi's cabin."

"Well, now, I did maybe hear somethin' about that."

Jennifer's scrubbing stopped, and her glasses slid down her nose as she gasped, "*What?*"

Stella burst into a musical laugh nothing like Mary Ellen's chortles. She smiled chidingly and gave a gentle poke to the dark glasses Jennifer wore, setting them back in place. Then she reached for the large light fixture to transfer to the rinse side of the sink.

"Wait, you've got to tell me!"

"Why, such nonsense going in your report?"

"No, but ... do tell. It does help ... *frame* the whole thing."

"Sure it does." Stella splashed some cool water over the glass she held. "It was probably nothing. Some old tales of how Silas' mama got tetched in the head after she had an encounter with some Creek Indians. They say Levi and his wife's first child, a girl, lived in that cabin. She had a reputation as a midwife and a healer. They say she wasn't like the others."

"The other what?"

"The other children. Grab that rag and you dry while I hold this, see."

"Yes. OK. Go on."

"Ain't no more to tell, 'cept I heard the daughter lived to an old age. I think she might have been an old maid, so you can imagine how local children back in those days of superstition might've been afraid on account of her."

Jennifer patted the cloth outside and inside the lighting fixture, thinking.

"Well, go on, hurry up. I've got to get home in time to take a casserole to a lady in the church who just came home from the hospital."

Jennifer actually liked the motherly way Stella bossed her that had nothing at all to do with the employer-employee relationship and everything to do with a lifetime of being the woman in charge. Stella could get away with it. She followed the older woman to the empty laundry room and arranged a thick towel on the floor in the back corner where the fixture could wait for Earl.

"Where can I find out more?"

"Maybe in the local library. They have a genealogy section."

"Won't you tell me more, Stella?"

"I just told you all I know." Stella swatted her on the arm with her rubber gloves.

"About the whole family. If you know that much about people from 1800, how much do you know about Michael's great-grandparents?"

A sharp glance met her curious gaze. "A sight more than he do, that's for sure."

"Let's take a break and have a cup of tea. I'll run get my notebook, and I can interview you. This cleaning can wait for an hour."

"Honey, the things I know have no place in your historical report, at least most of them. Shame on you for trying to lure me from my cleanin'. Come on back in here. No, the stories can wait. They'll come out when it's time, just like the layers of everything else in this house."

CHAPTER FIVE

Jennifer peeked out the door, unsettled. Some sort of lab-boxer mix rooted through the contents of the trash bag she'd set out on the back porch the night before, including what must be a still-fragrant Chicken Express box.

She'd spent her first night in the double-wide. Yesterday, as the roofing crew first appeared at Dunham House, she Tided and Lysoled in a successful and well-timed trailer attack, popping over to the adjacent yard as needed. Things had gone well until Stella came by to invite Jennifer, Michael and James to church the next day, reminding them it was Easter Sunday. Jennifer stammered excuses about her week of classes causing her to need the full weekend to clean and prepare her renovation plan. That led to questions about who might be missing her back home, and in an effort to not offend Stella, she revealed too much about herself. The whole conversation took place in front of Michael and James.

Thanks to repeated dreams of the roof above her being ripped off with a horrible screeching sound and the rain pouring down on her, the previous day's dark mood lingered into this early April morning. The old feelings of self-loathing crowded to the surface, and the mutt would not get off her porch. She didn't even have enough authority to control a dog. How could she hope for success in this or any restoration job?

"Shoo!" Holding open the storm door, she waved her arm. The dog backed up to the top step and lowered its head. It wasn't a humble lowering. Its tail also went down, its limbs stiffened, and it maintained eye contact, alerting her to possible danger. "Go, go home!" When it didn't budge, Jennifer stomped out onto the deck. That sent it running. Jennifer cleaned up the mess and retied the trash bag in a tight knot.

She grabbed her rain jacket, pulled it on and raised the hood against the faint drizzle. Locking the back door, she started across the yard. Then she realized the dog followed her. She yelled at him to go home again, presumably to the bungalow of the old man next door. If only the canine shared the reclusive tendencies of its master. He ran back a few steps but then started following her again. Creeping, more like. She grabbed a fallen branch and charged, yelling. Finally, he scurried across the property line. As Jennifer scanned the house next door for signs of habitation, a curtain in a rear window stirred. Well, thanks a lot. Instead of coming to call his dog in, the man probably sat there and steamed she hadn't set up a picnic on her deck.

Chosen today because the yard was a muddy mess, Jennifer's boots created cookie-cutter imprints in the soft ground. Michael wanted most of the roofing crew's work done and sprinklers installed before sodding the front and side yards, and seeding the back. Yesterday, a truck towing a trailer with spaces underneath delivered twenty- to twenty-five-foot long, three-foot wide coils of metal roofing, freshly painted at a Texas factory and shipped via Danielsville. The process of removing the early 1900s roofing initiated in sections, replaced on the high pitch areas with double-single-double Georgia rib pattern and on the porch and bay window by standing seam style for better run-off. V-strips created rain beds between the gables, while folded ridge covers crowned the top.

The faded metal created a startling contrast against the new metal even in today's overcast weather. Even more surprising had been how vulnerable the rough cut wood beneath the old roof had looked, making it easy to picture the house's appearance with its original wood shakes. No wonder leaks here and there plagued Michael and James. No doubt about it, yesterday's metal was vastly more effective than the shakes, and today's metal than yesterday's. Adequate protection for a structure was always step one.

Come to think of it, humans needed protection, too. When they were vulnerable to the elements, emotionally as well as physically speaking, they started to fall apart. Some people put stock in material things, others in family, and still others in religion. Jennifer had concluded from life that the only thing she could count on was herself. Rather like the roof renovation, as an adult, she'd gone to great lengths to build emotional and physical barricades to prevent a recurrence of those times she'd been unable to protect herself as a child. To stop the leaks, so to speak.

Hopefully by tomorrow the rain would let off and the workers could return. The buzz of electric screwdrivers, the calls of the five-man crew, and the rattle of saws on metal would provide the reassuring sounds of a project running on schedule. The house and apothecary both would be roofed in no less than several weeks. For now, the place seemed deserted, although Jennifer noticed Michael's F150 in the driveway. She didn't need to disturb him to check out the storage shed.

As she unlocked the door, she noted the overhang on the building would give her more space to create temporary discard piles without the items getting wet. The shed was electrified just as Michael had said. However, the single dim bulb in the center of the crowded space provided less than ideal lighting. She glanced around for rodents, then selected a broken child's stool near the entrance to prop open the spring-loaded door, allowing more light while blocking most of the damp, cool wind.

Jennifer drew in a musty breath, surveying boxes and old furniture. Most of it indeed appeared to be from Ettie Mae's era, roughly 1950s to 1960s. Since Ettie Mae was not a close relation to Michael and had no direct descendants of her own, Jennifer had his permission to toss any personal memorabilia, of which there appeared to be a lot. Garden party and Junior League programs, etiquette and cooking books, broken china, pillbox hats and stained gloves, and ribbons for cooking and gardening competitions provided silent proof of a Southern lady's life.

Anything Ettie Mae disliked or deemed flawed had found its way into the shed, including a Formica-topped table with matching, red vinyl chairs, one of which was ripped. A whatnot from the late 1800s might have served post-renovation if they were going for Victorian, but Jennifer guessed Michael would find it fusty, if not downright ridiculous, especially stacked with nick-nacks according to its intended use. One American Empire table, disassembled and scratched, held promise. Its heavy mahogany silhouette would look grand in the embrace of the bay window, or even in the middle of the parlor flanked by chairs. A shadow appeared in the doorway as she wrestled with the top of the table, scaring her.

Michael stood there in work-out pants and a T-shirt, a fitted Nike jacket outlining his fit physique. He held keys in one hand. "I thought I'd see if you were already out here before I left."

"Hi. Yep, I got an early start. Looks like you're not going to church, either."

"No, I thought I'd go by the Y in Athens, hit the gym, and swim a few laps before stopping at Lowe's. I've measured for new counters and want to look at appliances and hardware. Do you need help with that?"

"Oh. No, thanks." Jennifer wheeled the table top into her "keep" stack and brushed off her hands. "Isn't it wonderful? I thought we could use it inside later."

Michael inspected the wood. "It's great. Should be easy to repair."

She smiled, pleased by his approval. "I'm separating things into stacks—throw away, hold for Mary Ellen to see if she'd like to buy for her shop, and keep for possible future use." Jennifer indicated the areas as she talked.

Michael nodded. "Sounds good. I won't argue with making a buck instead of spending one for a change."

"There are some good things here, just not the right time period or style. So ... you swim?"

"Yeah. Since middle school. I just joined the Y in East Athens so I can use their indoor pool."

"Seeing as how there's not one around here," Jennifer joked. "Although you might find a pond come summertime."

To her surprise, Michael gave a relaxed laugh. "Right. Dad owns a house on Lake Oconee. Even the water there gets a little murky for me sometimes. I'm not much of an open water swimmer."

"Well, enjoy yourself. It's good to get a break from all the work here."

"You're not getting much of a break. Seems you're here every day you're not in class."

"Isn't that what you expect?" Jennifer had hoped her commitment would impress him.

"I expect you can take Sunday off. Especially Easter Sunday."

"You didn't."

Michael lifted a shoulder. "I live in the middle of this mess. It's hard to ignore unless I leave. Frankly, I want out of that camper."

"I guess you do." Jennifer pushed a strand of hair out of her face, suppressing irritation at the humidity and stuffiness in the shed. "You

64

didn't want to go to Hermon Baptist today with your dad and Mary Ellen's family, though?"

"Nah." Michael shook his head. "I'm not much for that these days."

"Me, neither."

"I kind of picked that up yesterday."

"I used to go." Jennifer didn't know why her defenses were rising. It wasn't like he had criticized her. In fact, he shared her view. But something compassionate about his glance now reminded her of the way the church crowd used to look at her in her hand-me-down, ruffled dresses that she'd hated. "We went to the Baptist church in Lumpkin, where I grew up. But my stepfather wasn't a church-goer." She didn't mention that dropping out of the church had almost come as a relief. Pretending to be something she was not had been exhausting.

"You said yesterday your mom had been married a couple of times, and she started to feel like the people at the church looked down on her."

"Yeah. Three times, actually." Jennifer ticked off the disasters on her fingers. "My brother Rab's—that's short for Rabon—father was stationed at Fort Benning. They had a whirlwind romance just out of high school, and Mom got pregnant with Rab. They got married, but he was killed in action, so Rab has the distinction of having an honorable man for a father, whereas I ..." Why was she wandering on, adding insult to injury from the day before?

"You what?" Michael prompted gently.

Jennifer turned back to an open box and started unwrapping figurines. A mouse nest cradled in the bottom appeared. She needed gloves. Shuddering, she added, "I got the truck driver who abandoned us."

"Oh, God. I'm sorry, Jennifer."

She shook her head. "Doesn't matter. It was a long time ago. Mom remarried when I was ten."

"The current father. The one who doesn't like church."

"Right."

"Did he like *you?*"

She felt like an arrow pierced her heart. Now why would he ask that? "Sure," she said, dead pan. "He liked me a lot."

"Did you like *him?*"

Jennifer glanced up. "More importantly, he and my brother like each other. They're birds of a feather, always under the hood of a car, planning some drag racing outing or going fishing. Roy owns a garage near Ft. Benning. Mom figured she wouldn't pick a guy who would leave her this time. My brother works for him now. Roy and Rab." She laughed and started unpacking another box to hide her face. "Sounds like a sideshow, doesn't it? They don't even notice when I'm gone. Have you been to Stewart County? There's nothing to go back to anyway." Oh, dear. Why was she was still trying to explain her lack of family cohesiveness?

Suddenly Jennifer realized she felt *guilty*, guilty for not being in church on Easter Sunday when Stella had invited her. And also a little mad at Stella for putting her in that position when otherwise she'd not have given spending her Sunday in this dreary shed a second thought.

"I understand," Michael said softly. "I don't have anything to go back to, either. So we're here for the same reason."

"Nothing in Atlanta?"

He shook his head. "Nothing in Atlanta. Hey, would you like me to bring you back lunch? It might be a little late, but better late than never, right?"

"Oh. Thanks, but no. I'll be fine. I stocked my pantry with some staples. I hope to finish up here this afternoon, and I have some homework waiting when I return to the apartment in town."

"Are you sure?"

Jennifer nodded and smiled. His thoughtfulness surprised her. "But thank you," she said again. "I might even be gone by the time you return."

"Dad won't be back for a while, either. The McWhorters invited him to lunch." Michael stubbed the toe of his tennis shoe against some loose siding on the shed. "Well, good luck."

"Thanks. I'm hoping to find some older things Ettie Mae stored, anything that will give me more history on the house and your family. If I don't find anything, I'd love to make a trip to the other storage shed your dad mentioned." Hopeful, she glanced at him.

Michael nodded, shifting his weight and looking up at the darkening sky. "Sure. I think it's going to rain again. I'd better be off. OK, see you later."

After he left, the silence thickened, making Jennifer aware of her aloneness whereas she hadn't been before. Usually it didn't bother her, but now she stifled the unreasonable wish that he could have stayed and gone through the shed's contents with her. How silly. He paid her so he didn't have to do every little thing himself. If only the privilege and adventure of discovering his own family history excited him. Fortune had given him an impressive legacy, whereas she would bury her own redneck roots as deep as a magma chamber if she could.

"What a mess," she said out loud to break the silence.

To her shock, she heard a reply. *Like the inside of you.*

Jennifer whipped her head around, although she knew no one had spoken out loud. No, it was more like someone had dropped the words straight inside her own brain. Spoken a certain way, the phrase could have implied criticism, but instead, a sense of compassion, of protection, wrapped Jennifer, as though someone caring hovered close. Deep, smooth and warm, the voice almost sounded like … like she had once imagined Jesus would sound, should his picture in her childhood Sunday school room come to life. Strange. Very strange. She shook her head to clear it.

Moving a battered Edwardian chest of drawers, Jennifer discovered what appeared to be a snake hole past the soft floorboards. Ugh. As much as she loved old buildings, she could list several positive qualities of modern metal storage buildings about now. Thankfully any occupant probably still hibernated.

Behind the chest she found a trunk from an earlier era, with green brass hinges flattened on decayed leather straps. After she forced the prongs and hinges, the box yielded its contents. "Oh, wow," she breathed.

A musty wedding ring quilt enwrapped a yellowed, intricate christening gown and bonnet, several hand-knit pieces of baby clothing and a pair of tiny, stiff Edwardian shoes with button hooks. Whose were these? Jennifer laid out each treasure with care, barely registering the fact that fat rain drops started to plunk on the metal roof.

Jennifer lifted out the quilt to find an old black family Bible. A photograph had been placed atop it, face down. She turned it over to reveal a framed sepia photograph of … Dunham House. She gasped and held it up to the light. The metal roof had been applied, but the overgrown boxwoods, closed shutters and clothing of the people indicated quite an early period. Perhaps 1905. A man with a full beard and a dapper suit stood at the foot of the porch steps, alone, but behind him, a woman on the top step perched amidst a group of small children. A black woman, though dressed quite nicely for the time. And the boy and two girls at her sides were also colored, but the smallest one in her lap, too small to be identified as boy or girl, looked … white.

Jennifer frowned over the unusual subject arrangement. The man had chosen to be in the portrait with the woman and children, yet he stood apart from them. Perhaps the black woman, a mammy, held the employer's child while her own children, playmates, joined them. But where was the mother, in that case? Deceased? And who were these people to Michael?

She nestled the picture atop the quilt, as awed by this discovery as if she had been unearthing her own family roots. With shaking hands, Jennifer opened the heavy leather cover and parted the front paper-thin pages of the Bible. Yes, true to custom, brown, spidery scrawl recorded a family tree.

The next moment, the shed door banged shut. Jennifer's head jerked up. Without windows, the single bulb provided her only light. Then that, too, went out. With a sickening feeling, her memory recreated the image of the switch … on the outside.

"Hey, I'm in here!" she yelled, clasping the big book to her chest while she stumbled forward. "Michael? James?"

No human sound answered her. Only the soft sighing of the wind, surely not strong enough to blow the door shut, along with the ever-increasing tattoo of raindrops. Her heart pounded, and she felt her way toward the door. "Hello? I'm in here!" Her voice came out high-pitched, indignant. And frightened. Finally her hand encountered the metal door knob and turned. *Locked.* Jennifer twisted and rattled the knob, pushing on the door with her shoulder, then beating on it. There was no use. She was locked in.

In complete darkness, without her cell phone, Jennifer had no idea what time her watch read or how long she had been in the shed.

After the door shut, she'd yelled for a while, until it became apparent that no one was coming to her rescue. Though Jennifer never heard thunder, it poured for a while, then settled into a steady rain.

Was it possible that when Michael had left he'd knocked the stool so that it no longer provided a wedge for the spring-loaded door, and then the wind or just time and pressure caused it to close on its own? Who would have wanted her locked in a shed, anyway? It was silly to think this was some sort of attack. She had no enemies. She'd just moved here!

Jennifer sat on the child's stool. It felt better to at least be near the door. There was no need to panic. Michael or James would return by at least mid-afternoon. Michael would probably come check on her. Or when she heard James pull in she'd yell so that he heard her before he went into the camper. Only what if he didn't hear her? And what if Michael just assumed she'd finished her work and returned to Athens? They'd see her car … only she'd pulled it so far to the other side of the double-wide it would not be visible from the house.

Fighting a sick feeling in her empty stomach, Jennifer forced herself to breathe slowly.

"Oh, my God, oh, my God."

But, no. Praying would accomplish nothing. A God she hadn't talked to since elementary school would have no interest in her pleas. If He hadn't helped her then, He certainly wouldn't now.

Michael and James might not discover her predicament until the first of the week. No, she'd told them that she would be busy with school until Wednesday, when she'd drive back out to oversee the roofing progress. That meant … she could spend not only the rest of today and tonight in this shed, but several nights. By the time they found her, she'd be like one of those wild-eyed, wild-haired humans deprived of companionship from birth. Jennifer let out a nervous giggle, struggling to apply her go-to defenses of humor and sarcasm in a difficult situation. *Feral*, that was the word. No, she wouldn't have the energy to be feral. She hadn't even brought a bottle of water. How long did one last without water? Tears eased out of her eyes, and she brushed them away. Now she was just wasting what little moisture her body had, and being dramatic to boot, but the dark confines of the shed triggered her fears of entrapment.

She'd spent the night in a strange place before, of course. Her initial overnight at the Lockwood Plantation merited an almost-blue bottom, courtesy of her mother. That outing defined creepy in a whole other way, but she took along her sleeping bag, food and water, and she'd had the option to leave any time she'd wanted to. After the fierce punishment she received, whenever she absolutely had to get away after that, she took care to lock her door and sneak back in by daylight through her window. The safety her truancy provided proved well worth the risk of discovery. And after a while, her mother no longer checked on her. Kelly's assumption that Jennifer had fallen in with the wrong crowd or crashed at a friend's house without permission offered easy excuses for perceived rebellion.

This was different. The abandoned antebellum mansion had been a refuge. This shed was a prison.

Minutes and hours ticked by, and as the rain abated, unwanted memories played themselves out in the blackness in front of her eyes. She covered her head. Was that a rustling noise? It sounded like things moving in the dark. She remembered the snake hole and bit her lip. Yes, the darkness was alive. It always was.

Distantly, what could be the rumble of an engine came to her sharpened hearing. Jennifer jumped up and started beating on the metal door. "Michael! James! Michael! Help! Help me, I'm in here!" She hollered until her throat hurt and her ears rang.

Was that the sound of a key in the lock?

The door popped open, and Jennifer fell into Michael's arms.

"Good heavens, what happened? How did you get locked in?" he asked, enfolding her in an embrace. He smelled so good, like manly bar soap and aftershave, not like cheap cologne and sweat. And he was solid and real, really there.

She did something terrible and humiliating. She started to cry.

Michael smoothed Jennifer's tangled hair back from her face and tried to wipe her tears away. He repeated his questions, saying he was so sorry this had happened to her.

"I don't know," she hiccupped. "I was back in the corner going through an old trunk when the door banged shut and the light went off. By the time I got over to it, it was locked. I yelled, but no one answered."

"Could it have blown shut?"

"I thought of that. Maybe if the stool wasn't wedged in well."

"But it wouldn't have locked."

Their eyes met as they both absorbed the unspeakable truth that if anyone had locked her in, they had done so knowing she was inside, since they would have heard her immediate cries for help. Michael tugged on her glasses. She removed them and wiped her face on the tail of her jacket. After he handed them back, he started searching the ground.

Jennifer sniffled and ducked her head as a cold, stray raindrop baptized her right in the part of her hair. "What are you doing, looking for prints?"

"Yeah." He bent down, shifting around to examine various sections of the ground. A jumble of footprints did exist, but puddles of water now filled the indentations. "But it must have rained here while I was gone."

"It did." She hung her head and hugged herself to recover her calm.

Michael attempted to trace his own shoe prints back to the house and her boot prints back toward the mobile home. A moment later he gave up and returned to her, shaking his head. "If someone did this, that rain couldn't have been timed better. With all the work that's gone on around here, there are too many partial prints heading in every direction, even back into the woods where Dad's been clearing. But it's too wet to distinguish the old from the new. Any idea who would have done such a thing?"

She shook her head. "I don't know. I did think of that old man next door to the mobile home, the hermit."

"Calvin Woods?"

"Is that his name?"

Michael nodded. "Yes, that's what Dad said. Why would he lock you in?"

"Well, his dog was on my porch this morning, in the trash. It wouldn't leave. Even when I started to walk over here, it followed me. I chased it off with a big stick. I think the man was watching."

Michael's face screwed up in skepticism. "And it made him mad enough to lock you in a shed where if I hadn't heard you yelling you could have been stuck for …"

"Days." She'd just dried the tears, but the memory of her fear and consideration of the worst case scenario caused the shameful, hot liquid to gush forth again. She firmed her chin, willing herself to stop.

"You're OK. It's OK. That didn't happen." Michael patted her arm, uncomfortable now. "Next time you're anywhere alone, you should really take your cell phone."

"Yes, you're right. I will, although I didn't think I was in any danger in your shed."

"Did anyone else know you'd be working in here today?"

Swiping her cheek, Jennifer thought a moment. "Um, some friends at school, and I probably mentioned it to Professor Shelley. And I went over yesterday to make sure Mary Ellen would be interested in looking at any finds. Amy Greene was in visiting her and said if Mary Ellen wasn't, she sure would be. I can't imagine any of those women would have it out for me."

"Me, either. Well, listen, you've had a real scare. Why don't you come into the house and let me fix you a cup of hot chocolate? Dad will be home soon, and we can all talk about this. OK?"

That sounded good, too good, and he was being nice, too nice. Jennifer put her glasses back on and glanced toward the mobile home. She ought to take herself there, and right away, before a vulnerable situation caused her to lower her guard even more to this man who would only ever be her employer. "Thanks, but I'm all right. There's really nothing more to talk about. I'm sure it was just an accident. Old doors can have crazy locks on them. I shouldn't have gotten so upset."

"I don't—"

"Besides, I have a lot of work waiting on me at my apartment, and a lot of time was wasted this afternoon. At least I'm mostly done here. Oh!" Jennifer turned toward the shed, then held out a hand. "If you'll hold the door, there's something I should show you."

"Of course." Michael stood in the frame as she picked her way back to the corner of the room, returning with the quilt and baby items. He managed a look of polite bemusement. But when she placed them back in the old chest and returned with the Bible and photograph, his eyebrows raised. She rested the heavy book in his open hands and turned to the family tree.

"I didn't have time to decipher it before I got shut in the dark," Jennifer told him, "but I think this may be your family. See, it starts with Levi Dunham, 1763-1837. It looks like he married a woman named Verity Miller. And here are their children, Selah, Comfort, *Silas*. What amazing Colonial names. Wish I had time to study this. What a valuable resource."

"Well, take it. You can look it over at your place." Michael held the Bible out to her.

She pushed it back. "No way! Do you have any idea how many people would love to have a family Bible with their genealogy, even if it appears to be a late 1800s edition someone copied the family tree into from an earlier Bible? This is yours and ought to stay in your house."

"Jennifer, in case you hadn't noticed, my house is bare, filthy and a construction zone. It would be safer with you."

She bit her lip, resisting temptation. "It isn't mine." *Even though I wish it were.* "Find a place for it in the camper, even if it's crowded. It ought not to be exposed to the damp one minute longer. Look at how the cover's finish is flaking off."

"OK. But you can have a good look at it next week."

"Agreed." And she'd think about it until then. Even now she noticed something intriguing, how the last name in the book, Hampton Dunham, born in 1861, had no marriage or children recorded. The line appeared to end with him, yet Jennifer found that odd. She laid the photograph she'd been clutching on top of the Bible. "And look at this."

"It's the house. You have an early photograph."

"I do indeed. But I'm confused by the people in it."

"Yes. I see what you mean. It looks like parts of two families put together."

Jennifer shook her head. She knew better than anyone that a house, or a family, was not always as it appeared on the outside. "Why don't you ask Stella to look at these? She knows more than she lets on. I think she just doesn't want to seem nosy, but I hear her folks have been in this area forever. She'll have some answers for you."

"Someone stole the mantel!"

Jennifer's screech rose above the grinding whir of electric screwdrivers on the roof, bouncing down the empty hallway to the rear of the house. As she stared in horror at the violated front bedroom fireplace, all embarrassment over the prospect of seeing Michael in the wake of her tearful meltdown fled. She ran to the parlor, where she faced another lipless maw of gaping, blackened bricks. She covered her heart with her hand. "Michael? James? Something terrible has happened!"

"What?" James met her in the dining room. "What's happened, Jennifer?"

Thank goodness the office and dining room retained their 1840s mantels. She gasped, "The mantels in the front two rooms are missing!"

As James frowned, Michael emerged from the laundry with a hammer in hand, tool belt slung over his hips. "No need to get worked up. I took them over to Mary Ellen's this morning."

"You did *what?*"

"Well, it's not like I stacked them in the trash heap, torched it and did a dance around the bonfire. They were too frou-frou for this house. We decided we were going for the earlier period, didn't we? Mary Ellen said she'll have buyers with no trouble, and she can find some earlier mantels more like these." Michael tipped the hammer toward the dining room surround.

"But—I made clear in my report …" Jennifer paused for breath. She was having trouble forming words. "You did *read* the report, didn't you?"

James cleared his throat and shifted his weight. "I, uh, did mention to Michael that I thought you'd like to keep what's in the house intact."

Jennifer stared from father to son, then threw up her hands in a gesture of defeat. "*One* of you read the report."

"I know what I need to know." Like a gunslinger after firing off a fancy round, Michael slid his hammer into the belt riding low on his slim hips. "And I know you're making much too big a deal over something trivial."

Jennifer's eyes bored like lasers straight through her glasses and into Michael. "If it's trivial, you won't care if I go over to the antique store and retrieve them, if it isn't already too late." She didn't pause for his response. One didn't discard such important parts of the house as though they had no value. He'd agreed to her expert plan, now he needed to trust her expertise. She heard an animated discussion break out between the two men as she marched down the hallway and out the front door.

Mary Ellen saw her coming before the bell on the glass door jangled. Her eyes popped open wide as she hopped off her stool behind the cash register. "I tried to tell him he oughta check with you first," she explained, placating hand extended as though she were attempting to deter a charging steer. "But he said it was his house and his call. What could I do?"

"Do you still have them?" She tried to calm her breathing.

Mary Ellen tipped her head. "They're in the back."

Jennifer sagged in relief. "Oh, thank goodness. We'll take them right back. I'm sorry, Mary Ellen, for the confusion and inconvenience. How much do we owe you?"

"Nothing. I hadn't made payment yet. I knew I'd need to discuss their value with you first. But what about what Michael said?"

"Michael signed an agreement which apparently he didn't read. If he had he would have known that for preservation purposes nothing was to be removed from the house unless I agreed it was beyond saving."

"But, Jennifer—"

Jennifer put her hands on her hips. "Mary Ellen, please just take me to the mantels. I'll deal with Michael."

Mary Ellen took an uneasy breath that said she wouldn't want to be in Jennifer's position. "Very well." She led the way into her storeroom, and with the air of a Roman convict taking up a cross, shouldered the heavy mantel surround. Then she trailed Jennifer, with the other mantel, to a rear door. As she opened it, something caught Jennifer's eye. The ability to focus had returned with the realization that the fireplaces could be saved.

"That painting, the one of the town." Jennifer gestured with her head to a gold-framed piece of art. "It's quite good. Why is it back here?"

"Why, Stella just brought it over. I have to price it before I put it out."

Jennifer examined the painting. "She wants to get rid of it?"

"She wants to sell it."

"Stella painted this?" Jennifer gasped.

"She did indeed. And there's more where it came from. We thought we'd see if there is any interest."

"*I'd* say there will be. It's excellent. She's a lot more than a wall painter, that's for sure." The oil-on-canvas scene, which captured the remains of Hermon in evening light, imbuing the old brick and glass of the buildings with a rustic charm, held Jennifer's gaze prisoner. The picture created the nostalgic, lost-in-time aura she'd experienced upon her arrival, and did so with far more skill than most of the art she'd admired at showings at the university and downtown galleries.

Jennifer's momentary distraction dissipated as they approached Dunham House. "I can come back for that," she offered as Mary Ellen rested, panting under the dogwood tree.

"No. It's all right. Girl, you must be stronger than you look."

I'd say, thought Jennifer, *or I would have broken a long time ago.* However, she knew determination provided her strength in this situation. She couldn't set a precedent this early on of Michael veering from the plan any time he took a hare-brained notion. She must be in charge of this project, or there was no reason for her to remain.

As she struggled up the front steps with the mantel, she looked up to see Michael lean on the door frame and cross his arms, a scowl darkening his features. His father came up behind him, and, seeing the women, hurried out to assist them. Since the younger man didn't budge, a faceoff occurred on the porch.

"OK," Mary Ellen puffed. "Y'all let me know what you decide. I've got to get back to the shop." So saying, she took off walking so fast that her white, capri-clad bottom resembled that of a cotton-tailed rabbit.

Michael didn't spare her a glance. "I appreciate the workmanship on the mantels, but I don't like them. They're elaborate and sissified, nothing a real man would have in his home. Let's get it straight right now that I have no intention of living in a dollhouse."

Jennifer braced one of the carved surrounds with her hand. "They're beautiful and original, and the report I submitted called for everything that was physically part of the home to remain. Michael,

I don't mean to be stubborn, but the very incongruity of the home is what lends it uniqueness. Everything does not have to look exactly the same to have worth."

"I think she has a point, Michael," James put in, his voice low.

"Just because the mantels are Victorian-looking doesn't mean we have to furnish the rooms that way," Jennifer continued. "I understand your concerns and will work with you to achieve the look you want when that time comes, if you'll listen to me now. These mantels are part of the historic renovation of the house. You should no more rip them out than you'd rip this millwork off the porch. Please don't throw them out just because they're different or you think they don't reflect you."

Something happened as she spoke. Michael studied her with interest and some amount of surprise. He uncrossed his arms and straightened, coming over to stand a few inches from her, close enough that she could smell his aftershave. "Fine," he said, and his breath whipped across her face as he stared into her eyes. "But I'll hold you to it."

Not to be one unnerved by challenge, Jennifer struggled to understand her flustered response. Then she realized that, for the first time, she'd sensed something from him besides aloof acceptance of her presence as a contractor. For the first time she felt like he'd looked at her not just as a person, but as a woman.

CHAPTER SIX

The last Friday in April, Stella and Mary Ellen both greeted Jennifer when she pulled in at the double-wide with her first load of personal belongings. They worked until ten p.m. carrying boxes, lining shelves, unpacking and decorating. Michael and James dropped by to deliver Subway sandwiches and to promise their help and the loan of the F150 for the furniture she intended to bring back on her next trip. When Stella ascertained Jennifer planned to stay the weekend in Hermon, finishing measurements and photographs of the house for her report and appropriating the country peace and quiet to study for finals, she made Jennifer promise to come for tea at three the next afternoon.

"You'll need a study break, and some fortification. I'll make my cranberry oatmeal cookies. Besides, Earl will be workin', so I'll have time for a visit."

Jennifer knew Earl had already sanded down the old plaster at Dunham House and repaired cracks and chips in the walls. He'd soon be ready to apply the first coat of joint compound. But tea she did not know about. What did one wear to tea? And as comfortable as she felt with Stella while working, would Stella find Jennifer's tea manners lacking?

On Saturday, she paid her overdue visit at Stella's house. When Jennifer walked up the entrance path to the Gothic Revival cottage complete with tulips blooming in well-cultivated beds, porch furniture with floral cushions and coordinating pillows and lace curtains at the windows, she knew Stella's sense of style extended beyond her personal appearance. And Jennifer wished she'd changed into something better than her solid red T-shirt, khaki capris and sandals. Maybe a sundress and hat.

It didn't matter. Stella knew she was working today. More importantly, Stella wanted her around, not just for work, but for a personal visit. A sweet strain of warmth and happiness played like a calming tune over her nerves as she rang the doorbell. She adjusted the satchel strap on her shoulder, evidence that she brought along the job, nevertheless. Michael's silly mantel fiasco and the demands of upcoming graduation had thrown her off, but she'd learned Michael had not asked Stella about the Bible and the photograph, and she fully intended to rectify his lapse today.

A very tall teenager with Earl's darker complexion opened the door. He held a wiggling Pomeranian under one lanky arm. When Jennifer introduced herself, the boy's free hand jutted out in her direction. "Hi, I'm Jamal."

"Nice to meet you, Jamal. You're ... fifteen?"

A bright grin lit up his face. "That's right. Hey, come on in. Mom's in the kitchen."

Jennifer followed as far as the living room, where she stalled like she'd just laid eyes on Starbuck's new fall menu for the first time, looking around with wide eyes. "Oh, my."

"Yeah, Mom said you loved antiques, that you're going to be redoing and decorating the old Dunham House. She also said you might need some help with yard work?"

Jennifer struggled to focus her attention on him. What appeared to be an 1860 Steinway piano squatted beneath a fully dressed Lambrequin window, the kind where a straight curtain fell from a stamped brass cornice board. A lace shawl and fresh flowers in an Italian porcelain swan, the type of souvenir Victorian people used to bring home from the Grand Tour, topped the instrument. "Uh, yes. Some brush needs cleared at the back of the lot right away. And soon, we'll have mowing, planting and pine straw to throw out. I can pay ten dollars an hour. We could put you to work any evening you're free or next weekend. Sound all right?"

"Yeah! I mean, yes, ma'am. I'd love that. I can ride my bike over, and when Gabe is free, he can drive me and come, too. That is, if it's OK."

"It would be great, thank you for asking!"

"Yoo-hoo, come on back, y'all. I'm ready to pour the tea!" came Stella's sing-song voice from the rear of the house.

"I can write down my number in the kitchen." Jamal dumped the dog on the ground, and after a preliminary sniff at Jennifer's shoe, it scrambled off toward its mama with toenails tapping.

"Uh, Jamal, forgive me for asking, but do you really kick back and relax on all those antiques?" Jennifer stared at the size of the boy's Nikes, envisioning their potential damage.

He laughed. "No, ma'am. That's mama's fancy room. She calls it her parlor. She likes to read or paint in there—when she puts down a drop cloth, that is. Luckily, we menfolk have all *this* to hang out in." He spread his arms to indicate a den with a fireplace, wide screen TV and leather sofa arranged adjacent to the eat-in kitchen.

Jennifer nodded. "I'm glad for you," she said, although she hoped Stella used the parlor for tea, too. She'd managed to tear her eyes away from the furnishings and paintings in there, but she longed to examine them at a much closer range.

A loose floral blouse and bright slacks draped Stella's lithe figure, while straight hair turned up on the tips behind sparkly earrings. She hugged Jennifer and led her to a display of tea boxes on the counter of a renovated kitchen. "Pick what you want and tell me if you prefer lemon, sugar, Splenda, or cream. Or all of the above!" She laughed, then her face transformed into a threatening cloud as she swatted Jamal's hand, intercepting the boy's attempt to pilfer not one but two cookies steaming on a plate on the oven.

"Aw, Mama. They're just little."

"Go on. Take *one* and leave me and Miss Jennifer to our talk."

"Can I watch TV in here?" he asked as he recorded his phone number on a sticky note and handed it to Jennifer.

Stella frowned. "If you keep it down low, baby."

"Thanks, Jamal." Jennifer held up a box of vanilla rooibos. "Splenda and cream, please."

"Ooh, this will go great with my cookies. Get you some," Stella said, placing the tea bag in an Old Roses china cup and reaching for the tea kettle whistling on the burner.

With tentative gestures, Jennifer served herself on a china plate, taking a cookie and adding a spoonful of diced fruit presented in a cut glass bowl.

"Stella, I'll be honest. I've never been invited to tea before. I'm afraid I don't know quite what to do."

"Drink it, silly girl. This isn't a proper tea, anyway. There's nothing more fun that goin' to a real tea room and eatin' clotted cream and scones and mini-sandwiches. We'll have to do that some time."

"For real?" The picture that evoked was so foreign to Jennifer's upbringing that it struck terror into her heart.

"Honey." Stella fixed her with a firm look. "For a girl who loves antiques and old houses, it's a crime you haven't been to a tea room."

"I don't think there were any around in Stewart County. Although there was a nice old hotel. I went in there once or twice, for parties for Westville staff."

"Westville?" Stella doctored her own tea, a ginger peach green variety, and listened as Jennifer described her teenage job. Then she said, "Let's go into the parlor. Jamal's making too much noise." She nodded toward her son. Only his head was visible, silent and reposed on the arm of the sofa. A baseball game emitted barely audible babble and applause. But Jennifer sure didn't argue. She allowed her hostess to lead the way, the Pomeranian snuffing at her heels.

Stella resumed the thread of conversation, turning to comment over her shoulder, "Westville sounds wonderful. I guess that's what got you started in preservation??

"Yes, that and the old plantation that was near my home. It was an antebellum mansion still in fairly good repair, probably caught up in some family squabble over a will or something. I used to sneak out and go there. I'd dream of buying the place and fixing it up when I grew up."

"Why didn't you?" Stella settled on a rosewood sofa with peach silk damask cushions. She spread a throw next to her, and the dog jumped up. She petted its silky head.

"Wow, you have him trained! What's his name?"

"Truffle. He knows my house rules, just like the other boys." She winked, then circled back to her inquiry. "Speaking of which, your family must want you to be closer to home."

Hadn't they already covered this topic Easter weekend? Jennifer shrugged. "That isn't realistic. All the houses in Westville are already restored, and there isn't much demand for experts to renovate those remaining in the surrounding area. It's very rural. You really have to go to bigger cities for work in my profession. Excuse me, but I have to ask, is that a John Henry Belter you're sitting on?"

"Well, it sure is. Mary Ellen found it for me in an estate sale not far from here. We located some cheaper reproduction fabric since reupholstering was necessary, but I think it turned out real nice."

"I'd say." Jennifer gaped. Belter's steam press curved single sheets of wood into chair backs, propelling him to prominence as the premier American furniture maker in the 1840s and '50s. His invention gave him an edge over competitors, who did their best to copy his designs, but with one or two seams and far less durability. A single chair bearing his mark could run upwards of $20,000. To find a sofa by the artisan in this woman's cottage on a side street in Hermon was the last thing Jennifer had expected.

Stella waved her hand. "Don't worry. I didn't pay near what you're thinking. The folks who sold it had no idea what it was worth. And Mary Ellen didn't fill them in." Her eyes twinkled. "Earl gave it to me for my twentieth anniversary present."

"That's a good present. What made *you* love antiques, Stella?"

"I guess I've just always had that artist's eye for anything beautiful and well-made."

"The eye." Covering her smirk at the further irony of Barb's phrase finding expression in Hermon, in Stella, Jennifer turned her attention to her refreshments. Feeling transported to another dimension of delight, Jennifer sipped her tea and bit into the moist cookie tasting of cinnamon and tangy cranberry. "Mmm. I can't imagine any tea room to be better than this."

"Oh, hush. It's my mama's recipe, anyway. But ... thank you. I'm glad you're enjoyin' it."

As she chewed, Jennifer's eye roved to various landscape paintings on the light green walls, similar to the style of the print she'd seen in Mary Ellen's storeroom. "Stella, did you do all those paintings?"

The older woman seemed surprised. "What makes you ask?"

"I have to confess, I saw the one you did of the town at the antique store." Jennifer rested her tea cup on the coffee table and rose to admire a depiction of overgrown railroad tracks disappearing into an autumn sunset. "They are remarkable. Did you go to art school?"

Stella smiled. "A long time ago. UGA."

"Really? And you never pursued your art?"

"I pursued being a mother. The art came out of me when it had to, like any of the gifts God graces us with. For a while, I taught lessons. I loved it. But then I just got busy with the boys and helping Earl with paint jobs. Those paid the bills. Most folks don't have any hankering for—or money for—fancy art."

"I think you're wrong. If not around here, your paintings would sell like hot cakes in Athens, Augusta, Madison, Greensboro … all the touristy historic towns around the Piedmont."

Stella chucked. "Well, maybe someday. We'll see if anyone takes a liking to it first."

A brainstorm hit Jennifer. She whirled around, unable to contain her excitement. "It's a waste to have you just paint plain walls. If Michael approves, would you consider doing something special at his house? I could see some stenciling, Gothic Revival style—or even a mural—something in the Ohio or Hudson River Valley tradition, but portraying a local scene, much like you already do."

"Like Robert Duncanson," Stella said.

"Yes, Robert Duncanson. You know who he is?"

Stella pressed her lips together, containing a smile. "Sure I do. The first free black man to make his mark paintin' landscape murals in the 1800s up in Cincinnati. But Miss Jennifer, don't you think that'd be a bit fancy for a country home like Michael's?"

"No, I don't. I'm learning that house and this community are both full of surprises. Maybe the hidden treasure isn't gold, but the people."

Stella nodded, and Jennifer experienced a wash of satisfaction when she realized Stella approved of what she'd just said. Not only that, but a golden warmth entered the room with the truth of her statement, oddly making the image of the Jesus painting flash into Jennifer's mind. "There you go, Miss Jennifer. You catching on."

Another realization followed. The country Southern speech of the residents of Hermon demonstrated just one of many apparent contrasts to their real education, experience and talent. Suddenly she felt ready to leave Athens and be here among these gentle and in-telligent folks, even if it was for just a short time. Talk about irony again: that Hermon might teach her more than the university. "So," she prodded. "Will you?"

"You talk to Mr. Michael about it, and if he agrees, we'll chat again. No sense in stirrin' him up none if he isn't interested, though." Stella sipped, smirked, and didn't meet her eyes.

Jennifer bit her lip. Stella had heard, somehow, about her fireplace debacle. Probably Mary Ellen. "Agreed. I'll talk to him tonight." And she would be very charming and convincing. "That reminds me, in going through the shed in back of the property, I came across an old trunk with baby clothes and this Bible and picture. I wanted to ask you about it." Jennifer dug in her canvas satchel and handed the contents to her new friend.

"Mmm-*hmm*," Stella said, gazing at the sepia portrait.

"Well? What does 'mmm-hmm' mean?"

"That sure is the house." Stella pursed her lips, pinching anything else back.

"Yes, and who's in front of it?"

"Look like Bachelor Hamp to me."

"Bachelor Hamp? You mean Hampton Dunham?" Excited, Jennifer scooted onto the sofa next to Stella, picking up the Bible and thumbing open to the family tree. Her short fingernail underlined the name. "This same Hampton Dunham?"

"I expect so."

"Whomever had the Bible didn't fill it out past Hampton. Do you mean to say he never married?"

"That's what I hear."

"So that line just ended with him?" Jennifer bent forward, chewing her lip as she studied Hampton's parents, Stuart and Charlotte. Stuart had had two brothers and a sister, Theodore, William and Anne. "I guess one of these is Michael's line, then. I'll have to go to the library like you said. Even if you can tell me which one, I'd need all the dates, names ..."

Stella sat back from her. "Jennifer, let me ask you something."

"Yes?"

"Is Michael as interested in his family history as you are?"

"Well, I admit I'm the one pressing it, mainly for the report I'm writing. I need to know who built the houses and when, and which ones were doctors and so on."

"It's my understanding Dunham House was built for this man," Stella said, her finger pointing to Theodore's name. "The older brother of Stuart, but he died early. So his brothers took up the practice for him."

"They were doctors, too?"

Stella nodded. "They meant to expand the business into town, have their own practice after their daddy, Silas, died. I believe Miss Anne stayed at the big house with her husband once she married. They couldn't all be needed to run the plantation and sanatorium, now could they, especially after the war when times were hard? Not if they wanted to doctor instead of farm."

Jennifer reached down for her notebook when the wail of a siren nearly made her jump out of her seat and Stella to rattle her teacup on the saucer. A flash of bright red and blue lights pierced the lace curtains.

"Oh, my Lord," Stella gasped, hand on her heart. Then she broke into laughter. "Why he always have to do that? Come on, Jennifer, and meet my scalawag brother."

Suppressing irritation at the interruption—just when she was getting somewhere —Jennifer set aside the notebook and followed Stella into the front yard, where a handsome man hung his arm out the window of his patrol car. White teeth grinned beneath mirrored sunglasses in his honey brown face.

"What you doing, Jake? Can't you see I've got company?"

"The company's why I'm here, Stella."

"Oh. Did I do something wrong?" Jennifer peered anxiously at her Civic, parked neatly in Stella's short driveway.

"No, ma'am, I'm just here to meet you," Jake said, climbing out of the car.

"And harass you, too," Stella put in jokingly. "He loves to come sound his siren outside my window just to scare me."

In a gesture of mock offense, Jake placed a hand over the badge on his uniform. "Now, Stella, I'm here to offer my services. I heard this young lady had an incident last week. I wanted to ask her some more about it." He approached with his hand extended. "I believe you're Jennifer Rushmore. And I'm Sheriff Jake Watson."

Jake's strong grip engulfed Jennifer's mouse-boned hand. "Pleased to meet you, but really, if you're talking about me getting shut in the storage shed, it was nothing. I can't imagine it was intentional."

"Just the same, I'd like you to describe in your own words what happened."

"My goodness, Jennifer. I want to hear this, too. Come let's sit on the porch," Stella said. "You want some tea, Jake?"

"No, honey, I don't want any tea. Thank you."

Embarrassed by Stella's concern and the sheriff's professional questioning, Jennifer recounted the shed incident, ending with repeating, "It really was nothing. Just an accident. Old doors can be persnickety, after all." At his request, she numbered off all the people aware of her work in the outbuilding, again minimizing any danger. Then she answered questions about the footprints and how the rain had dissolved them. Reminding her that he and his boys were trained to make sense of such scenes, Jake frowned and scolded her for not calling them, then handed her a card.

"Well, we'll leave it at that for now, but I want you to put this on your refrigerator, and if you have any more trouble, just give me a call, OK? Even though the community's quiet, any girl living alone needs to be careful. I live up in Lexington, but me or one of the boys will be out in a jiff if you need us. All right?"

"Sure. Thank you." Jennifer ducked her head.

"OK, I'll leave you to your visit," Jake said, standing up. "We're real glad to have you in Hermon." The radio on his shoulder crackled, and a voice registered a code. He shook hands again with Jennifer, hugged Stella, who thanked him for coming by, then strode out to his patrol car. He grinned and waved as he pulled away.

"What happened with that door doesn't make any sense," Stella told her. "I don't like it one bit."

"Please. It could happen to anybody stupid enough to leave their cell phone at the house. I learned my lesson, believe me. It does make me feel better to have this, though." Jennifer fingered Jake's business card. "I've never lived alone before, so it'll give me peace of mind."

"Any time you need something, you can call me, too." Stella touched her arm. "I'm right here."

"I know. Thank you. What I really need is to understand that photograph and family tree. You said Hampton was a bachelor, but why is he in that portrait with a bunch of children, at least one of whom appears to be his?"

"Miss Jennifer, you said yourself things are rarely as they seem around here. I said Hamp was a bachelor, not that he never had children. But I think this is a conversation we should be havin' with Michael. I've been watchin' that young man, and his mind is not here yet. It's on something else. I don't know what, but something heavy. Something that makes him blind to the family in front of him. You give him some time for the Lord to work. When he's ready, you bring him, and we have this conversation all together."

When Jennifer passed Dunham House on her way back to the double-wide, she saw a strange sight. Not just Michael, but his father as well, crouched on their hands and knees, peering under the apothecary shop. In case whatever held their attention was an item of architectural importance, she parked and walked across the property, parallel to the main road. When she reached the building, James had disappeared but Michael was still there, calling in a soft voice reserved for small animals and babies, "Come here, come on out."

She suppressed a giggle, guessing the funny falsetto meant she could safely assume Michael did not cajole a snake. "What is it?"

At her question, he jumped, bumping his head on the bottom of the apothecary raised from the ground by the pilings.

"Sorry."

Michael rubbed the offended area. "It's OK. It's a kitten. We were talking about what we wanted to do with that car ramp in the back when we heard this little sound—a meow so small you could hardly hear it. We've been calling it for a while. A big truck whooshed by just when it was about to come out and scared it. Dad went to get some milk."

"Really? Where?" Jennifer plopped down next to him and flattened onto her stomach for a better view, now glad she'd not gotten too dressy for tea. Her mother had never allowed pets, saying they were a waste of money, but sometimes, when Jennifer first visited the Lockwood Plantation, a big gray tom cat had come by. Once or twice, he'd even slept near enough for her to hear him purr. Because of that comforting memory, cats retained a special place in her heart.

"There." Michael pointed into the darkness, near a support stack of stones.

Jennifer barely made out the shape of two raised ears. "What, that tiny bump? Why, I've never seen a kitten so small! Any sight of its mother or other babies?"

"No. We even checked the woods nearby and in the boxwoods. Our best guess is that it was abandoned here. Maybe something happened to the mother, or maybe she's one of those wild cats we've seen around who just had one too many to nurse."

"Oh, my goodness. We've got to get it out. If we leave it here it will definitely die."

Michael shot her a wry glance. "No kidding. Why do you think we're out here like two fools trying to coax it over to us?"

"Kitty, kitty, kitty," Jennifer called. She made sweet kissing sounds which made Michael grin, but she ignored him. All she got in response from the kitten, however, was another tiny meow. Then she felt a shadow beside her as James crouched next to them.

"I've got some milk in a bowl and a spoon," he said. "It's all I could think to grab quick."

"No offense, but I don't think a cat that small will know how to lap it up," Jennifer said. "Here, let me put some on my fingers and hold my arm under the building. Maybe the smell will lure it." James held out the bowl so she could do as suggested. Then she extended her arm and wiggled as far as she could with her head and shoulders under the apothecary shop, all of them calling and coaxing. As her eyes adjusted to the darkness, she finally saw movement.

"It's working!" Michael hissed.

His low, gentle tone packed with joy made Jennifer's heart soften. Then she felt a light motion at her fingertips and realized the kitten's dry, raspy tongue licked off the milk! She shifted so that she could angle her hand around the body and grasp it.

The creature she pulled out into the sunlight made them all gasp. It lay easily within her opened hand, a fuzz of dark gray fur sparsely covering the ashen skin. The eyes shut against the bright light appeared swollen and mucous-covered. Jennifer wondered if they'd ever opened past slits. The kitten's legs dangled, limp and little bigger than toothpicks. Ears so prominent as to be comical poked up from a triangle-shaped head. But there was nothing funny about the shivers wracking the tiny animal even in the late spring warmth.

"Oh, my goodness," she said and closed her fingers in a protective shield around the skeletal frame. As she did, she heard the voice again, the same one that had spoken in the shed, both big and at the same time, silent.

My child, this is how I see you.

A shiver wracked Jennifer, an emotional, not a physical reaction to the same warmth she'd felt when she heard the voice in the shed. No one had ever spoken to her so tenderly. The alterations in her life must be unhinging her mind, allowing desperation from her past to generate voices. Her heart wrenched as, regardless of its dirty and pitiful state, she held the kitten up to her face, knowing in a deep part of her soul that same helplessness and vulnerability, and wanting to warm and comfort it. An unguarded tear dropped onto her fingers.

The men stood watching, uncommonly silent. Then James said, "Well, it would appear we have two choices. We can leave it, and it would be dead within a day or two, or we can get in the car and ride up to Lexington to the vet."

Her own mind already made up, Jennifer opened her eyes to gauge Michael's reaction. He watched her with a solemn expression. "There is no choice," he said.

1918
Oglethorpe County, Georgia

I was black at school, black at church, but white when I went into Athens with Daddy. And white when I looked in the mirror. I stayed out of the sun so my skin would reflect my name, and my hair, while jet black, fell to my waist in long, silky waves. My full lips I didn't consider a disadvantage, since men liked that. By age fourteen, I understood I had to follow certain rules at certain places. Anybody who thinks the time between the World

Wars was a simple time didn't live it. Our world exploded daily with so many little bombs of change it made everybody afraid, and fear breeds danger.

The same year after the Germans torpedoed the *Lusitania*, Georgia senator Hoke Smith announced there was no need to go to war to avenge the deaths of a few rich Americans, the boll weevil first turned up in the state, women agitated for the vote, and someone murdered a little white Marietta factory girl named Phagan. Out of the ashes of her death, which they blamed on her Jewish boss and a black janitor, and publicity surrounding some film Daddy said was horrible, rose the robed specter of the second Ku Klux Klan. I knew Democrats in bed sheets had scared the beJesus out of black people after the Civil War. Now they were back, saving the South again from tyranny and corruption in any form that threatened white Protestants. They burned a fiery cross atop Stone Mountain to announce their resurrection. They preached pure living at a time when bootlegging, joy riding, rising hem lines and dance parties threatened tradition, and they even said they wanted the women to vote, because women were the moral compass of the home. The punishment of white men who didn't do right by their families fell within their power, too. But they did believe in keeping the races separate, which made it hard for people like me. I couldn't help it that Daddy had fallen in love with Mama when he'd rescued her from a cruel overseer on the tenant farm her family worked. And I couldn't help it that the law forbade them to marry. So we were the "outside family" of Dr. Hampton Dunham, only we were his only family.

The Klan's eyes roved everywhere. Folks said everybody in the courthouse in Atlanta belonged to the Klan. The University of Georgia and the *Banner-Herald* would not condemn them. The war undergirded their power, because people so feared spies, treason and communism.

The October Revolution, when communists took over czarist Russia, scared Americans. People feared it could happen here, when citizens were needed to support freedom and the war effort. Athens even set up a local vigilance corps made up of Elks and Klansmen to held stamp out "the multiple-headed Red menace" by listening in for "Red utterances" at shops and offices.

In an attempt to do away with the attitude of "humble contentment" they said blacks here possessed, the NAACP also came to Athens in 1917. Not everybody was content. Mama told me with some pride that in 1914 the Athens black women had refused to sit in their designated area at the Atlanta convention of the Women's Christian Temperance Union. Black people no longer wanted to do domestic work for whites. Education opened the way for skilled black workers to earn as much as white people. It bothered many of them to see blacks driving around in cars and wearing nice clothes. The lines began to blur, but when they got crossed too far, vigilante justice re-established them. Black men were never to commit any crime against white people, or certainly not to mess with white women. The lynchings that happened in Watkinsville in 1905 and to Rufus Moncrief in Oconee County's Whitehall Road in 1917 reminded us of that. Daddy said the note pinned on Moncrief's bullet-riddled body that read he'd assaulted one white woman but would never touch another offered a red herring for a gambling quarrel, but it made its point nevertheless.

These things made my parents teach me how to stay within the careful boundaries of my sphere.

Daddy didn't go to church. We went to church with Mama, at the local African American Baptist Church, although I didn't like the long services in the intense summer heat. I did find it interesting, though, when during an especially powerful sermon or a revival, kids my age would "come through," becoming overtaken by the rhythms and preaching and shouting, until they sometimes fainted. They'd end up at the mourners' bench asking Jesus to cleanse their sinful hearts, and after a month or two, if the religion "stuck," they'd be dunked. Observing these rituals diverted me too much for me to "come through" myself, or maybe I had too much of Daddy's blood, like Minnie and Hazel said.

Local black children walked to the one-room school where one teacher instructed a whole bunch of them using textbooks worn out by the white children. But Daddy's money and status allowed him to send us to Jeruel Academy in Athens, which was supported by the local Baptist Association and the Negro churches in surrounding counties. From Jeruel, my oldest sibling Cecil attended Meharry Medical School in Nashville, the first medical college in the nation to educate black physicians. In 1893 they'd graduated the first two black women, a fact I pointed out to Mama and Daddy. Daddy nodded and looked thoughtful, but Mama said that even black men doctors were leery of black women doctors. They wanted to know what those women thought they could do that the men couldn't. If they put up with them at all, they showed their "support" by referring their middle-of-the-night patients. Cecil didn't help my case by pointing out how medical specialization now required internships and residencies and only a small number of hospitals in the country would take either blacks or women. Their few slots went to one or the other, but not to someone who was both. I didn't care. It had been I who sat under Daddy's compounding table for hours on end, listening as he told me what each medicine was and what it did, and I who could name all the bones and organs of the body from his medical textbook. I knew what I wanted to do, and I could do it better than Cecil, who in my opinion went to Nashville half-heartedly.

I waited on the right moment to convince Daddy that he should override Mama's reservations, and it finally came in late October, 1918, when one boy's misfortune became my good luck.

An influenza outbreak that fall had spread from the military camps near Augusta, so I was in the apothecary soaking Daddy's instruments in alcohol when I heard the shouting. Nate Washburn, a local farmer from just up the road, jumped off a heaving horse out front. I ran to meet him. I already knew I'd have to go get Daddy, whom we feared might be coming down with the flu himself, even though he was napping in the house— and quite possibly contagious.

"I need Dr. Hamp to bring his car and stretcher," Nate yelled. "Somethin' startled the mules when my son Frank was mowin' in the south field. The blade cut his leg real bad!"

"Where is he?"

"My wife has him on the porch with the wound staunched with her apron. The kids are boilin' a cotton sheet."

"I'll get Dr. Hamp, and he'll get the car. Have your wife apply tincture of iodine drops on the skin around the cuts and wrap the leg in the sheet. Does she have any McMunn's Elixir of Opium?"

Nate looked like he wasn't sure he could trust me. He shook his head. But I was certain. I ran in the shop to get the medicine and pressed it into his hand. "Ride back quick. We'll be right there."

We both took off, he to his boy's side and me to my daddy's. Papa launched out of the bed like a jack-in-the-box when I came in shouting, ignoring Mama's shushing. He ran a hand over his face, now clean-shaven in the style of the day, pulled on his suspenders and hurried out of the house. Sunlight glinted off the gray at his temples, evidence that he was much older than Mama. At the steps, I steadied him when he paused and reached for the hand rail. I felt his forehead, which was hot.

He brushed my hand away. "No time for that. Georgia, can you get the operatin' room ready? Soak some thread and gauze in carbolic acid, and lay out my tools."

"I just cleaned them, Papa."

"That's good. If an artery has been severed and the damage is too great, I might have to amputate."

My stomach soured. I'd pray that wouldn't be the case. Frank was my age, and for a white boy he was fairly kind to me. A farmer without a leg would be like a doctor without an arm.

"Did he say if the injury was above or below the knee?"

"I'm sorry, I didn't think to ask that, but I know they stopped the bleedin' with an apron. I told them to use iodine, and I sent some opium with Mr. Washburn."

Daddy put his hand on my shoulder. "Good girl. You did exactly right. Go on now. I fear I'm going to need to rely on you today, Georgia Pearl."

With a nod, I ran ahead to do my father's bidding while he went for his car. He pulled up to the shop, and we loaded the stretcher.

When Nate and Daddy brought Frank in twenty minutes later, I knew I'd done right to send the opium. The boy's shaggy blonde head rolled back, and he moaned when the men transferred him to the examining table. I'd laid back the table and elevated the foot. Daddy checked the sheet wrapped below his cut-off trousers to make sure bleeding had stopped, reminding me aloud that bright red blood and the fact that it had pumped in time with the heartbeat meant arterial rather than venous bleeding.

"It's a good thing the injury occurred below the knee. We may be able to avoid an amputation. Now, Nate, as I very carefully remove the bandage, I'm going to ask you to apply pressure here," Daddy said, pressing his thumbs in below the young boy's groin on the left wounded leg. "And hold it, no matter what."

The man did as he was told. As the wound was revealed, Nate Washburn turned positively green. I had a sudden memory of the man throwing up in the bushes when Daddy delivered his youngest daughter.

"Forceps."

I handed him the sterilized instrument and said, "I think Mr. Washburn needs to sit down."

Daddy glanced at him. "Nate, would you object to Georgia Pearl assisting me?" He knew he had to ask. Some people acted like we kids and

Luella weren't visible, but they sure would notice if we tried to touch a white person. One old lady had declared she'd rather faint dead away and risk splitting her head open than have a black boy manhandling her, that black boy being Cecil when he offered her a hand as she left, tottering woozily following a minor procedure.

"No-no." Smoothing his son's hair, Nate whispered in Frank's ear, "It's going to be all right, boy. I'm right here. Just you call out iffen you need me." Frank's eyes were rolled back in his head, so Nate stumbled over to a chair and hung his head between his legs.

I kept pressure on the artery with one hand and handed my father what he needed with the other while he cleaned debris from the wound, managing to do so without restarting the bleeding. Despite Daddy's efforts, which were impeded by his need to squeeze shut his eyes a few times to right his own fevered vision, I knew Frank would probably get an infection and fever as well. In those days before antibiotics, people accepted the likelihood. The grave danger of tetanus also loomed, with its subsequent lockjaw. No, just because Frank might get to keep his leg hardly meant he was out of mortal danger.

"It appears, Nate, that the bone wasn't broken. I can see where the blade grazed it, but I don't think you'll need to go to Augusta for x-rays," Daddy announced, and Nate sighed. In those days, with no worthy hospital in Athens, the expense of a trip to Augusta for a man without a car, not to mention the cost of treatment, was prohibitive.

"It's a good thing the blade wasn't serrated, because it's easier to sew up when the edges of the wound are straight, right, Daddy?" I asked.

He didn't even seem to notice my lapse. We didn't call him "daddy" in public, even though everyone knew. "Right, Georgia Pearl," he said with pride tinging his tired voice. "Bring me the thread, and can you please thread that needle for me today? It's all right to release the pressure point now."

"Yes, sir."

My father could have been the fanciest tailor on Fifth Avenue. Even sick as a dog, his stitches were perfect, small and even. He applied a sterile carbolic acid plaster when he was done. "What else could I have used today, Georgia?" he quizzed me.

The war with Germany was teaching our doctors many things, including the first ever blood transfusion. Since we weren't set up for that, I suggested bipping, which was smearing bismuth idoform paraffin paste on the wound.

"Very good. Mr. Washburn, I think your boy will recover just fine. I'd like to keep him here overnight. We should attempt to keep him still, quiet and as comfortable as possible. Your wife can stay and can call me if there's any need."

I knew Daddy would stay by Frank himself if he weren't afraid of making him sick. While he'd already exposed the boy to whatever he had, there'd been no help for it in the face of the greater emergency, but Hampton Dunham would take no further chances.

"I think she'd be real grateful, doctor."

"Georgia Pearl will sit with Frank while I drive you back and fetch her. We'll give her the report."

I put cool cloths on Frank's head after the sound of the Roadster motor died away. Frank's hazel eyes flashed open and a faint smile lit his dirt-streaked face. "That you, Georgia Pearl?"

"Yes, Frank Washburn."

"Am I gonna live?"

"You're gonna live, and walk again just fine, too. Here, take this sip of water while you're awake. You've lost a lot of blood."

He complied, then, dragged down into the haze of opium, fell asleep, but not before muttering, "You're awful pretty, Georgia Pearl."

I didn't put no stock by a white boy's words. I'd heard them before. Mama said I shouldn't listen.

Later, once Daddy had gotten some cod liver oil and aspirin down Frank and Mama had brought Mrs. Washburn supper and water for washing, I got Daddy to take some aspirin, too, and helped him back to the house. He felt hot and limp, and I took his arm around my shoulders to help support him up the steps. Nevertheless he said, "You did real good today, Georgia Pearl. You weren't even put off by all that blood."

"No, Daddy, it's like I've been tellin' you. I wanna be a doctor. Will you talk to Mama now?"

"Would you settle for bein' a nurse?"

"I might. If I had to."

"If you will consider it, I'll talk to your mama. I don't believe she'd send you to Nashville, but she might just send you to Atlanta."

So that proved to be one of the big turning points of my life. The other one happened a month or so later, when I met Glenn Swanson.

CHAPTER SEVEN

Having prepped Michael and received a positive reaction to Stella adding some special touches on the walls of the house, Jennifer had not expected him to be difficult on the interior painting walk-through.

Of course, neither had she expected her professor to show up. She'd invited Amy Greene, since she needed to know what color samples to bring on her next visit. But Barbara volunteered to ride along when Jennifer stuck her head in the professor's office after classes the Tuesday before graduation. Jennifer intended to give a passing report, but it slipped out that she was on her way to Hermon.

"The work on the roof is finished, and I'd like to consult with everyone before the fireplace crew arrives and makes a mess of everything," Jennifer explained. "Earl, Stella and Amy all had time tonight, so it made sense for me to drive out today."

"Don't you have graduation planning?" the professor asked, one eyebrow raised.

"Nope, it's not a big deal for my master's. Not like with high school and undergrad, invitations and family and parties and everything. I intend to work right up to it and right after the ceremony."

"Well, why don't I ride with you? We can leave straight from here."

"Oh, no, I wouldn't want to inconvenience you. It would take your whole evening."

"I don't have plans, and I'm due to check your progress on your big project. It will be fun." Barbara smiled brightly, stood and started packing up her books, planner, phone and purse. She paused and fixed Jennifer with a scolding gaze. "You don't mind, do you? After all, you haven't once invited me out to see how things are coming along."

"Oh. I didn't realize you wanted to go." That might be a partial truth. She didn't know because she hadn't asked, on purpose.

"Of course if you don't want me to go …"

"Why wouldn't I want you to go? I just assumed you were busy with—you know—professor things." Jennifer shifted her weight.

"If you're sure." Her teacher pinned her to the wall with her sharp eyes.

Jennifer put on a smile. "I'm sure. You can follow me back to the apartment and leave your car there." If she must be shanghaied, at least she'd drive this time.

"I have to admit, there's another reason I want to go to Hermon," Jennifer confessed once they parked Barb's car and, after passing several exits, turned onto Lexington Road.

Barb leaned her head back and rolled her eyes. "Oh, no. I thought I warned you."

"No, not a person. A kitten."

"A kitten?"

Jennifer nodded and described the feline rescue on her last visit. The vet had examined and wormed the tiny feline, declaring it was too early to tell if it was male or female, and instructing them to feed it warm goat's milk with a medicine dropper for a few weeks.

"And Michael's doing all that?"

"Yes, whenever I've texted to check on the kitten's progress, he's said he is."

"I bet his father's doing all the work."

"I don't think so. He mentioned getting up a couple times a night the first two nights." Jennifer felt pleased to defend Michael, although if she were honest, his tenderness and patience with the cat had surprised her as well. "He did say, though, that he's counting on his investment. He wants a good mouser when it gets bigger. They're calling it Yoda, like from 'Star Wars' … on account of the big ears."

Barbara and Jennifer found Yoda in a box in the kitchen, sleeping on a towel, with a litter box nearby. Jennifer stroked the kitten's side with one finger and sent Michael a satisfied smile, pleased at the improvements. He returned the expression with the barest curve of his flat mouth, evidence of the pique which had descended the moment he'd caught sight of Barbara behind Jennifer.

"We can't leave him in the camper," James told them. "He goes crazy, trembling and crying. Although he'll have to stay there when we have work crews in the house. The noise would scare the poor thing to death. He really likes Michael." James cast a teasing grin at his son.

"I don't even like cats," Michael muttered.

Moments later, Earl, Stella and Amy arrived. Yoda stirred and opened his eyes a crack.

"Oh, they're a blue-gray!" Jennifer cried from the position she'd never left on the floor.

"You might as well hold him now that he's up. He won't stay in his box," James told her. "Let me heat some milk before we start the tour."

Barbara sent Jennifer an "I told you so" look. Jennifer ignored it, scooping the tiny bag of bones and fur into her palm. But once the milk was ready, as everyone gathered around, it was Michael who took the cat in his hand, sat it on a towel on the island, and put the tip of the medicine dropper in its mouth. Yoda proceeded to suck down the milk with a noisy smacking sound that made everyone laugh.

"He still doesn't have much energy. Since he's been fed, I think he'll stay put for a while," Michael said, placing the cat in the box and washing his hands.

And now here they all were, an awkward crew of no less than seven in a country house, crinkling from room to room atop the paper and plastic put down on the floors to protect them, and consulting like they were about to paint the next Sistine Chapel.

Michael started the tour on the wrong foot by remarking, "I just think we should paint the whole house the golden-brown that was in the foyer and front rooms, and do the trim white. It's easy, it's neutral, it works." He said "was" because the walls were now covered with Earl's first sheet of drywall mud.

"Well, then, we can all just go home." The words came out of Jennifer's mouth before she could stop them.

Amy, who had produced her printed paint swatches, looked shocked, then crestfallen.

Michael edged his body so that he was facing her and partly blocking the others and spoke in a low but intense voice. "Do you remember our discussion? On the porch? About the mantels?"

The fact that moments before he'd been feeding a kitten with a medicine dropper made it difficult to picture him as threatening. She whispered back, "Do you remember our *last* discussion? About doing something special with the interior painting?" Jennifer cut a sideways glance at Stella, who watched them with poorly veiled amusement.

"We can have stencils and murals with brown walls."

Earl spoke up in his calm, sensible manner. "We got to redo the latex paint with somethin' better. We might as well hear what ideas Jennifer has."

"Yes, let her tell us what she has in mind, then when you hear it all, if you don't like it, you can just say so," Stella said.

James nodded. "Sounds reasonable to me."

Disregarding the irritation that Michael dammed up behind his scowl, Barbara stepped between him and Jennifer and began, "Speaking from a period aspect of decorating, houses of the 1840s tended to apply different color schemes to each room. That way they could refer to 'the green room' or 'the blue room.' They liked to use colors next to each other on the color wheel to accomplish this, and I think—"

"Since everyone is sharing their ideas today, what colors would you be envisioning, Dr. Shelley?" Michael gave her a tight, polite smile.

"Well, it's really what would be period correct, wouldn't it? Shades in vogue then included pea or sea green, or even apple green. Then you might consider burnt umber, yellow, pink and lavender, to provide variation from your standard grays and browns, which would have been most common in an entrance hall."

His mouth tightened, then relaxed as he stepped back and wagged a finger at her. "You're baiting me, Dr. Shelley. You know good and well I would never consider any of those."

"But now perhaps you'll hear my best student out. Jennifer, I think you were telling me when I came in that you'd like to take the color scheme for this room from the mantel, which has already been painted gray." She smiled in a self-satisfied manner.

Flabbergasted with Barbara and irritated with herself, Jennifer knew she had to take charge. With stronger personalities present, why did she lose her sense of self? And her voice? This was exactly why she was so good at research and evaluation, not interpersonal dealings. She gave her glasses a shove. "Uh, yes. Exactly. The shelving by the fireplace should match the fireplace, as should the baseboards. This wall would look best a flat white to coordinate with the white cabinets. Um … I'd also like to keep the ceiling white."

"The cracks in that ceiling let in a lot of air from the attic," Michael stated.

"Your father and I agreed that blowing in insulation will help."

James nodded, glancing up from pouring himself a cup of coffee.

"What would help even more would be to finish off those rough boards. Put some caulking up there," Michael said.

Jennifer's mouth popped open, and her voice rose in pitch. "But that would destroy the bead boarding!"

"Jennifer is right," Barbara chimed in. "If you sand and caulk that, you'll lose all the character."

She could afford to speak in a quiet tone. Even the suit and pumps from her day teaching worked to convey authority. Next to her, in Mary Janes, faded leggings and shapeless dress with a knit vest, Jennifer made a conscious effort not to hunch her shoulders. How fast one's college wardrobe became obsolete. And how destabilizing she found even professional arguments years after listening to all her parents' fights.

Jennifer frowned, realizing the professor's words would make Michael feel ganged up on. She just had to remind him of the terms of the agreement. "As one of the structural elements that convey the historic character of the house, I do feel it's important to preserve the ceiling as is, but we can table that for later. Let's concentrate on the walls today." Praying the delay would work, she moved into the dining room without looking back. Stella gave her a tiny nod which encouraged her to continue, "Bolder colors and wall papering often showed up in dining rooms, as one of the more public areas. In here I've discovered both, that beneath two layers of red and burgundy paint, dark red wallpaper existed."

Jennifer showed Amy a section of wall where she'd asked Earl to leave an example. Amy let out a happy exclamation.

"See the small diamond print? I wondered if you could locate a reproduction for us, Amy. Bradbury & Bradbury once made such prints, called diaper patterns. If you can't find diamonds in the dark red, Gothic leaves or Fleur de Lis and rose would be appropriate." Focusing on details instead of the opposing forces of Michael and Barbara helped Jennifer center.

"Sure I can. I'll get right on that," Amy agreed, snapping a picture with her cell phone camera. Then she pulled out a copy of the floor plan and made notes on the dining room space.

"How are you with applying wallpaper, Stella?" Jennifer asked.

"She's a whiz." Earl smiled and patted his wife's shoulder.

"Michael? James? You good with a red dining room?" When they both nodded, she sighed with relief and led them on. "I agree that the brown-gold is a nice shade for several rooms, including the office," she told Michael. "It's your room, and I think you should be most comfortable there and in the den."

"Why, thank you."

Jennifer nodded, not sure if that was that sarcasm.

"I guess the bedroom doesn't matter since I'll have my eyes shut the majority of the time."

Yep, it was sarcasm, but rather funny. A quick laugh escaped her while James rolled his eyes.

"If the front bedroom will be for guests, a different color would set it apart," Barbara offered. "Maybe a blue-gray?"

Jennifer honored the professor's attempt at diplomacy with a nod, but before moving on to that discussion, she said, "First, I wanted to suggest that Stella might stencil a border in the office."

Barbara began, "The best style would be Goth—"

But Stella grabbed Jennifer's hand before she finished speaking. "A trefoil."

"How did you know?" Jennifer gasped, while Barbara stared at them in a mixture of impatience and amazement, and Amy with a blank look. "It's like you read my mind, Stella. A trefoil or a quatrefoil would be perfect, although Rococo Revival floral stencils would also reflect the time period."

"No way," Michael said.

102

Jennifer shot him a quick smile to let him know she agreed. "I thought something Gothic would be more masculine."

"Not a quatrefoil," Stella argued. "A trefoil. It's the symbol of the Trinity."

"Just as long as you don't go painting any doves," Barbara said.

"What's a quatrefoil?" James looked confused.

Stella reached for her notepad. "It looks like this," she said, and sketched the design with a few pen strokes. She held it up for the men to see, and they nodded their reluctant approval.

"You could also stencil in the kitchen," Jennifer continued, ushering Stella before her into the bedroom.

Michael waved his hand, more teasing than combative now. "What happened to manly?"

"A stencil can be manly."

He cocked his wavy dark head and was about to argue when Jennifer's phone rang, causing the group to react with surprise. Hermon received such poor cell reception that people frequently emerged onto their porches or pulled off the road with their phones to their ears. Only at several spots in and around Dunham House could one text or receive calls. Jennifer took the phone out of her pocket and saw her mother's name and number on the screen. She said, "Excuse me. I need to take this."

The others continued their conversation, Barb taking the lead, as Jennifer stepped out onto the front porch. "Mom?" she said into the phone, her heart pounding a thick rhythm.

Her mother's high, nasal voice, mingled with a painful South Georgia drawl, pinched through the invisible line. "Hi, honey, how are you?"

"Fine. I'm ... in the middle of a walk-through with my clients." She hoped that sounded important enough.

Apparently not, for Jennifer's mother uttered the infamous four words that invariably proceeded a long monologue. "I won't keep you, but I jus' wanted to let you know I've changed my mind about comin' up this weekend. I know you said I don't need to see you for a third time with that crazy hat on your head, but it's a master's degree. It's a big deal! First one in the family. I never would have thought it. I really oughta be there for my baby girl."

"Oh, Mom, thank you for feeling that way, but honestly, I'm in the middle of a move. I have everything but the bed out here in no man's land. I don't know where you'd sleep!" Jennifer chewed her lip, hoping the excuse was enough to deter her.

"Aw, that's no problem, honey. I've got my tips cash from the steakhouse. I'll just get me a cheap hotel room for one night."

"Mom, it's graduation. Every hotel in town will be full by now."

"Well, it's not like I don't know how to sleep on a floor. I'll bring Roy's air mattress he uses for camping."

Jennifer sank down on the swing and held the phone close to her ear. Her stomach churned with dread as she pictured her stocky, balding stepfather. His loud humor which she mistook for good-natured when she'd first met him now drove her out of the room. "Is he ... he's not ...?"

Kelly pretended to think Jennifer's question signaled impending disappointment. "I don't think so, honey. He's backed up at work, but if things change and he can get free, you know he's got an extra air mattress Rab uses when they go camping. Don't worry about us."

The mere idea of seeing her mother and stepfather again, not just their sleeping arrangements, pitched Jennifer an emotional curve-ball. She needed time to fortify herself for such a surprise. Even with warning, Jennifer couldn't see them staying anywhere in the small apartment. "That won't work, Mom. There are no spare rooms in the apartment, so if Roy came, he'd have to sleep in the living room, and it's all girls. It would make them uncomfortable."

"Well, then, we could stay at your new place. The double-wide."

"It's way out in the country. I think this time it would be better if just you came." Even though that was more than enough. Jennifer avoided visiting her family except for brief visits between semesters and at Christmas. The last time they'd been in Athens had been for her undergrad graduation ceremony.

"OK, well, we'll see. It will probably just be me, but if Roy takes a notion, you know how he is. He'll get offended if I try to talk him out of it."

Jennifer knew all about that. Roy had always been quick to fault others for ruining his mood or hurting his feelings. Blame was one of the many ways he manipulated the gullible to his advantage. He was the most accomplished person she knew at freezing someone out with complete silence.

When she hung up with her mother, she leaned her head over, feeling sick. The uncertainty and dread would keep her stomach and mind in a state of upheaval until Saturday, and steal any rejoicing she might have experienced over receiving her diploma. For now, she had work to do, so she attempted to stuff her family problems into the back of her mind.

She must not have been entirely successful, however, for when her arrival interrupted a disagreement over trim color, Barb and Stella both looked at her oddly. "You OK, honey?" Stella asked.

"Yeah, sure. I'm fine." Jennifer managed a weak smile.

"Plans on track for this weekend?" Barbara pressed.

"Yes. It's just … that was my mother. She's coming up."

"Well, that's wonderful," Stella exclaimed. "Of course she is!"

"I just wasn't expecting her, and there's so much going on. But it'll be fine. Things will work out," Jennifer hastened to say.

Picking up on her inability to meet anyone's gaze, Stella patted her arm. "Sure they will. We'll all help you any way we can."

Michael watched her with arms crossed, his gaze guarded but contemplative.

Barbara gave a nod which meant she understood. Over the last couple of years, when it became clear that Jennifer preferred to stay in Athens between semesters rather than visit South Georgia, her professor deduced problems existed on her home front. Without asking myriad questions, Barbara made it clear she understood, and even empathized. She often stated, "In order to make something from nothing, you sometimes have to leave the nothing behind, especially when it constantly pulls you back." Jennifer sensed that

Barbara even guessed that her step-father was the main source of Jennifer's objection to Stewart County, although her mother and brother were reminder enough. She'd been sensitive enough to not ask the details, and Jennifer appreciated that blessing.

Now, Barb redirected the conversation. "What is your opinion on the color of the baseboard trim, Jennifer? Of course you know that in the 1840s white trim was only common in town houses. By the standards of that day, one could argue that this was a town house. However, given the size of this trim, that would be quite a lot of white. Don't you agree?"

"Yes. I wondered if the trim work might have been faux marble-ized. Or faux wood grain to look walnut. Both are options we could consider."

"That's a great idea." Barb's voice betrayed her surprise. "Very Gothic."

Michael uncrossed his arms. "I'd like to use the brown-gold paint in here. The faux wood grain would look more natural with that."

"Yes, it would," Jennifer told him, relieved they actually agreed. "Stella? Are you familiar with that type of treatment? Do you think you could do that?"

Amy looked up from her notepad and interrupted, "Oh, I know what you mean! The Stephenson house in Lexington has beautiful faux graining on the baseboards, the doors, even some doorknobs."

Stella nodded. "Right. There's a local artist who specializes in that. I took a class from her once, a while back. I think I could do what you're wantin', but of course you might prefer to call her in."

"I'd rather *you* try, Stella." Jennifer felt overwhelmed and round-ed her shoulders to try to shrug off the tension. She already strug-gled with the number of people she worked with. Adding one more personality felt like one too many.

Stella seemed to pick up on what she said, or more importantly, felt. "Sure, honey. Let me practice some at home. We'll see what I come up with."

"Thank you." After broaching one more major item with Stella, Jennifer anticipated stepping back and letting the others chat and plan. "Since we're papering the dining room, I wondered how you might feel about a mural on this back wall." Jennifer walked over to indicate where she intended to place the focus. "I spoke about it with Michael and James already, and showed them some examples of what we discussed at your house, Stella, and they approved. We all think it would be a great spot to feature your artwork. A Hudson River School style painting, Professor Shelley, but with a local setting, maybe the Oconee River. What do you think?" After the split second of explanation thrown in for Barbara, Jennifer turned back to her new friend.

After a glance at the men, who nodded their approval, Stella put a hand to her chin and narrowed her eyes, gazing at the wall. "What you think about the old sanatorium, Jennifer? With the plantation house and the cabins and Long Creek? Maybe late summer, with touches of autumn?"

The heaviness introduced by her mother's phone call lifted for a moment, and light and inspiration shone through. "I think that's perfect."

As Earl beamed at his wife with approval, Stella continued, "I got an old book at home with a photo of the plantation house before it burned down. And Earl can drive me out there to take some photos of the lay of the land, can't you, Earl?"

"Sure I can, honey. We go now if you want."

"The evening light would be nice. But I may need to see it in the morning, too, before I make a decision."

Michael fished his keys out of his pocket and took a tiny one off the ring, handing it to the painter. "Here you go, Earl. This unlocks the gate at the entrance to the property. Go any time you like."

"Thank you. I keep a good hold on this." Earl pocketed the key.

"You must be quite the artist, Stella," Barbara remarked, sizing up the woman with a skeptical eye.

"All I strive to do is use whatever talent the good Lord gave me, Dr. Shelley," Barb answered. "The outcome is up to Him. The way I look at it, no sense doing something unless it's unto Him and blessed by Him. And this, yes, I do believe He's pleased to bless."

Even though she covered her reaction quickly, Barbara could not have looked more startled had Stella broken out singing in tongues, which somehow wouldn't have surprised Jennifer one whit. Jennifer, by contrast, experienced a sense of calm that Stella felt God had confidence in their project.

Showing unexpected discretion, Amy took that moment to jump in, providing endorsement and redirection within a breath of each other. "Oh, there's no doubt about Stella's skill. Everyone in these parts knows that. I can guarantee you'll be impressed, Professor Shelley. Michael, goin' along with that color wheel approach, I'm picturing gold drapes in here, very elegant. Are you wantin' the same paint in your bedroom?"

"That and the sunroom both," he replied.

As they moved off to discuss the next room, Jennifer felt too tired to argue. Let Michael have his predominately golden brown palate. She'd accomplished what she'd intended today, a unified plan for the interior walls of the home, and a platform to leave a true local artist's mark on a historical canvas. There was satisfaction in that.

CHAPTER EIGHT

At the end of the tour, Jennifer confirmed that Earl planned to apply the final coat of joint compound right away. Then, as he completed his sanding, he'd accompany the fireplace crews coming next week in filling the house with a storm of sand, dust and noise. After he primed, they'd be in touch with Amy, who would bring paint samples in the color spectrum they desired for the rooms not part of the golden brown palate. She'd smear two-by-two swatches on the walls. While Earl and a friend of his painted the outside of the house, Jennifer, Michael and James could see which of the internal colors "grew on them" before Amy mixed the final interior paint. With Michael and James ready to burst out of the camper, Jennifer reminded them that patience was the word of the day. And month.

"While you and Dr. Shelley are both here, Jennifer," James said as they filed out the kitchen door past the kitten, who was once again sleeping, "I hoped you might offer an opinion about the outhouse. Given what terrible shape it's in, should we just tear it down?"

"Well, let's have a look," Barbara said. Her confident tone and her long stride as she took off toward the weathered, ramshackle structure located just behind the house showed her pleasure at being deferred to. Jennifer and the others followed.

"We could light one big bonfire when we take the addition off the back of the apothecary," James added, catching Barb's attention as she pulled the door open.

She paused. "You know, if you do, I'd suggest having it somewhere else, not right here. If you would permit, I'd love to bring a group of students out this fall to excavate the outhouse area as well as the compost heap that I noticed on our earlier visit, at the edge of the woods near the cook's cabin." She was too politically correct to call it a slave cabin in front of Earl and Stella.

"You wanna dig in the old outhouse?" Earl's eyes widened. "Why?"

"You'd be amazed what people throw down the hole of the outhouse or out in a trash heap. An archeology class would find all kinds of things that tell a lot about the people and their lives."

While Barb stood back talking, Jennifer took that moment to poke her head into the building. With her mother's visit monopolizing her thoughts, she failed to register an odd rattling noise and a movement in the shadows as she stepped in. Then she froze. A brown, diamond-patterned snake, its small, black-bead eyes focused on her, curled into a coil on the two-seater board in front of her! The sight of a snake focused every ounce of revulsion toward evil in all its forms. The coldest, basest type of horror jolted down her spine, and the scream she let out could have raised the dead in the Hermon cemetery. She bolted from the outhouse and, just like she had after being sprung from the storage shed, straight into Michael, who once again caught her in his arms.

"What?" he cried.

Barbara looked into the outhouse with wide eyes and let out an explicative.

"A snake, a snake, a huge, huge, snake!" Jennifer cried out.

"Whoo-wee, I'm not goin' near there!" Stella exclaimed, making a shooing motion with her hand while Amy, too, skedaddled back. "Earl, you gotta kill it!"

Her entreaty interrupted Jennifer's unchoreographed dance of revulsion. Oblivious to the gathered group, she wiggled, stomped and flailed her hands as if to fling off the memory of the disgusting reptile. When the others laughed at her, she cried, "It's not funny! It's horrible!"

"OK, ok, calm down." Michael took hold of her shoulders, and she grasped his muscular forearms. He looked into her face, his narrowed gaze not impatient for once. "You're shaking like a leaf. Earl and I will take care of it." His hands slid down to hers, like electricity running a path through a wire, then briefly held hers before releasing them with a reassuring squeeze.

Barbara, standing near them, studied them while keeping a wary eye on the outhouse. "Well, someone's got to do something before it slithers back into that hole. My degrees didn't include training on killing snakes."

Earl peeked into the building. "My, oh, my, he sure is a big one. Sure hope there ain't a nest down there."

"Oh, my gosh," Jennifer moaned. She stepped behind Michael, then, deciding she needed more distance, took off for the driveway.

"If you'll watch the outhouse, Earl, I'll go get my .22," Michael said. When the man nodded, he jogged off toward the camper.

".22?" Jennifer called. "More like gasoline and a match!"

"That wouldn't be a good idea until we've cleared the area," he yelled back over his shoulder. "I really doubt there's a nest. We probably just disturbed the rest of a lone rattler."

"Now how do you know that?" Amy asked. "OK, forgive me y'all, but I'm out of here. I'll be back with some paint on a day you've taken care of this little problem. Thanks for the notes." Waving, she tiptoed fast over to her Cadillac like she feared the ground beneath her wedge heels was accursed.

"Why don't we let the men handle this and go in the house, honey," Stella said to Jennifer, taking her by the arm and giving a sympathetic pat. "You're even more upset than I am."

"Better yet, we could just head on back to town," Barbara put in, crunching out toward them on the fresh gravel Michael had put down on the driveway. "It's getting late anyway. I can drive."

"Sure, we can go. Happy to. But I'll drive." Jennifer knew she was more upset than the snake incident warranted but not to the point of surrendering her keys. She gave Stella a brief hug, then unlocked her Civic.

As they pulled out of the driveway, a gun cracked. Jennifer eased the pedal toward the floorboard and sped toward Athens. A few minutes later, her phone dinged and Jennifer saw that Stella had texted, "They got him."

Jennifer shuddered. "Thank goodness."

"Oh, the adventures of the country," Barbara commented. "Are you sure you're ready?" Barb fingered through her short hair as Jennifer put up the windows, shutting out the ironically timed, pungent scent of freshly spread chicken litter.

"I'm just ready to get past graduation."

The older woman nodded, understanding she referred to more than exams and papers. "You weren't happy about your mom coming up. Are things that bad between you?"

Jennifer shook her head. "Not really. We get along OK now. It's just better she stays in Lumpkin with Roy and my brother. I don't fit in with them anymore. You know? It's hard to pretend I do."

"Hard to remember where you came from?" Barb prompted.

"Something like that."

There was a beat of silence, then Barb said, "I'm going to say something not as your professor, Jennifer, but as your friend. I think a lot of you and your talents, so I hope we can be friends now that you're graduating. Anyway, I have hard memories, too, so I think I get where you're coming from. Seeking some professional counseling when I was younger helped me. Maybe it's something you could consider, too. I could hook you up with someone in the university psych office. Now, don't take that wrong. It's not that I think you're unbalanced. Not at all! Lots of people talk over their feelings about their family of origin with a professional."

"Yeah, maybe." Jennifer threw out the words, having no intention of following through. Sort through the rubble of her past on the therapeutic couch of one of Barb's liberal, high-minded friends? No way! Jennifer reminded herself she'd be out of Athens in one week, and the subject would never come up again.

As usual, Barbara seemed to guess her intentions. "It would help more than running to a man, you know."

Jennifer's head swiveled toward her professor, mouth open. "I didn't run to a man. I ran *into* him." She didn't mention that had been the second time, and that for the brief moments Michael's arms closed around her, a sense of safety flooded her, probably the first time that had been true when a man held her, if she could count restraint during a panic attack holding.

Barbara's eyes flashed over to her in the dim light. "All right, but are you sure he isn't a little bit of the reason you're now keen on moving to the country?"

"No! This job provides a great opportunity. That's what you said, right?"

"Yes." She sighed. "I did say that. And it's true. I just thought I saw something between you and Michael Johnson today, which could be especially dangerous if you're working for him."

Jennifer started laughing. "That's ridiculous. We couldn't be more different. We step all over each other. I'm sure the only reason he's forced to notice me is that I annoy him so much."

"I doubt that. Just remember, men are different. There's no use looking for a soul mate in one. I learned that the hard way. I don't want to see you get your heart broken or ruin a good job situation. In the long run, it's much better to fill your life with interests, experiences and friends harmonious with the inner you, to learn to be self-sufficient and let everything else fall into place in its own time. I only mentioned counseling because it could make you stronger, Jennifer. That's what we do. We make structures stronger, don't we? Why not do that for yourself?"

"I am. Thanks. I'll keep in mind what you said."

As Barbara accepted Jennifer's bid for an end to the conversation, silence fell. Jennifer fumed, feeling like everyone was pulling shingles off her own roof and exposing the mess inside, a mess that made a lie of the words she'd just spoken. The worst part of it was, as she left the university nest for the unexpected and eclectic in Hermon, she sensed that, like in her dream, the reconstruction had only begun. But no human counselor was needed to make it happen. Question was, if God initiated this process as she'd begun to suspect, did she trust Him to be in charge?

Jennifer sat in her folding chair in the masters and specialists section on Stegman Colliseum's polished wooden floor painted with a large "G." A red sea of bleacher chairs occupied by proud family and friends encircled her section and the doctoral candidates across the way.

She fidgeted, crossing her feet in black pumps at the ankle and adjusting her black dress. Belted at the waist, the dress, the only one she owned, fell just below the knee. Since purchasing it a couple years ago as a go-to for anything from funerals to cocktail parties, Jennifer dug it out for any function she feared her typical shapeless, long skirts and dresses might garner those familiar looks of faint disapproval.

That morning as she got ready her mother had said, "It's so nice to see you in somethin' fitted. You really have a good figure, Jennifer. You oughta enjoy it and show it off while you're young. I don't know why you insist on hidin' it in hippy clothes."

An expert at dressing to accentuate her own lush curves, Kelly Jones frequently tried new diets, cleanses or pills to keep her weight down. Although her waist looked smaller than Jennifer's in the scanty, electric blue dress constricting her figure today, she'd complained that she looked fat, a phrase Jennifer grew up hearing. Her bleached blonde hair swirled into a tight up do, and more make-up colored her face than that worn by most teenagers. As she located her in the stadium, Kelly waved her hand in fast little motions. Jennifer lifted hers. Then her eye drifted upward.

No! She gasped. There, two rows above her mother, Michael and Stella sat talking, unaware she'd spied them. She couldn't believe it! Without an official invitation, how had they gotten in? As Jennifer realized they attended just for her, she looked away, embarrassed. She wrestled her phone out of her pocket and out from under her black gown and texted Stella, "What are you doing here? And did you know you're sitting two rows above my mother?"

An immediate text came back. "We didn't want to miss your graduation. When Michael and I asked, your professor got us in. Is your mom the blonde lady?"

"Yes. Her name is Kelly."

Putting her phone away, Jennifer saw Stella and Michael meet her mother. The thought of them all together made her nervous. She'd have to get to them as quickly as possible after the ceremony, or who knew what her mother would say. At least Roy and Rab had remained under the hoods of Stewart County's defunct automobiles.

Graduates and guests alike stood as the professors of all departments marched down the aisles wearing their robes and bright regalia. Watching this centuries old tradition, Jennifer thought about what it would take to earn her Ph.D. Maybe after she worked a few years and paid back her student loans. No one in Stewart County could look down on Dr. Jennifer Rushmore, now could they?

Jennifer stifled a yawn, deprived of sleep after a night spent listening to Kelly squeaking and sighing on her air mattress between Jennifer's and Tilly's twin beds. Her mother ought to have been grateful instead of complaining. Even that space had been available only because the room had been emptied of everything else belonging to Jennifer. This afternoon the bedframe, mattresses and comforter would also be transported to Hermon in Michael's truck. Kelly's whining and needs for this and that had prevented Jennifer from even absorbing the fact that it had been her last night in Athens.

Today, she accomplished what she'd set out to, earning an advanced degree, a certain ticket out of Stewart County. Jennifer waited for the resulting exultation. Instead, watching the graduates walk across the stage to receive their diplomas, fear began to sneak in again. It really was over. She was on her own. She would never move back home. And while the people she was getting to know in Hermon touched her by coming to support her today, they were just temporary acquaintances. The rest of her future loomed large, lonely and uncertain.

Instructed to save applause for the end, the crowd complied. The biggest outbreak so far could still be considered decorous. When Jennifer approached the stage, she prayed about her mother. *Please don't yell, please don't yell.* She bit her lip as she mounted the steps.

"Jennifer Lynn Rushmore."

With the eyes of hundreds upon her, a strange thing transpired. A strong emotion engulfed Jennifer, not adulation, triumph, relief, or joy, or pride … but shame. The same unworthiness sprung from her core to assault her any time attention centered on her. No matter how many A's she made or how far from home she moved, it stalked her. She guessed it would be with her forever. She just had to learn to cover it up. Now, Jennifer wanted only to cave in on herself, but she forced her feet to walk toward the president of the university instead. She took the diploma, shook the hands, and descended the other side, her hand on the stair rail shaking. Suddenly she realized the intense sensation had caused her ears to roar, drowning out any sounds her mother might have made. Moments like these mocked her desire to be a strong woman and the teaching of her professors that she had everything inside herself that she needed. Weakness from her past cycled upward to remind her that she didn't.

After the ceremony, she texted to pinpoint the location of her guests in the soaring glass lobby of the steel-arched building. Like a cheerleader at the banner run-through of her football team, Kelly jumped up and down when she spotted her.

"Oh, baby girl, I'm so proud of you," she cried, throwing her arms around Jennifer and drowning her in cheap perfume.

"Thanks, Mom." Jennifer disengaged from her mother and hugged Stella, who congratulated her, smelling by contrast of faint, sweet lavender. Michael shook her hand, his set features conveying he wanted to get out of the crowd as soon as possible.

Kelly turned to the others, beaming and ready to cash in on Jennifer's moment. "I never would have thought this shy little thing would one day get a master's degree and leave home for the great big world. 'Course I knew she was pretty passionate about those old houses, the way she always ran off to that one near our trailer park. I swear, she woulda moved in there if we'd let her. Her stepdaddy was forever lookin' for her. I can't tell you the times I told him to just leave her be, she wanted to be alone in her pretend world."

"Mom." Jennifer nudged her mother's arm.

"She drug her sleeping bag out there, along with all kinds of broken furniture. She'd take things folks'd set out for the trash man." Kelly giggled.

Michael asked, "So an old house near where you grew up inspired you, Jennifer?"

Jennifer explained about the Lockwood Plantation.

"And then there was her job at Westville," Kelly said.

"Yes, she told me about that, as well as the plantation," Stella said.

"I was glad when she finally got it. Gave her some people like her to hang out with. If you're gonna spend all your time in old houses, you might as well at least have company, right?"

"And money for college," Jennifer put in, smiling. "Why don't we get out of here? I can't hear myself think." Of course, her mother bore the fault for that more than the hundred or so other individuals laughing, talking and posing for photos around them.

Michael looked grateful for her suggestion. They filed toward the door, which Michael held open as Jennifer heard someone call her name. She turned to see Professor Shelley edging her way through the crowded lobby.

"Oh, just a minute," Jennifer said.

As the others waited, Barb came straight up to Jennifer and hugged her. She took her hands and looked squarely into her eyes. "Congratulations. This is the beginning of great things for you, Jennifer, if you'll just believe in yourself. I know you'll make me very proud. Before you know it, you'll be living in Savannah making lots of money doing exactly what you love, making us all jealous."

"Thank you, Dr. Shelley, for everything. I owe you so much."

"It's Barbara. Call me Barb now." The older woman squeezed her hands.

Jennifer tried to pull her hands away. "And thank you for getting Stella and Michael in today."

"Oh." The older woman just then glanced at Jennifer's companions. She smiled. "No problem." She leaned forward to whisper, "I thought you could use the support." Then she turned to shake hands with Jennifer's mother and friends and accept their thanks as well. To Kelly, placing an arm around Jennifer's shoulders, she said, "You really should be proud of your daughter. She's very talented."

"Oh, I am." But Kelly looked unhappy as she gazed at the professor. Even Stella pressed her lips together. They said nothing further as Barbara Shelley excused herself with a promise to Jennifer to be in touch and flitted off.

What had just happened? The mood sagged as they discussed how they should go out to eat together to celebrate before Michael picked up her bed. From the apartment, Jennifer and her mother could each follow in their own cars, since Kelly insisted on seeing where Jennifer would be living and working before she headed home. Jennifer just hoped she wouldn't invite herself to stay another night at the double-wide. She needed down time, and her mother never understood why Jennifer didn't want to know all about how the mean kids from high school were marrying and working and coaching Little League back home. Neither did she want to hear Kelly's reports of barbeques at the Moose Lodge and the latest Nascar race with Roy and Rab, or camping at the lake with her brother's latest girlfriend. The last thing she needed at this point of advancement in her life was getting sucked back into the details of her shoddy past.

During dinner, Kelly subjected Michael and Stella to an unending string of childhood memories of Jennifer. Their initial interest dissolved into sympathetic glances toward Jennifer as Kelly shared personal details. Spurning her Christmas baby doll and stroller at five, Jennifer took Rab's Lincoln logs. Oh, yes, Jennifer played with Barbie dolls in elementary school, but only after building houses for them out of old cardboard boxes and getting angry at neighbor friends who didn't want to play for hours. Rather than enter the Miss Richland pageant at twelve wearing the pink chiffon dress Kelly purchased for her using five hundred dollars of dearly earned tip money, Jennifer hung it up on the shower head and set fire to it with one of Roy's lighters. Kelly never understood that, since Jennifer had always loved to play dress-up when she was little. But by the time Roy came on the scene, Jennifer followed her brother and stepfather around until Roy taught her how to change oil and tires and allowed her to go with them on their fishing and camping trips. Only when she started her job at Westville had she been willing to dress up again, and then only for special events in the historical costumes made for interpreters. And she had looked so very cute in them when she'd worn her contacts instead of those awful glasses.

Jennifer cringed. The ability to ping-pong questions about interests and backgrounds with new acquaintances, something Jennifer learned to do by watching her superiors at Westville, her professors, and older students at UGA, ought to be a skill of any grown woman. But Kelly's spiel did provide her an escape from having to answer any serious questions.

In any case, her mother either didn't notice polite attempts by the others to turn the conversation or just refused to be interrupted. Jennifer could see Michael's eyebrows lowering as he studied her mother and ate his steak dinner. Stella smiled in her gentle way, listening and nodding, but Jennifer knew they both couldn't wait to leave. Her mother's nasal twang rang out over the restaurant and caused other diners to look at their table, a common occurrence when Kelly talked. The arrival of the bill brought relief. Michael quietly picked it up and slid out of the booth, ignoring efforts to help pay from Jennifer and Stella.

Arriving at the apartment, they found it empty. Before learning her mother was coming, Jennifer had suggested going out to celebrate with her roommates and some of their North Campus friends. But she'd learned finals scattered them to all points of the compass. With one more year to go, Tilly would complete her internship in Athens over the summer, but she had plans with her boyfriend. So, after clearing out her few belongings, Jennifer locked the apartment and slid her key under the mat as she left.

That was it. No going back. The finality and separation anxiety mounted as the miles rolled away. She remained silent as her mother talked in a loud voice accompanied by big gestures about how Roy was about to go down to the steakhouse where she worked and have a "word" with the new manager who'd been hitting on her. Someone always hit on Kelly, it seemed, and Kelly's ploy to keep Roy's attention from straying to younger women worked most of the time.

By the time Michael and Kelly helped set up Jennifer's bedroom and Kelly took a tour of the property, Jennifer had to fight to slow her breathing and heartbeat as panic set in. This was her home now, this place in the middle of nowhere with people she did not know or understand. Well, there was Stella. But there were things Jennifer did not understand about her, either.

She sagged in relief when, after drinking two Mr. Pibbs as she waffled back and forth for an hour over departing, her mother decided to go. Jennifer waved her off from the porch of the double-wide, then sank onto a plastic chair someone, probably James, had put there. Only birdsong and the occasional rush of passing traffic broke the silence. Lots of logging trucks used the road. Jennifer breathed deeply of air redolent with the sweet, somewhat overpowering, duo of honeysuckle and sweet shrub. She looked up past the azaleas blooming bright pink in a bed with pine trees to see Michael striding through the Leyland cypresses. She didn't bother to get up. He came and stood on the porch, leaning against the rail since there wasn't another chair.

"Hey there. I just wanted to make sure you didn't need anything else," he said.

"No, thanks, I'm good. I'll make the grocery run tomorrow to Bell's." Bell's in Lexington was the only grocery store in the county.

Michael grimaced. "They stock on Mondays. You might be disappointed."

"It's OK. I'll learn to appreciate the small things."

"That you will. So … you're OK?"

She nodded and rested her head back on the chair.

"It's been a long day. You're probably tired."

"Yep. Thank you for coming today, by the way. It was … helpful." She stared at her hands, venturing only a quick glance up.

"Sure." He gazed at her then with something like sympathy. Hooking his thumbs through the belt loops of his black dress slacks, which paired with a striped and collared shirt made him look amazingly suave, he added, "I know being here is a big decision for you, Jennifer. You could have gone a lot of places after graduation."

She smiled and decided to be honest. "Not really. Actually, this was kind of my only option for the time being. Not that I'm not happy to be here," she hastened to add. No need to make her employer think her ungrateful. After all, he was the one giving her a roof over her head, money in her pocket and the excuse not to be in a south-bound car with her mother right now.

Michael nodded. "Well, be that as it may, I just wanted you to know we're glad you're here." So saying, he ducked his head, waved and walked off.

Jennifer knew the effort had cost him something. She didn't know why. Perhaps what Kelly implied about Jennifer being burdensome and undesirable still rang true, and Michael felt saddled with the weight of enduring her now. But somehow Jennifer didn't think that was it, or he wouldn't have come over tonight at all. No, the hesitation, the block, existed within Michael himself. With the realization, Jennifer experienced a rush of relief, a stirring of curiosity that pushed her past the bleak borders of introspection … and an unexpected warmth. Michael's actions showed a desire to do what was right despite his feelings. If that was God at work, maybe they could both come out of this project stronger.

CHAPTER NINE

A 6:45 a.m. rapping on the door of the double-wide Monday first inclined Jennifer to not respond. It was perfectly acceptable to not answer the door when one was in bed, right? But the knocker persisted. Jennifer rolled out from under the covers and peeked out the blinds, muttering to herself, "No way am I opening that door if it's Michael."

A small, white-haired lady stood on her porch in a coordinated outfit in bright, floral shades of aqua. It took Jennifer a moment to place her. Then she recalled the figure watching them remove trees from outside the beauty shop. The woman held a quilted casserole carrier, which provided the inducement for Jennifer to pull a robe over her T-shirt and shorts PJs.

"Hallo!" called a sweet, sing-song voice.

"Coming! Coming." No time for the niceties, apparently. She ran a hand through her hair and scrubbed her eyes as she dashed for the living room.

"Good mornin', dear!" exclaimed perfectly painted red lips as soon as Jennifer cracked the door. "Rita Worley. Welcome to the neighborhood."

"Um, thank you. I'm Jennifer Rushmore."

"I know who you are, and I know it's early, but I wanted to catch you before you cooked anything." The woman put her face up close to Jennifer. "Oh, honey, is that your real hair?"

"What?" Jennifer put an uncertain hand to her head.

"I've never seen hair like that." The lady reached out a hand with a weighty, matching turquoise ring and bracelet as though to touch Jennifer's brown locks, then caught herself. "It's so perfectly full and cut so straight, the back and the bangs. I thought for a moment ..."

Realization dawned fast. *She thought I was wearing a wig.* Jennifer couldn't stop her mouth from falling open. At the moment, she knew her plain style resembled a tousled explosion, but really? Who wore a wig, besides cancer patients and maybe women from that very traditional sect of Jews? Were either true, she'd hardly wish the fact pointed out by a stranger. And not to mention Rita's unreasonably early and unannounced arrival, what gave her grounds to talk? Certainly not her own short white hair, so carefully fluffed, swirled and sprayed, it resembled a helmet more than hair.

Rita's next words pierced and deflated Jennifer's mental tirade. "I'm sorry, dear. It's lovely. You'll have to pardon me. You know I do hair for a living, and it's the first thing I notice. And I tend to say the first thing that comes into my mind. It's a terrible habit. Anyway, the reason I'm here is, I brought you an egg and sausage casserole straight from the oven, and what gave me the idea for that was these amazin' sweet rolls baked by my granddaughter while she was visiting yesterday." Rita opened the carrier to reveal a pan of cinnamon and frosting coated bread sitting atop the casserole dish. If the sight alone had not been sufficient to erase all offense, the heavenly smell certainly would have.

"Oh, my," Jennifer said. "They look delicious."

"She's a better baker than I am now, and she's only twelve. Like everybody, she heard about you being new to the neighborhood, and nothin' would do but that we welcome you properly." The older woman paused to accent her words with a bright smile.

If only Jennifer had anticipated making good on her pledge to emulate Southern graciousness so soon, and so often. She sighed, relaxing her tense shoulders. "How thoughtful. Thank you." Jennifer stood aside and held the door open. "Would you like to come in?"

"Oh, no, dear. I imagine you've gotta get ready for work next door. I hear you and Stella have a full week ahead priming over there." Rita tipped her cotton candy head toward the Dunham place, a knowing hint of a smile lingering on her thin, red lips. Her blue eyes sparkled.

If priming was the big news in Hermon, Jennifer really ought to be concerned. She reached for the casserole carrier. "OK, well, thank you again. I'm really going to enjoy this."

"I know you will. Just return the dishes and the carrier to my shop any day. I'm there Tuesday through Saturday, eight to six. And I tell you what, you schedule an appointment with me and let me put some layers and highlights into that hair of yours, and the first cut's on me." Rita winked to punctuate her offer.

Jennifer's eyes opened wide. "I'll keep that in mind."

"It'll look beautiful, honey. Really open up your sweet face."

"OK. Thanks." Jennifer wiggled her fingers and eased backward as Rita finally stepped her white orthopedic walkers off the porch. She breathed a sigh of relief and shut the door. Despite the woman's tactlessness, something well-meaning about the hairdresser made it impossible to truly be offended, not to mention her offer of a steaming hot breakfast. She eased it onto the kitchen counter and punched the power button on her Keurig before gratefully uncovering the welcome gesture or peace offering, whatever it was. The mingled, mouthwatering scents of coffee and cinnamon made her stomach growl in anticipation.

Jennifer was not exactly handy in the kitchen, although that was not entirely her own fault. Hamburger Helper and canned peas constituted Kelly's idea of a home cooked meal, which Jennifer had to admit was an improvement over spam sandwiches. She'd eaten so many spam sandwiches as a child, she'd learned to cower at the sound of the tabbed can slurping open.

By eight o'clock, Jennifer stepped outside, replete with the best breakfast she'd had in maybe forever, showered, and dressed in work clothes: baggy khaki capris and an old T-shirt stating "Westville Heritage Days" in Victorian lettering. James sipped coffee on the front porch of the house next door, watching a sprinkler sling water across the new lawn with a cheerful clicking sound. The sight and sound resurrected summer memories of darting in and out of old school sprinkler spray with a tanned Rab as a child, in the happier days before her father's semi disappeared for the last time into the setting sun of I-20. Knowing that particular day preceded a string of endless, other waiting days when she'd run to the window at the sound of every approaching truck engine, even after a red-nosed, hungover, tousled Kelly yelled at her to give up, Jennifer slammed the mental door on that recollection. Back to the present moment. The newly renovated kitchen now offered fortifying snacks and drinks aplenty, and with the day promising heat and length, James appeared in need of encouragement to get past his first pit stop. She'd offer a guiding hand rather than a shove, though.

"Good morning," Jennifer called as she came up the steps. "The sod sure took nicely."

"Yep, it sure did. Good to have something besides all that clay."

Jennifer gave a nod. "How's Yoda?"

A grin brightened James' face. "Oh, he's great, more and more playful. I had to make a bigger box to set the smaller one inside, and he *still* gets out."

"He can get out of the box?"

"Yep, one this high!" James bent over and held his hand at knee-level. "And when he hears the click of the gas stove, he comes running. Gamboling like a new lamb is more like it. I've never seen such a bow-legged critter."

Jennifer clasped her hands under her chin in anticipation. "Oh, I can't wait to see him."

"I had to put him in the camper today, with all the noise that's coming."

She pulled herself back to a semblance of professionalism. "Oh. Well, as you know I'm a little out of the loop since graduation. I'm going to need you guys to update *me* this time. What's on your agenda for today, James?"

"I thought that while you and Stella prime, Earl could use my help with the door frames. They're so gunked up it's been taking him a day per door with sixty grit sandpaper. Michael pressure washes the outside of the house today to prepare it for when Earl's friends come, later in the week."

"That sounds like a plan."

"Earl got all the ceilings painted with the sprayer last week. Go and see. He's in there getting things set up for y'all right now."

"Wow, he's early."

James smiled. "He's always early. Fireplace guys should be here by ten."

"Great." Somehow, living here already made her feel more connected. When her time had been split between studies and work this spring, she'd worried that Michael might feel cheated. Now she could apply herself to the restoration project whole-heartedly, get hands-on and give him his money's worth.

Michael emerged from the front door at that moment, shower damp hair curling at his neck and forehead. Jennifer swallowed. He smiled as he pulled the door closed. "Good morning."

Jennifer greeted him, and they talked a few minutes about the tasks of the day, then she mentioned, "While I've got you both here, I wondered if we could schedule a day next week to visit your grandmother's storage shed. I *must* finish up my research and get the report ready to mail in. And I wondered if your grandmother might have stored any antiques we might make use of?"

Michael looked thoughtful. "She might have. She did have some. But we're not near ready for those yet."

"No, but it would help me to inventory what we have and let Mary Ellen know what we'll be on the look-out for before the time comes to furnish the house."

James nodded, then turned to Michael. "You know, son, that's not a bad idea, and Donald should know before you go over there. Obviously he'll want you to take whatever you need for the house. It's not like he's doing anything with it, and your grandmother wanted you to make use of it. But we've not got down to see him in some time. On the last phone call he complained to me that no one's donated tomato and pepper plants this year for the VA home's garden. He'd be real pleased if you'd take some down for him and the garden club to put in."

Jennifer smiled and cocked her head. "Oh, that's so sweet."

"He does love his garden," Michael remarked. "And his candy stash. He keeps the nurses on his side with peppermints and Werther's. And he's probably getting low. Time for another Wal-Mart run. But it would have to be next week. You know how we discussed going to the lake this weekend."

James shrugged. "Sure, that's up to you. The lake thing was your idea. I told you, I'm totally flexible. You want to go to church, we'll go to church. You want to go to the lake, we'll go to the lake. You want to go to Milledgeville, *you* get to go to Milledgeville." He paused for a meaningful grin.

"You don't like visiting the VA home?" Jennifer asked him.

"Oh, I don't mind, but Donald hardly notices I'm there. Once the grandkids come along, son-in-laws are a thing of the past. I made the mistake once of going without Michael. I'll never make it again." James laughed, then he added to his son, "You could pick up the plants at Wal-Mart when he's with you. That way he'd feel like he was part of the selection process, even though he can't half see."

Michael nodded.

"Sounds fun," Jennifer blurted. At the surprised reaction from the men, she shrugged. "I love old folks ... *and* gardens." And, something told her too that she might learn far more about her brooding young employer and his Dunham ancestors on such an outing than she'd been able to in weeks in Hermon.

Michael glanced at her. "There would be no need for you to go to Milledgeville. By the time we drive there and take him out to lunch and Wal-Mart, we'd be lucky to get back by dark! We'd have to go to the Lawrenceville storage unit another day."

He was right. There was absolutely no reason she needed to go visit Michael's grandfather. Jennifer lifted a shoulder again in an attempt to show impassiveness, but she couldn't quite hide how much she wanted to go. "It's time to put a few basic plants in here. We could maybe pick them up at the same time. And I thought we might use the ride to discuss a more detailed, long-range landscaping plan."

"There you go," James exclaimed. "Take her with you, Michael. I mean, think on it, you'll have someone new to help keep up the conversation with him. You know how shouting everything wears you out. Besides, after a week in Hermon, Jennifer will need to break out for a day, or she might leave permanently." He winked at her, rising from the swing with his empty coffee mug and giving his son a good-natured slap on the arm.

"Aren't you going?"

"I don't see why." So saying, James went into the house.

Jennifer followed him, pausing at the open door to glance back at Michael. As she caught sight of his unguarded, stricken expression when he didn't think she was looking, her stomach sank. Was the idea of being trapped in the truck with her for two hours that excruciating? Or did he fear his grandfather would get the wrong idea about their relationship if she went with him? "Never mind. It's OK," Jennifer said.

"No, if you want to go—"

Jennifer waved her hand. Whatever felt stuck in her throat caused her to not trust her voice in that moment. She got out, "It was a silly idea. I'm sure I'll be of more use here." And she shut the door before he could say anything else.

Going to find Stella and Earl in the front parlor and waiting while Earl set up their ladders, Jennifer berated herself. Why had she opened her stupid mouth? She knew to keep silent, to not let her desires or emotions show, especially where men were concerned. Anything else always led to heartbreak and shame. If Michael hadn't come to her graduation and walked over to assure her of his welcome Saturday night, tricking her into thinking they might become real friends, she never would have presumed to reveal so much. Now the cheery mood of belonging generated by the sweet rolls and beautiful May weather curdled. She didn't even want to talk to Stella, though Earl set them up near each other to allow for conversation over the blast of the pressure washer which Michael started farther down on the outside of the house. Stella cut in with the brush and Jennifer swiped big sections with the roller.

Of course Stella refused to settle for two minutes of Jennifer sinking in her morose self-examination. "You OK?" she asked right away as she dipped her brush, climbed her ladder and with fast, expert strokes, outlined the front, top corner of the parlor.

"Sure, just a little tired." Pouring paint into her roller tray, Jennifer sent her a weak smile.

"Didn't you get to rest up yesterday?"

"Yes, but Rita Worley knocked on my door before seven."

"Oh, my goodness, that woman has no shame. What did she want?"

"To bring breakfast. So I forgave her." Jennifer smiled again and proceeded to tell Stella about the visit and how the hair dresser seemed to know all about what they were doing at Dunham House.

"Well, that's not surprising. She's the typical beautician, knows everything that goes on from Lexington to Union Point. Nice lady, though."

"Seriously, Stella, what does go on around here? I mean, what do y'all do for fun?"

"I imagine the same things you did for fun in Athens. We've just got to drive farther to do them." Stella paused as they laughed. "But no, we have things here in the county to do. Fresh Oglethorpe in Lexington hosts local musicians on Friday nights. Lexington throws a nice Fourth of July festival coming up. Then let's see, the historical groups probably interest you more than the Woman's Club or local bridge group."

Jennifer rolled her eyes. "I'd say so."

"Our schools and churches also stay very active," Stella added. "Singings, BBQs, revivals, festivals. You ought to come with Earl and me to Harmony Grove this Sunday." She brightened, peeking over the shoulder of her denim over shirt. "Michael and James are visiting."

"They are? I just heard them say they're going to the lake." Jennifer paused to check her phone, exclaiming, "I can't believe I got reception in here!" Barb's text touched base to see how things were going and if Jennifer needed anything.

"What? Well, Earl and I invited them this weekend. We talked to Michael Saturday. Michael said he had plans for yesterday, and James was goin' to church with the McWhorters again, but he said they'd plan for the next week, which would be this comin' Sunday."

"Well, apparently he changed his mind. James said going to the lake was Michael's idea."

Stella shook her head and painted a moment in silence. That laden silence was the closest Jennifer had heard her get to mad. Finally she murmured, "That boy is runnin' from somethin', or I'm a fool. And nothin' like the Lord to fix folks, if they'd just ask for help." Then, louder, "Well, you can come on, anyway, right?"

Jennifer, in the process of texting Barb back that all was well, bit her lip. Her mind flip-flopped like a trout on the bank, searching for an excuse that would satisfy Stella under the circumstances. She found none. "Uh, sure. I guess." Her professors taught that to restore or reconstruct a structure with wisdom, one must study the social, economic, political and religious topography of the surrounding culture. That was what she'd be doing, attending church to help figure out the culture, she told herself. If she looked at this like an assignment, she was less libel to panic at the thought of putting herself in a situation where she could be weighed and found wanting again.

"Good. You got something to wear?" Stella cut a sharp eye over the denim shoulder again.

"Well, yes. Of course." The black dress. Of course.

"Good." She paused, frowning at Jennifer's phone as it dinged again. "Who's that?"

"Uh, it's Barb, just reminding me if we need any help she's happy to come out. I think she has extra time before summer semester starts."

"Maybe this ain't my business to point out, but I think she needs to let you handle it and find something else to do."

"You don't like her much, do you, Stella?"

Stella painted fast, the pale white covering the sanded-out golden-brown. "I don't know her well enough to pass judgment. God tells us He's the only fair judge, but He does give us discernment about people and situations sometimes, and it's true she doesn't give me the best feeling."

"Why, what do you think is wrong?"

"I don't know, honey. Maybe she's a little too controlling. Listen, we'll pick you up at 10:30. And be sure to eat a good breakfast that morning."

"Why?"

"'Cause we won't get lunch until two. It's Mother's Day, so we may get lucky and get out by 1:30."

Jennifer almost croaked. What in the world would the people do all closed in together in that building for that long? Seizing on an excuse, she blurted, "Maybe I should wait and go when Michael and James do, being that it's Mother's Day. I mean, you probably have plans with your family."

Stella switched a now-dry brush back and forth in a chiding gesture. "Uh, uh, uh, you ain't gonna weasel outta this, Miss Jennifer Rushmore. Just you be ready or we'll beat on your door and drag you outta bed like Miss Rita did, only without the cinnamon rolls. And remember to send your mother a card. Even though you might not be close with your mama, and maybe for good reason, Miss Jennifer, don't mean she didn't do the best she knew how to do. It's only the Lord Jesus who makes any of us fit to be had." When Jennifer's phone announced another incoming text, Stella added, "And there's one good thing about bad cell reception. It comes in awful handy for people who don't know when to stop dingin' your phone. Just remind them you won't always get their messages. Then, whether you do or not, *they* won't know."

Mindful of her current duty, Jennifer stuffed the phone away and climbed back up her ladder. Stella might appear to some as controlling as her former professor, but Jennifer knew Stella acted in her best interest and with love. And something told her Stella was right.

At ten, the fireplace crew arrived. The fact that they required an introduction to the job and the noisy brick saw they set up right outside the bedroom where Stella and Jennifer were painting relieved her of the need to sustain conversation. In the interim, Jennifer decided she wouldn't ask Michael again about going to the storage unit, much less Milledgeville. He'd have to come to her to pick a day and see if she could go. If not, whatever antiques he brought from Lawrenceville would have to do, but if he waited too long, she'd just go shopping. As for gathering information for the National Register historical sketch, the one photograph and the family tree from the Bible begged that trip to the local library to produce additional documentation. She'd rather spend a week there than ask Michael again or try to convince him to talk to Stella. Who knew what it would take for him to fully engage with his past, rather than just drifting through the motions of a renovation. She only knew she couldn't force it.

At eleven, the pressure washer shut off. Everyone released a sigh. With the noise of the brick saw also absent, the sudden silence throbbed. Steps sounded on the front porch and in the hallway. Jennifer turned on her ladder as Michael came in, dripping on the plastic that covered the floors. His T-shirt clung to him in a way that was positively indecent. She whisked around to resume her painting, making it clear she assumed he must have come to speak with Stella.

Stella didn't give him the opportunity to choose. "Young man, what's this I hear about you goin' to the lake Sunday instead of to church with us?"

Jennifer stifled a snort, glad somebody could get onto him for something. She expected him to hedge, act awkward, insist he'd forgotten, or make a joke. But she didn't expect his quiet, firm response, without excuses.

"I'm sorry, Stella. We did decide to go to the lake. My aunts, Patricia and Mary, and their families, have the weekend open, and I thought it would be some good family time since we hardly see them anymore. They're coming up from Atlanta."

Jennifer peeked over her shoulder. Stella's discerning eye fixed on Michael, initiating a quiet stare-down. Neither one retreated. Finally

Stella said, "Well, we want you to come another time. It's important to get involved in a community church, whether it's ours or someone else's. Nobody supports you like your church family in hard times, and there's no better place to get closer to God. And you know, in Him we find all we need."

My, my, maybe she ought to give Stella the roller today! She looked away, relieved the woman's crusading now focused on someone else.

Despite her direct words, her sincerity pierced Michael's armor. The lines of his long body softened, and he said quietly, "I know, Stella. Thank you. And we will come another time, just not yet. Not this weekend."

"OK, honey." The black woman reached out and touched Michael's elbow.

Jennifer thought she heard his voice waver slightly as he asked, "Can I talk to Jennifer a minute?"

Jennifer's hand stilled, but her heart thudded, then rushed.

"Sure. I've got to go get more paint." So saying, Stella took her brush and tray and went down the hall.

"Can you come down the ladder just a second?" Michael asked her.

She did so, descending to stand before him. "Yes?" She made sure the question sounded business-like, not hopeful or needy, although that was difficult when he looked like he did right now, wet, contrite and undeniably gorgeous.

"Er ... I think I came across the wrong way earlier and gave you the impression I didn't want you to go because I didn't want your company. It's not that." Michael sighed, looking off to one side like he was trying to choose just the right words. "It's just ... my grandfather is around ninety. His moods and what he says can be kind of unpredictable. Not that he's crass or curses or anything, just more that he's unreliable. He doesn't exactly have a filter. You know what I mean?"

Relief that he hadn't dreaded being with her opened the door to a quick rush of humor. "Sure I do. Sounds just like my mother."

Unexpectedly, Michael laughed. Small lines around his eyes creased, and a dimple appeared in one cheek. The effect transformed him, providing a vision of what he had been like before ... before his mother died? A sudden thought hit her. When he'd declined the James' invitation to church, he'd said, "Not this weekend." Because it was Mother's Day? After all these years, the death of his mother still brought such pain? Or was there more to it? Maybe finding out what had changed him was the key to understanding him. If she questioned James with tact, he might tell her more about his wife's death. And as for Michael, he'd showed again that an inborn or inbred conscience eventually won out over whatever made him withdrawn. Jennifer made a tentative peace offering of a small, return smile.

"I just don't want you to put a lot of stock by what he says. And please don't be offended by anything. But I'd like you to come."

"Really?"

"Really."

CHAPTER TEN

After Jennifer and Michael agreed on a tentative trip to Milledgeville the next Tuesday and Lawrenceville the day after, the week progressed with everyone absorbed in their work. The brick saw shrilled outside, and the electric grinder threw sparks inside as the fireplace crew cut bricks and new metal lintels to size and carefully daubed fresh mortar into gaps. Michael completed the pressure washing of the house and moved to the apothecary. Stella and Jennifer covered the walls with primer while Earl finally tackled the last interior door, then went outside to start sanding. James returned from checking in at their Atlanta construction office in time to take off for the lake Friday night with his son.

By Saturday, Jennifer was ready to crash, just praying no new neighbor would knock on her door. Barb's invitation to come into Athens for dinner and a visit, which Jennifer turned down, took her by surprise. She assumed her former professor desired a full update on their progress.

Instead, Jennifer basked in a lovely day alone, sleeping until ten, padding barefoot across freshly cleaned carpet, kicking back with her newly installed Dish and Bell's Morning Fresh brand of moose tracks ice cream, and lingering in a hot bath. Best of all, she took charge of Yoda's care when the men brought the kitten, boxes and supplies over to the double-wide before departing for Lake Oconee. When he or she, whichever it was, woke up, Jennifer saw antennae-like ears poke up above the edge of the cardboard box. The gray-blue eyes soberly watched her every move until she reached in and lifted the kitten out to play. If she stirred around in the kitchen, he clawed and sprung his way over the precipice and clamored across the linoleum to wait at the foot of the stove. She let the kitten sleep on her and play with a ball and her shoes while she watched TV. She found the cat so entertaining that she didn't even touch her computer. She went off to bed certain that in her relaxed frame of mind she'd sleep just as well as she had the night previous.

However, around midnight the barking of a neighbor's dog woke her. *The* dog. She turned over. Ugh. Why didn't the old man put him up? The barking ceased, she started to drift, then it resumed. Groggy, Jennifer stumbled to her window, which provided a view of the direction of canine concern, her back yard and those adjacent. She blinked. Was that a faint light, like a small flash light, behind the Dunham place?

More awake now, Jennifer cracked open her back door, peeking through the storm glass. She thought she saw some shifting in the shadows in that vicinity, so she eased onto the back deck. There, a chill passed over her that had nothing to do with the temperature. The faint light shone again in the pecan grove. It brought to mind girlhood tales of the South Georgia swamp will-o-the-wisps, spirits that would reveal themselves as lights in order to lead people to disorientation and eventual death in the tangled bog. Of course she was just being fanciful, and the real danger was that a person could be back there. She remembered Sheriff Jake Watson's card on her refrigerator. But what would she say, "Um, I'm seeing lights, can you please go investigate?" By Monday, everyone in town would know the preservation graduate might be a little loco.

She turned to go in when the dog barked again, and something zinged by her head. A bat? She yelped, and someone else started cursing. A very definite shape, this one low and solid, shot through her yard, and behind it materialized the form of a man carrying a gun.

"Otis! Get back here!"

Jennifer ducked for the door. What was going on?

At that moment, her neighbor noticed her. "What are you doing outside, girl? You coulda got kilt."

"I'm on my own deck, and you're in my yard, in case you hadn't noticed! What are *you* doing with a gun, for heaven's sake?"

"I'm tryin' to keep my stupid dog from contractin' leprosy or some other rare disease from that dad-blamed armadillo he's chasin'!" Off in the distance, they heard a fresh explosion of barking. Jennifer guessed Otis had driven the creature back into its den. Calvin Woods stalked across the yard and returned in a moment, dragging Otis home by his collar. He yelled above the panting and scraping of his dog, "I'm sorry 'bout that shot, but if you hear him carryin' on at night, next time stay inside. Nothing will kill those varmints but a shot between their two beady eyes!"

"It would be better for you to refrain from firing your gun on this property. Good night!"

Jennifer slammed her door and stood there fuming. After almost shooting her on her own back deck, he had the gall to tell her to stay inside?

Then she realized the incident could well have happened in Stewart County among some of the country folk she'd known. When had she gotten so high and mighty? After six years of life in a university town with Starbuck's and lecture halls, that's when. Picturing the scene again, she burst into laughter. She might as well own this reality, at least until she moved to Savannah. Then, realizing that what had come so close to her head had been a bullet, she quickly sobered and went back to bed.

Jennifer still fixated on that bullet the next morning when Stella and Earl picked her up. Both were dressed to the nines, Stella in a bright floral skirt, blouse and jacket, and Earl in a royal blue suit and striped tie. Stella took one look at Jennifer's black dress and Mary Jane flats, pressed those lips tight, and gave her a hug. It seemed no matter where Jennifer went outside life at the university she didn't fit, but she didn't have proper dress clothes like Stella's. To further increase her discomfort, Earl invited her to sit up front with him in the car since both teenage boys sprawled in the back seat, dressed like their father, except if possible, in shirts of even brighter hues. They offered Jennifer polite greetings. She'd not been at Dunham House when they had come over to clear brush and re-establish the borders of the front yard beds, but she commented on what a good job they'd done and asked if they'd be available at the end of the week when the pine straw was delivered. Both boys responded with eagerness to work, and the warmth of the family soon began to relax her nerves.

Various shiny vehicles filled the lot of Harmony Grove by the time they arrived, forcing Earl to park in the grass. Sunday school had begun earlier, Stella told her. Jennifer wondered if her presence had caused them to miss their usual class. As they walked in, she swallowed. The clothing of those in the pews exceeded the formality that she remembered from her childhood in a white church. Some of the older women even wore hats. Even though she tried to hide behind Stella, everyone smiled and greeted her. The handsome pastor who shook hands at the door acted like he didn't find it strange that the Jameses brought the only white person in the building. She met a couple of men hired to help Earl paint the exterior of Michael's house, then Stella introduced her to various cousins, aunts and uncles, and even her mother, Dorace Watson, a tiny, adorable woman with silvering curls and a neat polyester suit. Dorace held onto Jennifer's hand a long time, patting it rhythmically and assuring her of how welcome she was. She sat beside her son Jake, who, accompanied by his wife and two middle school-aged daughters, sported a cream-colored suit. He gave her his bright smile and asked if she'd had any further trouble.

About to shrug off the previous night's misadventure, Jennifer remembered she was in the house of the Lord. Sliding into a pew behind Dorace and Jake and between Stella and her boys, Jennifer gave him a brief recounting, attempting to add a humorous spin on the unusual night happenings.

"You want me to come out and check on the place?" Jake offered.

She waved it off. "No, not unless Michael and James notice anything amiss when they return. I'll tell them."

"Well, you give me a call if there's any question. As for the neighbor, that's Calvin Woods for you. He's as country as they come. But a lot of people hunt armadillos at night, especially those that care about their yards."

"I'm sure he was more concerned about his dog."

Jake nodded and laughed. "No doubt about that! That man do like his privacy. I'd lay odds on him being the only one stupid enough to create a ruckus tryin' to stop the Firefly Trail."

"The Firefly Trail?"

"Yeah, the biking trail running out from Athens. They'll bring it all the way through Hermon to Union Point if they can get clearance. And you know how many bicyclists there are in that city. All our local organizations are pushing for it."

"That sounds wonderful. I can't imagine why anyone would want to oppose it. Hey, don't we need to leave room for Earl?" Jennifer asked as she noticed they had filled up the pew, while Stella's husband made his way toward the front, greeting people and shaking hands.

"No, today we get a treat. Our men's choir sings on special occasions, like today, Mother's Day," Stella told her. "Earl's an elder and sings with them. When the service starts, he'll sit up front."

"Speaking of which, we've got to go up," Jake hissed over his shoulder. "Come on, Mama."

What, was Dorace an elder, too? Jennifer noticed that between the congregation and the podium and choir loft two small sections of pews faced each other. On the one side older women of the church gathered. Jake seated Dorace there. The other side remained empty. Jennifer presumed the elders would take their places there momentarily in the tradition Stella had referenced. As Pastor Simms circulated through the congregation greeting every family, Jake disappeared through a side door in search of the men's ensemble.

Minutes later, the choir filed in wearing bright robes, musicians took their places at the piano, keyboard, drums and guitar, one man took up a tambourine, and an explosion of joyful music almost as startling as the sun breaking through the stained glass windows filled the church. Everyone stood and began clapping and singing.

At Jennifer's bemused look, which she didn't conceal quickly enough, Stella said, "You probably won't know the songs. Just clap and smile." And giving her a reassuring squeeze around her shoulders, Stella broke into a lovely alto, swaying and patting her hands together.

Jennifer attempted to emulate her, minus the singing. The fact that the tunes were unfamiliar wouldn't have been surprising even in a white Baptist church. But the liveliness of the unique worship style unsettled Jennifer. Strongly rhythmic and passionate, the minor key lent this music a mournful quality. At times the song leader would call out a line which the choir and congregation would echo. Many people raised their hands or shouted "Yes, Jesus!" or "Thank you, Lord!" at unexpected moments. Their transported expressions confused her. They acted like God stood right behind the pulpit. Then again, a strange energy did fill the room.

Half an hour later, they finally sat down. Jennifer flexed her toes, glad she'd worn comfortable shoes. As the men's chorus sang a special, a man in a dark purple suit spaced four chairs across the front of the sanctuary. When the music ended, several men from the choir, including Earl, moved to stand behind the chairs. The elders, Jennifer assumed. During the next special, they knelt and, with fists pressed to furrowed foreheads, appeared to be in prayer.

At the next break, one of the elders prayed aloud. "Oh, Lord, we bless You for the opportunity to be in Your house. We ask Your blessing on each and every person here today, that they might hear from You. We ask Your anointing on Pastor Simms as He brings Thy word. Strengthen our homes and families represented here today. May Your truth shine forth, and may we rise up to do Thy bidding. Amen."

When the music ebbed, the elders shook each other's hands and went to sit in the empty, side pews, except for Earl, who announced from the pulpit that money from the two buckets now being set in place of the chairs went for the support of the ministry and the pastor. As the entire congregation rose and trailed up to the front row by row, Jennifer panicked. She had not brought a purse. Now she'd look ungrateful and embarrass Stella and Earl.

Stella whispered, "Don't worry about it, honey. Nobody expects you to put money in. Just walk by with us."

Jennifer could only think of one other sacrament over which she'd be certain to embarrass herself further: communion. Hopefully the bread and wine wouldn't be pulled out next. She followed Stella up front, nodded and smiled awkwardly at the ushers behind the buckets as her friend dropped in a big bill, and finally sank into the pew with a sense of relief.

Moments later Earl led the announcements. "We have here a letter of invitation from our brethren at Joyful Baptist. May tenth. 'Our dear brothers and sisters in Christ at Harmony Grove, we write to extend an invitation for you to join us for our 100th homecoming celebration to be held Sunday, June 30 at eleven a.m. After many weeks of rehearsal, a community choir will render praise unto the Lord, Reverend Paul Overhower of Thankful Baptist in Winder, Georgia, will fill our pulpit, and following the services we host our annual dinner on the grounds.'"

When Earl completed that and several other, equally formal pronouncements, he joined the elders while Pastor Simms took the stage.

"Today I'm sharin' with you what God put on my heart this week about how our Lord Jesus, in the course of His life, provided wisdom for mothers. Only by drawing on His help and example can a woman be the kind of mother God intends."

"That's right," someone exclaimed with enough fervor to draw a smattering of laughter.

"Yes, sister. I hear you. Many of you in here today are mothers, some in the midst of raisin' your babies, some with teenagers you're about ready to boot out of the nest—" good-natured chuckles of agreement arose— "and some with grown children, but even you, my dear mothers up here close to me, in the twilight of your lives, you perhaps more than the young mothers can be that example to your children and grandchildren, bringin' them up in the nurture and admonition of the Lord." The hat-clad heads on the side pews nodded sagely back at him.

As he talked, Pastor Simms walked the stage and down into the congregation to point people out. His glistening hair, pin-striped suit and red handkerchief mesmerized Jennifer. She just hoped he wouldn't focus that charismatic attention on her.

"But you say, 'Jesus was a man, Son of God. He is Father to us.' Yes, He is! But the Good Book also makes it clear that God possesses the qualities of a mother. It says He knows everything about each of His children. I said *everything*! There is nothing you can hide from God, my friend. He knows it before we know Him! He knows every hair on our heads ... and every thought in them, too. And He loves us the same! Which is just amazing! Can I get an 'amen?'"

"Amens" and appreciative nodding followed.

"In the Gospels Jesus told His disciples how He wanted to gather His chosen people to Himself like a mother hen would gather her chicks, but they would not let Him. I tell you, the Israelites did not have anything over on us. Are we not that way? Stiff-necked in our rebellion against God?"

"Mmm-hmm," some older women said.

Pastor Simms directed, "Turn to your neighbor and look them in the eye and say, 'Are you stiff-necked in your rebellion against God?'"

On the other side of Jennifer, Jamal and Gabe elbowed and pointed their fingers at each other. Stella could only turn to her. Jennifer cringed as Stella smiled softly and repeated the question. At the kindness, not accusation, in her voice, Jennifer made a show of laughing like she was playing along, but the question made her uncomfortable, and she could not ask it back.

"Now say, 'But He loves you anyway. So soften your heart of stone.'"

Jennifer's stomach sank. She wished the floor would open and swallow her. "But He loves you, Jennifer," Stella told her. Something in her eyes pierced Jennifer through and made her feel vulnerable and exposed. The older woman reached out and took her hand and gave it a reassuring squeeze before returning her attention to the preacher.

"That's right. The prophet Isaiah tells us that Jesus inscribed our names on His palms. Inscribed where those nails were, that's where!"

A man near the front shouted, "Thank you, Jesus!"

"Because of that, He will no more forget you than a nursing mother could forget her child. Whoever you are today, wherever you are today, God knows you. God loves you, even though we are all born in sin. Sin is like a cancer that will always make us choose our own way. It puts self on the throne instead of God, and it always bring us to pain and ruin." The pastor pumped his fist downward, accentuating each point. Like a naughty child being chided, Jennifer curled her toes in her shoes. "Someone had to break its power. Someone perfect. To take away the stain of that sin, who was the only acceptable sacrifice?"

"Jesus," called the congregation.

"He went to that cross to die so He could have that love relationship with you, to restore the fellowship with Him we were created for before sin entered in the garden. He wants to be that friend that sticks closer than a brother. The one who will carry you through trials and pain. The one who will never leave!" Pastor Simms' voice rolled like a wave toward a crescendo, and along with it, murmurs and sighs and hand raisings issued from his flock. He came to his point. "And who does that sound like more than a mother?"

"Yes, that's right," some of the women agreed.

"Sacrificial, faithful, selfless: the traits of a good mother. Not just in His Word but in His life we see this motherly love." For the moment, the pastor's voice returned to an even keel. "Think of how patiently Jesus taught His disciples and the crowds, using parables, stories, they could understand. And He still had to explain them further. Mothers, you have to explain things more than one way sometimes, don't you? And how patiently He did that! When the crowds pressed around Him when He was tired and hungry, He did not rebuke them. And who received the greatest patience? 'The least of these,' the children. He told His disciples, 'Suffer the little children to come to me, for such is the Kingdom of God.'" Pastor Simms paused. "There is something else a mother does. She heals. When the blind man came to Jesus, He healed. When the paralytic was lowered through the roof by his friends where Jesus was preaching, He healed. When the woman with the twelve-year flow of blood touched just the hem of His garment, He healed. Over and over He healed, because He is Jehovah Rapha, our Healer. His nature is to heal. He heals our bodies, and He heals our souls. The psalmist David said there is healing in His wings. Under His wings we should take refuge. In that image can't you just see the protective embrace of a mother with her child?" Pastor Simms' hands made a tender, cradling gesture close to the breast of his fine suit.

Jennifer wiggled. Too bad Kelly had taken to dropping off her children at church when she imagined the whispers and stares judged her. Otherwise she might have absorbed some of these wonderful nurturing and protective qualities Jesus modeled in the Good Book. Bitterness shot from somewhere deep into her chest, flooding it with heat. Well, she might have to sit in this service today, but at least she didn't have to pretend warm affection for the woman who most definitely had *not* protected her. And she didn't have to listen anymore, either. This really didn't have to do with her, after all. She'd finally put the miles between herself and her mother. Neither was she about to become a mother any time soon. As Pastor Simms went on to assure the mothers present that they, like Jesus, should withdraw to their prayer closets to recharge their batteries, Jennifer occupied herself by studying those around her. Gradually the swirl of emotions banked. It was always better when one put oneself outside a situation.

Stella and Earl invited her to their house for a cookout—Earl was grilling steaks, and there were potatoes in the oven and a cake the boys had made for their mother—but Jennifer was not about to crash their family time. She was eager to be alone. All the noise and strange concepts and pretending wearied her. She didn't need a prayer closet to recharge, though; a frozen meal and some ice cream with reruns of "This Old House" would do.

"Thank you so much for coming. You made my Mother's Day," Stella told her warmly. Jennifer didn't understand that, either, but she smiled and returned the thanks for the opportunity. "I hope you'll come again sometime. We'd love to have you any Sunday."

Jennifer nodded, but tamped down mixed emotions. On one hand, everyone had welcomed her with great warmth, and the peace and joy in the church had lifted her spirit. On the other, she'd felt so conspicuous, not just because of her pale skin, but because a far deeper separation existed between her and those people. They knew what the pastor was talking about. They lived it. And it was totally foreign to her.

Several episodes of "This Old House" later, Yoda fed and sleeping on her lap, Jennifer felt herself again. Placing the kitten in his box, she went to the window and looked out. The late afternoon sun warmed the back deck, and the bees buzzed around the knock-out roses. Some of those would look pretty beside a white picket fence where the driveway turned into Dunham House. Eagerness to talk to Michael this week about the landscape plans for the front yard stirred. The bark of a more distant neighbor dog reminded her of last night's adventure, and curiosity stirred, too. Had someone really been in Michael's back yard? Had they left any evidence of their trespass? With the ground dry, it was not likely, but on a whim, and wanting fresh air, Jennifer put on her boots and went outside.

She investigated the area right behind the home. Some prints appeared near the outhouse, but given the "friend" she'd encountered on her last visit there, she didn't care to open the door. The thing was, anyone could have made these prints. Then she noticed with some surprise that Michael's truck was back in the driveway. She didn't want him to come out and ask what she was doing. She wanted the rest of her Sunday to herself. A quick stroll over the back part of the lot to look for anything unusual, and she'd return to the double-wide.

The chirp of crickets and the song of birds calmed her spirits. Past the pecan grove and the well, a heavy section of blackberry vines sagged, thick with white blooms. These and some wild blueberry bushes she spied promised tasty rewards in about a month. To her left, Jennifer noticed a shady trail winding into a field behind the abandoned lot between Michael's and the antique store. If anyone wanted to trespass, they could park a car unnoticed in the thick trees at the front of the lot. She decided to follow the trail and was about to step out into the open field when she heard a sound that stopped her cold. She couldn't have reacted with greater heart-pounding alarm had a rattlesnake rattled. No, this sound was even more foreign, even though the only danger came from embarrassment should her presence be discovered. Michael sat on a fallen log at the edge of the woods, dressed in khaki shorts and a faded blue T-shirt. He didn't see her, and wouldn't have even if she hadn't ducked back onto the trail. Because his dark head hung between his hands, and he was crying.

Crying? Did such a man cry? Did men cry at all? Jennifer knew they did, but she'd never seen one. And he wasn't just sniffling. With his elbows braced on his knees, he wept like his heart was broken. That wasn't the way someone cried over a mother who had died twenty or even fifteen years ago. No. Jennifer recognized the keening sound of deep pain and aloneness, because it had howled out of her, too, many times, when no one was around to hear.

Breathing fast, confused and upset by what she'd witnessed and aware that it would change the way she looked at the man even if she didn't want it to, Jennifer hurried back home.

CHAPTER ELEVEN

"Good morning," Jennifer offered in a voice not quite up to strength. She smiled and clutched her travel coffee mug. The beautiful day promised opportunity for an enjoyable road trip. But as Michael responded in his polite, low-key manner, the awkwardness of knowing deep reserves of emotion lodged behind this man's aloof exterior washed over her. She climbed into his F150 and pulled the heavy door shut. She reminded herself that theirs was a work-based relationship, so whatever caused Michael such hidden grief did not concern her.

Besides, a little sadness lingered for her this morning, too. Yoda had kept her company since Michael's and James' return from the lake, but since the kitten needed tending while they traveled today, she brought Yoda and his box and accessories to James. And the look on his face told Jennifer she'd not be getting the pet back right away. Even the older man had grown attached to the unexpected and amusing addition to their lives, and for Jennifer, the prospect of returning to an empty house loomed so much less appealing now.

As they pulled out of the driveway and headed south, Michael glanced over at her. She'd looped her hair back in a clasp, and she wore one of her cuter blouses with capris and sandals. After all, today work did not demand clothes that could get dirty, and even she knew one dressed decently to meet someone's elderly relative. To cover her discomfort at his attention, she flipped through her notebook. Locating her landscaping notes, she pushed up her glasses and was about to speak when he did first.

"Can I ask you a question?"

"Sure."

"Why don't you wear contacts?"

She wasn't expecting that one. When she took a minute to respond, he added, "It's just that you seem to always be messing with the glasses. I'd imagine they get in your way sometimes with the kind of work you do."

"I do have contacts. I've just not worn them. When I spent most of my time in a classroom, it wasn't an issue." Glancing over at him, she made herself smile to appear relaxed. "But you may be right. I should probably wear them more now." Agreeing was easier than telling him that contacts posed unnecessary expense while her limited funds had always been consumed by rent, food and books ... and that the few times she'd worn them, she'd felt bare, exposed, without the familiar barrier through which she viewed the world. Yep, best to change the subject. "So I've jotted down some ideas about the property landscaping, if you'd like to hear them."

Michael's quick shift of attention back to the road, as he hung a hand over the steering wheel, made her wonder if she'd come across too abrupt again. "Yeah, sure."

"OK, well, first of all, I should have talked about this with you before you put the grass in, but something more immediate always demanded my time while I was in Hermon. But anyway, since it's in, I assume you want to keep it there."

"Uh. *Yeah*." Michael shot her an incredulous glance.

"It's just that a lot of 1840s homes included a parterre garden in the front yard."

"A what?"

"Parterre means a formal garden on a level surface with planting beds in symmetrical patterns. Gravel or sand pathways connected the beds and different themed areas, and tightly clipped hedges or stone edged the gardens. The Thomas Grant House in Athens provides a great example of parterre, if you're familiar with it."

"No, I'm not."

Of course he wasn't, she reminded herself. He hadn't lived in Athens. She decided to provide more explanation. "Often a white picket fence enclosed boxwoods in a diamond pattern. Sometimes the owners placed potted shrubs around but never allowed them to grow tall enough to obstruct the parterre view."

"No, Jennifer, that is definitely out. I do not want to tear up my expensive sod and put in a bunch of shrubs and dainty pots that I'll just have to maintain. Historical accuracy is OK, but I need it to blend with easy living."

"Of course. I figured you'd feel that way." She swallowed. Despite her words, his displeasure, communicated in a tone of sharp, exaggerated patience, still made something inside her ache. "So here are my alternative thoughts. Picture this: a section of picket fence on either side of the driveway where you turn in, pine straw in those beds and around the house, and naturalized under the magnolias because there's no way to keep it perfect otherwise."

"Yes, and we must be perfect." Michael grinned briefly.

She frowned at him. "I'm trying to work with you here."

"I know. Thank you. Go ahead."

"I'd like to see what Wal-Mart has in today as far as a few basics are concerned, some knock-out roses for the turn-in, crepe myrtles, gardenias, Sweet Williams, dwarf phlox, azaleas and so forth. These are all appropriate to the period and the area, having been documented to places like Westville, the Tulle Smith House in Atlanta, and Ferrell Gardens in LaGrange."

Those locales registered the exact same amount of recognition the Thomas Grant House had, but to his credit, Michael just said, "I'm good with that."

"I'd set these out in the beds as needed and keep it simple. The landscaping should not overwhelm the house."

"Agreed. Is that all?"

"Well, I have in mind some rarer varieties, too, like quince and historic roses. An 1817 climbing rose called Seven Sisters would look lovely mixed with the jasmine and wisteria on the trellis archways. Then maybe a Rose Campion and Cherokee Rose or Old Blush. What do you think?" She hoped he wouldn't object. She'd spent hours on the computer, supplementing her knowledge from previous classes with extra research.

"I think I have no idea, and I'll leave that to you. I'll be there to dig the holes."

Now they were getting somewhere. But Jennifer grimaced, afraid her next statement might upset the balance. "I'd probably have to visit a real nursery to find those."

"If you need a few plants from a nicer nursery, I'm all right with that. I expected as much. Just remember I don't want to spend every waking moment watering and pruning, and I don't want to have to hire a full-time gardener. Whatever you do, so long as you keep those stipulations in mind, I don't care. Within reason, of course." This last caveat contained a quick warning glance that promised grim repercussions should she go berserk with his checkbook.

"Got it. Not to worry. Not a big shopper, remember?"

Michael nodded. "You should go to Greatness Grows Nursery in Lexington. They should have what you need. Just let me know when you want to borrow the truck."

Jennifer offered him a smile. "Thank you." Then, like the famous squirrel from "Ice Age" when he spotted his beloved nut, Jennifer's head whisked around as they drove past a Federal-style house, half-hidden in a grove of trees and cloaked in that intriguing air of abandonment. Before she could stop herself, her finger jabbed the glass of the window and her neck craned. "Oh, look!"

"Shall I turn around so you can get a better view? Maybe knock on the door and offer to help them get a nice green sign for the yard?"

"No. You're not funny, either. Besides, I think it was unoccupied."

"Ah, even better."

Jennifer straightened and peered ahead down the highway, trying not to notice Michael's crooked grin that really was quite charming. *We're not friends*, she reminded herself. *He's my employer. And I've mistaken harassment for flirtation before.* As for the house, maybe she could get a better look on the way home. "So, another thing I wondered was about the old well. It deserves a well house in keeping with the trellis and millwork on the place. Maybe some elaeagnus vine and boxwoods at the base. What do you think?"

"I think when there's time that would pose no problem and would be a good task for Dad."

Jennifer nodded. "Then the last thing is, it would be historically unforgiveable to not reconstruct a medicinal herb garden behind the apothecary. There's plenty of room there, and I can figure most of it out, but it might be helpful to consult with a local expert."

"I've heard about a lady living in the county who knows a lot about medicinal herbs. She'd probably help you choose what to grow, but Jennifer, who is going to tend this and keep it going? This isn't going to be a house museum. I don't have staff. And I have no interest in puttering around in an herb garden."

Her countenance fell. "I hadn't thought of that." Suddenly Jennifer realized she'd made plans like *she* owned Dunham House, or at least like Michael planned to employ a year-round staff! Begrudgingly, she saw his point. "I'll have to figure that out later."

"That's fine. No hurry, really. Today's simple. Wal-Mart and basics."

"Yes, that's right. So tell me a little about your grandparents." Surely it wasn't too personal to learn something about the man she was going to meet today. To keep it casual, she looked out at the endless growth of second-generation pine whizzing by her window rather than at her companion.

"Well, Donald fought in WWII. After the war, he spent his life as a postmaster. It didn't pay much, but enough and with good enough benefits that his wife, Gloria, could stay home with the kids."

"The aunts you met at the lake this past weekend."

"Yes, they had three daughters. Patricia was the oldest, then my mother, Linda, then Mary."

"Do you have cousins in Atlanta, too?"

"Yes, I do. They helped make up for being an only child growing up."

"Did you always want to be in construction with your dad?"

Michael fell silent a minute. Jennifer glanced over to witness an apparent internal struggle manifest on his face. "Grandma always wanted me to be a doctor, and for a while I thought I would, but that didn't work out."

His expression made it so clear that he didn't want to talk any more on the subject that Jennifer banked the next question that came to her mind, which was if he felt like he was letting his grandmother down. She nodded and said, "I'd love to hear about your grandfather's WWII experiences."

"I'm sure you would, and that's a great question to ask him to get him started reminiscing."

"Duly noted. I'll save it for him. And something just occurred to me."

"What's that?"

"The herb garden at the apothecary: if someone else tended it, you'd have no objection to it, would you?"

Tilting his head in thought, Michael pursed his lips. "I don't guess I would."

148

Jennifer smiled to herself, enjoying a view of the sun shining off Lake Sinclair. Michael refrained from inquiring why she looked so satisfied. Their conversation from that point on centered around Jennifer's story of seeing lights behind Michael's house and almost getting shot by Calvin Woods. Michael assured her he'd found nothing amiss upon his return home but promised they would look around at the cypress trees today.

After following a circuitous route across Milledgeville, Jennifer stretched and groaned in relief when she climbed down from Michael's truck. Donald waited for them on the bench just outside the sliding entrance doors of his wing of the VA home, a walker parked in front of him. He greeted Jennifer by standing, taking her hand and gazing at her from under busy white brows. The origin of Michael's bright blue eyes became clear. Even dimmed with macular degeneration, Donald's eyes recalled a mischievous and charming younger man.

"Is this sweet little thing your girlfriend, Michael?"

Jennifer laughed and withdrew her hand while Michael said, "No, Grandpa, this is Jennifer Rushmore, the lady with the expertise on old houses helping us restore Georgia Pearl's place near Athens."

"Oh! Well, pleased to meet you." Donald sought her hand again with his leathery one and shook it. "What are you doing down here?"

"Why, I came to meet you."

"What? Why'd you do that?"

"Because I wanted to. And I like plants, and we're going to pick out plants for your garden today."

"We are?" Donald cried with glee and rubbed his hands. He glanced at his grandson, who nodded. "Well, isn't that sweet of you? I don't know why you'd want to come all that way to see me and get plants. Come here, you big, ugly thing, give me a hug." Donald reached out, and Michael bent his neck. The older man completed the embrace by ruffling his grandson's short, dark hair, which stood up in spikes. "Here, I done messed him up. Fix his hair," he told Jennifer.

She laughed in an uncomfortable manner and gave an obligatory swipe at Michael's head.

"Aw, you're too shy. I guess that isn't professional, huh? Has he been treating you right?"

A yelled summary of her disapproval of Michael's lack of appreciation for history, both personal or structural, especially mantels, was no way to begin an acquaintance, so Jennifer said simply, "Yes, sir, he's very nice." Overall that was true.

"Nice, is he? That isn't the Michael I know!"

Michael cleared his throat and asked with emphasis, "Grandpa, you want to go in and get anything before we leave?"

"No, I want to go. If we go in, all the old biddies in their wheel chairs will mob you, then you'll be all they can talk about for a week. You're far too handsome for this place. Let's go get some lunch."

"You just can't compete when I'm around," Michael teased him.

"That's right, and I don't like it."

"I was thinking Long John's," Michael said as he helped Donald to his feet, moving the walker in front of him. "I know how you like the fried fish."

"Oh, no, son, I've got a craving for a Big Mac today."

Jennifer laughed.

Donald turned to her and said in all earnestness, "You can't get a decent burger in this place."

Jennifer realized the inconvenience the truck posed when they went to load Donald into it, not just because it was too high but because it lacked an extended cab, meaning she had to sit by Michael to allow the elderly man easier access. The collapsed walker fit nicely in the bed, but Jennifer debated which moment that followed alarmed her more: when Donald teetered backward from his pose on the running board and Michael had to catch him and shove him into the cab, or when Michael came around and slid in an elbow's length from her side.

"Sorry," Michael murmured to her as he started the ignition. He gave her a rueful glance. "You didn't know what you were getting into, did you?"

"Nonsense, this is fine, just fine!" declared Donald. "Son, I need some more of them Little Debbies and some peppermints. We'll have time to get those, too, won't we?"

"Yes, Grandpa, plenty of time."

Jennifer smirked as she and Michael shared a glance. "Mr. Johnson—"

150

"Blankenship, honey, it's Blankenship."

"Oh. Of course. I guess I was thinking you were James' father for a minute there. Mr. Blankenship—"

"Just call me Donald."

"Donald. Michael told me you were in WWII. I'm a big history buff, of course, so I'd love to hear about what you did."

"Aw, I didn't do much."

"Sure you did! You served our country in one of the most important wars of all time! Were you in the infantry?"

"Yes, I was." Donald went on to tell her how he'd been assigned to drive a supply truck in Italy, often without headlights due to the threat of enemy fighters flying overhead. He waxed eloquent on the impressive wine and women until the Golden Arches came into view. Inside, once they settled Donald with his burger, Coke and fries, he asked them, "So how's it coming at the old place? I'd love to come see it, Son, but you know I can't hardly see anyway. Just far away," he told Jennifer. "That's why I had to leave my house and quit driving."

She nodded in understanding. "I'm sorry to hear that."

"I sometimes wonder if it was on account of the war. But I don't mind much. I like living at the home. We stay busy. I go visit friends in the other wings, work in the garden and lift weights in the gym. We have special events and play Bingo, and generally the food's pretty good. It's a lot better than living at home all alone since I can't get around anymore. Anyway, I bet it's looking good. Did you move into the house yet?"

"Not nearly, Grandpa. It's a big job." Michael filled him in on their progress, which, peppered with Donald's questions, took most of their meal. Michael impressed Jennifer with his patience. Jennifer cringed when Michael had to shout some of his answers, but Michael just acted like he didn't notice the indignant faces turning in their direction.

At Wal-Mart, they visited the grocery section first, where Michael picked on his grandfather about his extensive and unhealthy snack selections.

"Seeing as how I'll be eighty-nine soon, you can see it hasn't hurt me any," Donald pointed out.

"Well, I don't know about that!"

Donald pretended to run over Michael with his walker and said, "Oh, sorry, didn't see you there."

"Yeah, maybe that's why they took your driver's license."

While trying to stay out of their way and laughing at their banter, Jennifer couldn't help but glance twice at Michael's dimple. When sufficient Yoo-hoos and root beers filled the buggy to satisfy Donald, he turned to Jennifer and suggested, "Come on, let's leave him and go get the plants. He's too much trouble." So saying, he took off with Jennifer pushing the buggy and Michael trailing behind. Michael grabbed another buggy at the entrance to the garden section.

As she helped Donald select tomato, green bean, squash, zucchini, strawberry and pepper plants, discussing the merits and apparent health of each specimen, he acted like his grandson wasn't there. He clearly enjoyed the undivided attentions of a young lady, which made Jennifer feel unusually pretty and helpful. Her real father's parents had lived far away and died while she was still young, and Kelly's parents were wastrels, so she bloomed like the garden plants under Donald's grandfatherly approval.

"Will someone help you put these in?" she asked about the vegetable plants. Fearing Donald's energy might be waning, she made some quick selections for Dunham House.

Donald fingered the tender leaves of a tomato plant as though drawing sustenance from just its feel. "Yeah, there's a man who comes to help the garden club. He should be there end of the week." He lifted his fingers to sniff them and shook his head. "Time was, I thought a tomato plant smelled too bitter. Now I'd just like to smell it."

"Oh, Mr. Blankenship, I'm sure these will grow tomatoes delicious enough that you can at least taste them! Well, if you're sure about getting the plants in. Michael and I could always stay to help you plant them if we need to."

Michael raised his eyebrows at her, eyes wide. She frowned back.

"Oh, no, honey, all the garden club will want to help on the day we meet. Fridays. They'd be mad at me if we did it all without them. And some of them you don't want to get mad. You can say what you want about old people being senile, but that's one thing these never do forget."

"An offense?"

"Yeah, an offense." The blue eyes twinkled.

Jennifer laughed. "OK, then, we'll just make sure to water and put the plants in a good place before we go. We wouldn't want to make you any enemies."

"You're a good girl," Donald proclaimed unexpectedly as they stood in the check-out line. "Michael, you'd be smart to keep this one around after the work's finished."

Jennifer turned scarlet. "I'll probably be moving around Christmas."

"Moving?" He said it like she'd just announced she planned to commit a felony.

"Yes, to Savannah. I'm applying for a job there."

"Well, are you that sure you're going to get it?"

"No, but I'm hopeful." She helped Michael arrange the bar codes on the plants so that the clerk could scan them easily. The acrid smell of fertilizer wafted around the cash register. Michael pretended he didn't hear the conversation, but when his grandfather spoke again his eyes cut straight to Donald.

"Well, I'm hopeful you and this boy here'll hook up so you'll come see me again. After what he went through with that sweet little Ashley, I figure it'll take a miracle to get him—"

"*Grandfather.*" Not Grandpa, "grandfather."

Jennifer felt tension lash through the air like a whip. Donald looked angry at the silencing. To ease his hurt feelings, she offered, "I *will* come see you again. That is, if Michael will let me." She placed her hand over Donald's and smiled. He grabbed on, squeezing. His yellowed nails sank into her skin, but she didn't pull back.

"Of course I'll let you," Michael said, but the way he snapped it sounded more irritated than placating.

In silence, Jennifer helped Donald to the truck. They both got him in, then unloaded the buggies.

"Sorry," Michael offered tersely. "He knows there are things I don't like to talk about."

Things you don't need to know about, he might as well have added, although she merely gave a nod. Ashley. Was she the reason for Michael's broken weeping the other day? Didn't look like she was going to find out any time soon. And she had no reason to pry, not just because of the employer-employee relationship she'd reminded herself of earlier that very day, but when she also kept secrets she never intended to share, either. Hanging out with Michael and his grandfather lowered her defenses, she realized, because it sort of felt like family, at least like she imagined family should be.

Donald's thoughts traced a similar path, for once they got into the truck, he asked Michael with something of a grumpy defiance, "Have you met any of your grandmother's people up that way yet?"

"Not that I know of."

"You know Gloria wanted you to. That was one reason she willed you the house. Well, she had to will it to Patricia and Mary, too, but she knew what they'd do with it." When Jennifer turned to look at him, he added, "Gloria knew I had enough to live on with my own savings, social security and money from the house sale. So we agreed each of our daughters would receive one-third of their mother's estate. With Michael's mother already gone, that one-third went directly to Michael. Patricia and Mary had no need of that old house. They had their own lives in Atlanta, you know. But they knew Michael was spoilin' for a change, and his dad, too. This restoration gave them something to focus on. But it also gave them the chance to reconnect to the past, see."

"No, I don't see. You're saying Michael still has relatives in Oglethorpe County?"

Michael glanced over, frowning.

"That's what I gathered from what Gloria told me just before she died. On her death bed, she said her mama had broken with some of her family years ago and had always regretted it."

"Grandma never said anything like that to me."

"Well, son, you weren't quite yourself at that time, now were you? You had a lot else going on."

At that, Michael's jaw tightened. Jennifer sensed she sat smack dab in the middle of something she didn't understand. Apparently Michael didn't, either.

"Why did Georgia Pearl break with her family?" he asked.

Donald looked straight out the windshield. "I think that's something she meant for you to discover."

"Grandpa, this isn't funny. This isn't some scavenger hunt. If you know, just tell me!"

"I don't know all of it, son, and I don't know if you want me saying what I do know in front of Jennifer."

"Well, it's a fine time to mention that." Michael jerked the wheel into the driveway of the looming, three-building VA complex. He pulled the truck into a parking space and leaned over, tapping the elderly man's knee when he still wouldn't look at him. "Jennifer's been after me for the family history anyway, for this report she's doing. That's part of the reason I told you we're going to Grandma's storage shed tomorrow. So out with it. It can't be that bad."

Donald turned his head to face Michael, and compassion dawned in his rheumy eyes. Clearly he didn't think Michael was ready for what he was about to share. "All I know is it had something to do with Georgia Pearl's mama being part Negro."

CHAPTER TWELVE

The whole way back from Milledgeville, Michael stewed in an angry silence. Jennifer cringed away from the emotional steam emanating across the cab of the truck. When she suggested that he talk with Stella when they got back, Michael said thank you, he'd do so when he was good and ready.

Jennifer looked out her window. Was Michael upset because he had African American blood in his line, or was it something else? While a blended family would have caused major ripples at the turn of the 20th Century, the concept hardly shocked anyone today. True, perhaps mixed race families turned up less often in the country than the city. Jennifer noticed that where she grew up and in Oglethorpe, blacks and whites pretty much occupied their own spheres, despite occasional friendships like those between Stella and Mary Ellen. But Michael hailed from the city, where children with *café au lait* skin and corkscrew curls jumped rope on every playground.

A minute later, he answered her silent question. He knew he'd offended her. "Look, it's just that I'm upset to be put in this position. Grandma should have told me this a long time ago. I don't understand why she didn't."

"She was a child of the segregation era, though, wasn't she?" Jennifer asked. "Maybe she was afraid."

"Afraid of what?"

"I don't know, afraid if she came up here and tried to reconnect, it wouldn't go well. Afraid the family in Oglethorpe held anger against her mother, and by default, her, too. Afraid she wouldn't know what to say. Who knows? Lots of reasons could have kept her from acting on what her mother told her when she died."

"And we'll never know. There's no one left to ask. I guess that's part of what makes me mad."

Wanting to be supportive and realizing it showed progress Michael even shared this with her, Jennifer nodded.

"And the other part is, it's just like her to control things even after she's gone. In life she always manipulated but never really explained. What Grandma wanted, Grandma got. Now she's done the same thing, channeling me up here to Athens to restore this house I didn't even know existed and dumping a whole different line of ancestors on me she only vaguely alluded to, not to mention living family members. I mean, who are they? Do I already know them? And how stupid do I look to them right now?"

"I wouldn't think you look stupid at all," Jennifer murmured. Something told her to reach over and touch him, just a pat of reassurance. Acting on that strange prodding, or even wanting to, would defy all of her character and experience. She tried to ignore it, but it overpowered her. Touching his hand would be too personal, so she patted his forearm about like one would pat a squid, then jerked back into a crossed-arm pose.

Michael glanced at her in surprise, and his irritation softened momentarily to appreciation. "Thanks for understanding."

The rest of the way home he stared out the front windshield, moody and not attempting to share further. She left him alone, but when they pulled in the driveway and Michael put the truck in park, she ventured to ask, "Your grandma, when she pushed you to do things, were they generally for your own good?"

He sighed and grudgingly admitted, "Yes."

"Well, maybe she felt this would be, too. Maybe she thought bequeathing you the house opened the door to reconnect with the past. She knew you and your dad could take that step even if she hadn't."

"You may be right. I just need some time to sort it out. Would you mind ... I don't want to hurt your feelings or anything, but I really think I should go tomorrow by myself. I can take photos of any antiques and bring back anything that gives a history of the house and family for you to look at. But there's gonna be a lot of just ... junk ... to go through. And I really could use the time to think."

"Sure." Jennifer opened her door and got out, fighting mixed emotions. In her mind, the storage shed waited to fling its doors open to her, as inviting as a treasure trove. She wanted to see for herself what it held, but Michael was right. Its interior contained personal memories for Michael of his mother and grandmother, who had died just last year. He could deal with those more effectively if she didn't intrude, forcing him to focus on antiques and make conversation on the long ride there and back. As an introvert herself, she got that.

"You're not mad?" he asked as he let the tail gate down.

About to reach for the black plastic pot of an azalea, Jennifer paused and looked at him. He cared if she was mad. That was new. Awkward awareness caused her to flush as she assured him, "No, I'm not mad."

But Michael's request did force her to rearrange her plans. Somehow priming lost its appeal. Stella expected her to be gone anyway, and the mystery of Michael's family loomed in Jennifer's mind like a puzzle with gaping holes. So the next morning she drove to Lexington to the local library.

Silencing her cell phone as she entered, her hopes sank. The whole library consisted of just one large room, the various sections partitioned off by the tall shelving, and the girl behind the main desk didn't even look out of high school. But Jennifer walked up and told her, "I was wondering if someone could help me with genealogy."

"You're in luck. Our historical specialist is here today. Just a minute, and I'll go get her."

Jennifer perked up as the clerk retreated into an office and returned with a stately woman nearing retirement age. Her shoulder-length hair, iron gray and turned under at the ends, framed high cheekbones and an aristocratic nose. She modeled—not just wore—a loose-fitting tunic blouse, long skirt, and tasteful gold and diamond jewelry.

"I'm Grace Stevenson," she said, holding out her hand. "Are you by chance the young woman working on the Dunham house?"

Surprised, Jennifer shook her hand. "I am. Jennifer Rushmore."

"It's such a pleasure to meet you. I've heard such good things about you, and really, the improvements on the house speak for themselves. The way you took those trees out and replaced the roof really brightened the place up. Honestly, it makes the whole community more alive. Everyone is so excited about what you are doing."

"Really?" Jennifer collected herself. "Well, thank you." Grace's last name jangled a memory bell in Jennifer's mind. Wait, wasn't

Stevenson the family that owned the lot between Michael's and the antique store? She had to ask, but did so with delicacy.

Grace gave a modulated chuckle. "Yes, my husband's father, Bryce, owns that lot. I'm afraid their family fame precedes me everywhere in this county."

"I'm sorry. I know exactly how that is." Jennifer smiled, comforting herself with the thought that familial craziness did not confine itself to trailer trash.

"Oh, please, no apologies. You're here to learn more about the Dunhams, are you? I thought you might be coming in."

"Yes, I am. Can you help me get started? I'd like to see if there is anything on Hampton Dunham, who was born in 1861. Would you have records here, or would I have to go to the courthouse?"

Grace held up a slender finger. "Nope, I can help you. We have the wills for the county right here, some genealogy books, and old newspapers back to its beginning in the late 1800s. Come with me."

Jennifer followed to one of the portions of the library sectioned off by the high shelves, a table in the center. She just might uncover that treasure trove today, after all. "I'm sorry, I don't know when Hampton died."

"I believe it was in the 1920s. Let me pull that volume. I'm something of an amateur historian myself. My family has been in the county since the late 1700s. By the way, my dear, we'd love to have you visit us at our Historical Oglethorpe County group. And UDC if you're a member."

"Uh, no, I'm not a member." Jennifer almost laughed at the concept of any of her redneck ancestors being crowned with laurels of praise for gallant Confederate service. She set her bag on the table and settled while Grace placed several books before her.

"Well, HOC, then. And we'd love for you to speak on what you do. Many of us own historic homes and could learn a lot from you."

The idea of mature adults who lived in homes like she'd only ever dreamed of considering her an expert disconcerted her. As appealing as Jennifer found the concept of hobnobbing with distinguished residents who loved history like herself, Grace hailed from a different caliber of folks than her shotgun-waving, hermit neighbor, or even sweet but simple Mary Ellen, for that matter. Unfortunately, since Jennifer had no intention of telling her, Grace had no way of knowing the idea of speaking in public made Jennifer nauseous with dread. "Oh, um, maybe. I guess it would depend if it worked out with my work schedule between now and Christmas."

"What's happening at Christmas?"

"I aim to finish my work at Dunham House by then. Hopefully I'll be moving to Savannah to begin a new job for a preservation firm."

Grace clasped her hands together in ecstasy. "Oh, how delightful, to work in Savannah among all those beautiful homes. We visit Savannah at least once a year. We love it. But I'm sorry you'll be with us such a short time. Perhaps we can change your mind. Well, Historical Oglethorpe meets every second Tuesday. Before you leave I'd love to get your contact information so I can keep you informed."

Oh, goody.

"Now let me show you what we have here." Grace bent over to explain the volumes she'd selected, then finished by adding, "Let me know if you have any questions or if you want me to set up the microfilm machine so that you can view the historic newspapers. I'm happy to help."

"Thank you so much, I will."

Opening her notebook, Jennifer started with the 1920-25 wills as Grace returned to the office. A clerk had provided a helpful index by name in the front of the book. She scanned his spidery script until "Dunham, Hampton," leapt off the page at her. Flipping to the back to 1925, Jennifer perused the hand-written document. The doctor had left his house and land in town and on Long Creek to a woman named Luella Wright. She was to live off the proceeds of rented land and the money he'd left in the bank until her death, when the remaining funds would be equally divided among her three eldest children, Cecil, Minnie and Hazel. Georgia Pearl would receive the house and land. That explained how Gloria had come into possession of the deeds, but Jennifer found it strange that the oldest child, a boy, had not inherited. Could that have created resentment among his descendants, that the youngest girl, the most Caucasian in appearance, the favorite, had been preferred even after the father's death?

Jennifer decided not to waste time looking for Luella's will, since she already knew Georgia Pearl and Gloria had received the house and property. Instead, she opened a thick tome titled *A History of Oglethorpe County* and scanned the chapter headings. They included sections on schools, churches and towns, but most helpful, one on the families that settled in the area. She easily found "Dunham" and began to read with increasing excitement. Published in the 1950s, the manual used descriptive language and included interesting tidbits and folklore passed down through word of mouth, so was much juicier than the standard historical text. It began by verifying what Horace Greene had told Michael about his earliest ancestor in the county, Levi.

"Levi Dunham (1763-1837), son of a tobacco farmer and doctor from Virginia, came to the Long Creek area via Augusta and Greensborough after receiving a grant of 200 acres for his service in the Revolutionary War. His met his wife, Verity Miller, the daughter of a frontier lawyer, in Greensborough. As a newlywed, Mrs. Dunham remained with her parents in that township as her husband built a cabin on Long Creek, being still in Greensborough during the Creek Indian attack of August, 1787. She was said to be among the four women and two slaves taken away by Indians on the Augusta trail. After Levi received her back, they had three children, Selah, Comfort and Silas."

Jennifer paused. Her skin tingled when reading of Verity's capture. This was the stuff movies were made of. But where were the missing details? "After Levi received her back?" What a downer after a cliffhanger.

The account continued, "Silas Dunham (1798-1865) married Phoebe Smith, and from that union sprang Theodore (1822), William (1831), Anne (1833) and Stuart (1835)." It went on to describe how Silas went to Philadelphia for a traditional study of medicine, thus following in his grandfather's footsteps. He built a handsome plantation house and outlying cabins which were used to treat patients who came from all over the state, as he became known as an expert in traditional and herbal medicines, incorporating both

African American and American Indian remedies. The entry also verified the tale of him bailing out the Bank of Athens.

"All of the sons of Silas and Phoebe became doctors. More than a decade before the Civil War, the Dunhams purchased land and built a small house along the railroad tracks in the nearby town of Hermon to expand their practice. In the early 1870s, an apothecary was constructed at the same time the home was expanded. Stuart Dunham (1835-1870), noted for his medical service to the Confederate Army, returned from the war grievously injured in the head. The son of Stuart Dunham and Charlotte Ormond Dunham (1842-1900), Hampton (1861-1925), affectionately known as "Bachelor Hamp," ran the apothecary and medical practice in Hermon until his death."

Jennifer snorted. Bachelor Hamp indeed. My, what the history books left out. And that was it, the end of the saga of the Dunhams as recorded in *The History of Oglethorpe County*. Yet Jennifer knew that history still unfurled today.

The account raised more questions than it answered. She found the discussion of which Dunham doctors did what during the mid-1800s especially vague. She searched intently through the other books Grace had laid out for her, but found no more pertinent information. Still, the entry aligned with the family Bible and would provide much more official documentation than Horace's hearsay. She paid for copies, then knocked on the office door to ask if Grace would prepare the microfilm.

"I'm happy to," Grace said with a smile. "What particularly are you looking for?"

"When did the newspaper start?"

"Oh, I think it was in the mid-1870s. Want to start there?"

The book had said the apothecary was built and the house expanded in the early 1870s, but in case there might be a mention of the Dunhams and their doings, she nodded. Grace wound the tape through the appropriate prongs and showed her how to focus and advance before she departed. After scanning the first two years and coming up empty, Jennifer requested the films for 1919-1921. This time frame should find Georgia Pearl still living in Oglethorpe County and her father practicing medicine.

Jennifer's growling stomach reminded her it was past lunch time, but she ignored it, sipped from the water bottle allowed inside the library, and continued her visual feast instead. Her preconceptions of the 1920s as a peaceful valley between world wars evaporated. Social and political upheaval threw daily life into a tailspin. In the wake of Russia's 1917 Bolshevik Revolution, communists advocated revolution in Western Europe and the United States, leading to mail bombs, striking unions and race riots. In response, the Palmer Raids rounded up thousands of suspected anarchists, detaining and deporting many without benefit of being charged or represented. The newspaper declared that while "we have in America the seeds of the disease," local farmers would never be unpatriotic enough to consider striking.

On September 26, 1919, economic fears broadcasted in the headline, "Dreaded Boll Weevil We Now Have With Us: Makes Appearance on Several Farms in the County." Multiple articles gave directions for fighting the "elephant-like, with a long, curved snout" pest that threatened to devour Georgia's white gold.

Women in Atlanta were allowed to vote in the primary elections of 1919, but a July rejection of the Nineteenth Amendment delayed Georgia women getting to vote until 1922. Apparently, the state representative from Oglethorpe County, Phil Davis, opposed the amendment while his wife, Nancy Heard Davis, supported it. A May, 1920 editorial made Jennifer growl in defiance when it stated, "Wonder if those women who want to vote and otherwise take control of everything ever stop to think that womankind was an afterthought of the Creator and He used a second hand rib in the creation at that."

Really, the things a newspaper printed back then would have initiated a backlash of immediate lawsuits today. The "happenings in and about town told paragraphically" included personal information such as "an obstreperous tooth has made Mr. Rob Brooks fat on one side of his face for the past several days." And the belittling attitude of the editor reached beyond women and amusing observations about the neighbors. Klan articles declared the organization was a "patriotic, ritualistic fraternal order," its purpose to "inculcate the sacred principles and noble ideas of chivalry, the development of character, the protection of the home and the chastity of woman-hood, the exemplification of a pure patriotism toward our glorious country, the preservation of American ideals and the maintenance of white supremacy." Following a "fracas," one article referred to "three dusky sons of Ham" awaiting the outcome of the law. Another described how a colored man named Glenn Swanson had been dragged by a car after several white men from Athens accused him of stepping out with a white girl. Accounts of lynchings horrified Jennifer. One involved a black man named Obe Cox, who stood accused of raping a white woman outside Lexington, then beating her to death when she'd called for help. He hid in a local swamp but was eventually spotted by a young girl on a farm. As several thousand spectators gathered, Cox was chained to an iron post, riddled with bullets, and after having confessed to the crime as well as the recent rape of a black woman, burned alive.

She sat back from the microfilm machine. Even if he was guilty, she found it hard to imagine as recently as the fall of 1919 a man could be sentenced to death by mob law without judge or jury. It had been a hundred years ago, but still, one considered the 20th century part of the modern age. The language used to describe the man and the fact that the black community offered a humble, printed agreement with the lynching in tones of thankfulness that the community's ire had not turned against their race in force made her stomach sour. She knew from personal experience the humiliation of being powerless and victimized. Jennifer blinked and looked around, reminding herself it truly was 2016. This did put into perspective Georgia Pearl's exodus from the confusion of her childhood, and her daughter's reticence to attempt any bridge-building.

So far nothing about Hampton Dunham. Needing to lighten her mood, Jennifer scanned numerous baseball results, accounts of "frost on the pumpkins" and fox hunts, and reports of festivals with bucking donkeys and canning competitions. Ads abounded for women's clothing and hats, some of them by Gillen's Department Store in Hermon. But even the ads reminded her that 1920 had been another world. Grove's Tasteless Chill Tonic was recommended for children with worms, and an article described a judge scratched by a pet with rabies undergoing twenty-one days of Pasteur treatment.

She looked at her watch. Four o'clock, and she was starved. Based on the fact that she hadn't hit the "print" button once, she could have given up her exploration hours ago. Yet somehow she felt what she had gleaned from the newspaper articles had been intentional and useful. She'd opened the window on another world, this world, one hundred years ago. And it hadn't been as she'd expected. It had reminded her that people had thought and lived differently. One couldn't judge them using today's standards, because they hadn't known what modern people knew.

Thanking Grace, she tried to make a quick exit but was stuck writing down her cell number and e-mail anyway. Jennifer ducked into her hot Civic and piloted it toward Chicken Express, still in a mental fog. There she encountered another social commentary, a loud group of teenagers just released from the local high school, clutching twenty-ounce Styrofoam lidded cups and e-cigs as they perched on tailgates and hoods. The drive-thru didn't move for fifteen minutes, and she didn't find the local mating rituals entertaining. She was just about to give up and go to Subway when the line inched forward a car length. By the time Jennifer placed her order, she suffered visions of hopping out of her vehicle, dashing to the window and wringing the skinny kid's neck in a desperate demand for the nourishment of syrupy sweet tea and greasy corn nuggets. She inhaled them on the ride home, her chicken fingers exclamation points of hunger jabbed into honey mustard sauce.

At home, Jennifer enjoyed a cool bath and changed into a tank top and shorts before someone knocked on her door. She'd left the inner door open with the storm door locked, so she saw Michael's looming frame waiting there. She couldn't wait to share what she'd learned today in hopes of helping reconcile him to his great-grandmother's decisions, even though they didn't know exactly what factors led her tomake them. But when she opened the door and Michael stalked in, it was clear that he was in no mood for placating.

"What's wrong?" she asked, trailing him into the living room.

He stopped by the coffee table and threw down a sepia photograph of a very handsome African American young man in what appeared to be a WWI uniform. "I found this in a box that my grandmother had labeled with her mother's name. Georgia Pearl.

Who was this to Georgia Pearl? All right, I came to let you know I'm ready to talk to Stella."

Jennifer walked over and picked up the photograph. On the back, written in a flowery, faded cursive, was one word. A name. "Glenn."

1920
Oglethorpe County, Georgia

I first met Glenn Swanson in 1919 when White's Dark Town Swells played the Morton Theatre, on another of my outings with Daddy. I was fifteen. I remember I wore a new white chiffon evening dress with crystal and white beads. Mama let me use her almond lotion and Alyshia face powder and put my hair up in a fancy twist. I noticed Glenn, from the best seats on the floor, looking up at me in the balcony. The Division of Military Intelligence reported concern about the black soldier newly returned from the Great War "strutting around in his uniform." Well, that soldier strutting around was Glenn Swanson, and he was about the handsomest man I'd ever laid eyes on. Though light-skinned as African Americans went, Glen's color gave me hope Mama might approve. But how could he know I orbited within his reach, while I sat in the white section next to my distinguished father, clad in my finery?

Just the fact that I was there must have given him courage to inquire. I saw him talking to Ida Mae Johnson. Then he looked back up and smiled at me. I covered my face with my fan. Daddy had acquainted me with Mrs. Johnson some years before, so she was able to introduce us after the show. He kissed my hand. Ida Mae told us that Glenn's father worked in the government offices downtown, and he would be doing the same. Daddy looked approving, but when Glenn asked if he might call on me, Daddy said no.

"She's fifteen." He enunciated so clearly that he seemed to think the artillery fire in Europe had reduced Glenn to lip reading. Then he glanced down at me and noticed my pouty expression. "But we'll be seein' you around in the future, I'm sure," he added before drawing me away on his arm.

I couldn't forget Glenn. I dreamed of him in his khaki uniform. But over six months passed before I saw him again. The next time occurred at the Athens Automobile Show in December, which promised sixty lines of cars on display and daily aeroplane flights. Heavy gray skies almost made Daddy change his mind about going. The Oconee River swelled so high the mail carrier couldn't even make his rounds. But the newspapers told me R.F. Brooks in Lexington burgeoned with candies, fruits and dolls, and Toyland awaited at Davison-Nicholson Company in Athens. It was that time of year, and I knew what I wanted. The Dayton company displayed bicycles at the automobile show, I reminded Daddy, and it had been such a hard year. Wasn't it high time for a little fun?

He could never refuse my sugar-coated combination of charm and pleading. Doctor Hamp owned a much more practical but still luxurious Rolls Royce Silver Ghost now, so away we went to Athens in it.

It *had* been a hard year. In addition to the Palmer Raids, strikes and bombings, and the troubles caused by the men coming home and wanting back the jobs the women and blacks had filled while they were gone, the boll weevil had descended upon the local farmers. They tried everything to keep the little monsters away, geese, traps made with vinegar and molasses, then calcium arsenate. Children in the fields applied a pesticide mixture to the central buds of each plant with a mop every five or so days. Their clothing become sticky, then hardened, so that by the next day, it actually stood up on its own. The disembodied overalls decorating the porches of the tenant farmers' homes might have amused us had the situation not been so dire. As though this was not enough, a late fall fungus attacked the bolls before they opened, withering and decaying the plants. Even though we didn't farm our own land, the boll weevil had a galling effect on us all.

Daddy realized I didn't get to attend home "pound parties" sponsored by the white churches, where each kid would take a pound of refreshments. Girls strolled ten or fifteen minutes with the different boys in a series of "proms" before being assigned new partners. I couldn't go to the local hot springs hotel and do the one-step, two-step and waltz. I couldn't even frequent private parties and dance the Charleston to Victrola music or join in at the local hoe-downs, square dancing to fiddle music while the men sipped homemade moonshine out of fruit jars between Coca-Cola chasers. And Daddy didn't consider the local colored young men, uneducated as they were, suitable. So if I did any socializing, he had to take me. He was the key to opening whatever my future might hold, much more likely in Athens than Hermon.

He'd also noticed how that awful lynching of Obe Cox upset me. The three-day manhunt turned the county upside down. Blacks and whites looked at each other with fear and mistrust. Daddy could no longer convince me that my future would be like that of Mary Wright Hill, the black principal of an East Athens school who lived in a ten-room house, married in a fancy church ceremony, put all her children through college and treated her daughter to a European tour.

But that night I put all that behind me, because on the way there Daddy asked did I want to go up in an aeroplane. I almost had a heart attack of delight. I'd been hearing about the barnstormers, ace flyers from the war who'd returned to show their skills all across the country. Seeing an aeroplane was amazing enough. I'd never dreamed I'd go up in one.

When we finally entered Athens, a light rain began to fall from a darkening sky. Patting down my new cloche hat, I told Daddy we really ought to hurry. He drove me to the air strip, and I pointed as a yellow bird with propeller whirring at her nose lifted into the sky, wheels rendered useless. Another sat on the runway. We pulled up close so that Daddy could go talk to the men in charge, discussing the weather. Visibility would be poor, they said, but I didn't care.

Then a voice next to me said, "You're going up? I am, too."

And there stood Glenn Swanson again, this time in a sack suit with high waist, broad shoulders and stylish trousers they called Oxford Bags.

He helped me out of the Silver Ghost and continued to hold my hand, looking into my eyes. His eyes were a light golden brown, like a tiger's, but they were not predatory or scary, merely warm. "I'm glad to see you again," he told me.

"How's the job?" was all I could think to ask.

"Going great. Are you done with school?"

"Not until spring, remember." He must be five years older than me. Excitement tingled up from my fingertips. When Daddy arrived, he released my hand.

Daddy greeted Glenn, then told me, "You'll have to wait on the yellow plane we just saw. This red one's been booked."

"Oh, that would be by me," Glenn said. "And I'd be honored if you'd go ahead of me. I'd hate it if the weather worsened in the next few minutes."

"But what about you?" I asked.

"It's all right. I have an ex-soldier friend who works here at the air field. I can always go another time."

"That's very kind of you," Daddy said to him.

"Thank you," I cried. As Daddy ushered me toward the plane with a hand on my back, I jumped up and down again and clapped.

The pilot explained his bi-plane was a Curtiss JN-4 "Jenny," the American model that had done much of the work during the war. She was a trainer plane, meaning the instructor sat in the rear while the student occupied the front.

"Do I have to do anything?" I asked as he handed me a leather helmet which I was supposed to put on in place of my hat.

"No," the young man laughed. "All your controls will be powered off. I'll fly the plane from the rear."

"Oh, thank goodness." I took the thick goggles he offered and made a face.

"Believe me, you'll want them. You never know what can come at you up there. The windshields only provide partial protection. Now, we won't get up to her maximum speed of seventy-five miles per hour, but expect a lot of noise from the wind and the engine just the same."

I grasped Daddy's hand. "Seventy-five!"

"I don't know about this," Daddy muttered. "Maybe we should wait for a better day."

"Oh, there is no other day. Oh, Daddy, please."

"I'll take good care of her, sir. We'll keep it low so she can see under the clouds, and only a short pass over the area."

Needless to say, they handed me up and settled me in. The ground crew spun the propeller, and the engine in front of me roared to life. My seat vibrated under me, and I stared at a myriad of strange looking dials and knobs. I kept my hands to myself.

"Ready?" the pilot yelled behind me.

I made a thumbs up gesture, and we bumped down the runway. I managed to wave at Daddy as we left him behind. Glenn also waved. Oh, thank you, Glenn. Thank you, thank you. I couldn't have waited five more minutes for this.

Then I held on for dear life. The moment the wheels lifted off the ground I felt the freedom, leaving earth and its troubles behind. The rain had almost stopped, and I gazed in wonder as the buildings, cars and people of the auto show beneath us shrank to miniature proportions. Forests and fields of cotton surrounded Athens. How small it looked. I'd only been to Atlanta once, and I wanted to go now and fly over the skyscrapers, but our pilot said there would not be enough time for that. But seeing the land below from this perspective, I decided that I wouldn't stay in Oglethorpe County or even in Athens my whole life. There was more out there for me, and I would find it.

The wisps of fog thickened into low-lying clouds as we circled back to taxi in. I felt bad for Glenn, because, with a rumble, the sky let loose. But he didn't seem to mind. He hastened to help me down from the plane.

"Did you like it?"

"Oh, it was wonderful, so wonderful!" I jumped into his arms, and he swung me onto the ground.

"Georgia Pearl," Daddy scolded.

"I'm sorry, Daddy, it was just so exciting. I hate it for Glenn, though. His ride is ruined."

But a bright smile lit Glenn's face. "Your reaction made the sacrifice well worth it. And I'll consider myself paid back in full if you'll allow me to treat you both to dinner."

My parents could not disapprove of his manners. I looked hopefully at my father, who nodded. "Let's just get out of this rain."

I hadn't even noticed. After that, I didn't notice much else, either. Not the Model T's, fancy Pierce Arrows with their side-mounted wheels or boxy Dodge touring cars Daddy and Glenn appeared to be so engrossed in. Not the bikes which I could hardly choose between. Not the food at the outdoor vendor. Not the looks at our mixed company as we took shelter under an awning to eat hot dogs and drink the new orange crush sodas. Because Glenn Swanson, the most charming and handsome man I'd ever met, made it abundantly but tastefully clear he was enamored with me.

Glenn became a frequent guest at our house after that. He drove his father's Oldsmobile out most Sundays for lunch. Sometimes my parents accompanied us to the movie theatre at Hot Corner. That year, inspired by Henry Dudley, a failed farmer who bought the home of former Congressman William Howard in Lexington and visited South Carolina and Florida nurseries to learn the secrets of pecan trees, Daddy put in the grove behind the house. Glenn came to help.

Despite all this, I didn't see Glenn near often enough in my estimation, even after graduation freed me from high school. Bouts of flu, measles and mumps that closed Meson Academy for weeks at a time, followed by an outbreak of smallpox in the Negro settlement outside Crawford, occupied Daddy and the other doctors, and me along with them. Glenn couldn't take me to the white baseball games like Daddy did, and Daddy said it wasn't safe for Glenn to take me to the Negro leagues, either. I'd draw too much attention, as strangers supposed I was fully white. The Klan had shifted into high gear, their new publicity machine recruiting throngs of new members, and Daddy said we couldn't be too careful.

That warning still rang in late fall, when the boll weevil and race issues made everyone tense. Even after cotton growers dusted their crops every four days like the USDA told them to, cotton prices hung so low the farmers decided against selling. The New York Cotton Exchange sold cotton for under twenty-five cents when it was worth more than forty. The farmers blamed Congress. "Let the South today begin the fight," the Oglethorpe Echo proclaimed. You'd think they heralded the inauguration of the Second Civil War.

That description hovered not far from the truth. About that time, Daddy finally agreed to let me go on my first date alone with Glenn, but he took me to the Junior Civic League's Halloween Party himself. The event took place in a vacant room in front of the new barber shop in Lexington. I wanted to be there with Glenn, playing carnival games, sipping hot cider, and munching on homemade candy, popcorn and peanuts "arranged to suit the low price of cotton," just as advertised. But no way would the Junior League admit Glenn, and I was only accepted on Hampton Dunham's arm. In his presence, I became the county pet: a cute little thing no one knew quite what to do with. I had to content myself with our plan for Glenn to pick me up from there for the drive to a new jazz club near the Morton. As I often told myself, I had to make the best of both worlds.

I'll never forget what happened when I leapt over "the famous twelve candles" at the bidding of the be-turbaned, bejeweled Madam Juanita. An almost simultaneous gasp exhaled from the cluster of girls waiting in the black-curtained enclosure behind me. Madam Juanita clasped her ample bosom.

I looked down at my two-tone T-straps. All the candles still stood. But all the candles were extinguished. A chill went up my spine. "What does it mean?" I whispered.

The Gypsy woman took my arm and shook her head. She seemed at a loss for words.

"What does it mean?"

"Ill luck. A disastrous month ahead."

The bevy of junior leaguers stared at me goggle-eyed.

I locked down my heels. "Wait, take me back and read my palm," I insisted. "It will probably tell you something different. I don't generally have bad luck."

Madam Juanita seemed wary of me. "No, no. You go now. And be very watchful."

Something in her dark, glittering eyes caused me to take her seriously. But when Glenn pulled up down the street and stood waiting outside the car, I forgot what she said. I didn't even listen when Daddy fretted, wondering if he should accompany us.

Glenn held my door open, clearly anxious to have me all to himself. "It's a small club, Dr. Dunham, and I know the owners. A good crowd there. No trouble will be made."

"Well, if you're sure." And Daddy kissed my cheek.

"I'll take the best care of your girl. I put my life on it."

The corn stood in shocks, the orange autumn moon rose and the breeze tingled cool on my cheeks. Filled with anticipation as tangy as the apple cider, I wound my scarf tight and smiled. My heart skyrocketed as Glenn took my hand.

We discussed the newest rage, jazz, hot from New Orleans, combining earlier brass band marches, French quadrilles, ragtime and blues with its Deep South field hollers, chants and spirituals. African American musicians took the music to the north and west in the last decade.

"Livery Stable Blues" rocked the nation in 1917 as the first jazz recording. This year, 1920, Mamie Smith became the first black female performer to make a recording with her band, the Jazz Hounds. Jazz made me feel proud of my mama's people. We sang Mamie's songs, "Crazy Blues" and "You Can't Keep a Good Man Down," then warbled off-key and happy into Nora Bayes' hit from earlier that year, "How Ya Gonna Keep 'Em Down on the Farm (After They've Seen Pareé)?"

> How ya gonna keep 'em down on the farm
> After they've seen Pareé?
> How ya gonna keep 'em away from Broadway,
> Jazzin' around and paintin' the town?
> How ya gonna keep 'em away from harm, that's a mystery.
> They'll never want to see a rake or plow,
> And who the deuce can parlez vous a cow?
> How ya gonna keep 'em down on the farm
> After they've seen Pareé?

The crowd at the club caused Glenn to circle back to a parking lot that bordered the white section of town. Some men stood on the corner when he got out and walked around the car to my door.

"Hey, hey, you can't park there," one of them yelled.

I was scared to get out, but Glenn said, "Come on," in a gentle voice, just like they weren't even there. He offered me his arm as I stepped clear of the closing door. Then we started walking.

"Who does he think he is?" one of the men queried.

But as it became clear we were headed toward Hot Corner, the group fell silent, and I breathed a sigh of relief. "Aren't you afraid for your car?" I whispered.

He shook his head. "Nah, they'll be gone by the time we come out. Best thing is just to ignore such fools."

"You do a lot of ignoring, I guess."

"Yes, I do. And if you're with me, Georgia Pearl, so will you."

I clasped his arm. "I think it might be worth it."

Oh, the club. I loved it. I was relieved to not be the only light-skinned individual present. Glenn got us a table, and we ordered dinner. He told me of his plans to buy a little house near his parents' close to the street car tracks, making his job easily accessible. When he said he'd like me to meet his parents, I knew he deemed me old enough now for serious attentions and pictured me a possible keeper of that home. But did I want that? Was I ready to get married and start a family? What about my dreams to become a nurse? Grady Memorial Hospital Municipal Training School for Colored Nurses had graduated its first accredited class this past spring. They offered a dorm just for the student nurses, and Mama had agreed that I might go, but she'd said sixteen was too young. Next year, when I was seventeen, I might test my wings. I'd told Glenn. Had he not taken me seriously? Did he hope I'd choose him instead?

Too nervous to bring it up right then and possibly ruin the date, I released a sigh of relief when the band took the stage and flooded the room with piano and brass instrument music. A large, dark-skinned woman crooned husky tones into a microphone. Before long, the beat accelerated and people poured onto the wooden dance floor, bobbed hair, sequins and beads flying, and heeled shoes stomping out the cakewalk and the Charleston. I was not an accomplished dancer for obvious reasons, but I loved watching with Glenn's arm around me. I think I felt him kiss my hair several times, too.

He kept his arm around me as we walked through the chilly night to the car. My apprehension melted when I saw that the stragglers from earlier were nowhere in sight, just like Glenn had predicated. It felt exciting to be out with a man after dark. At the car, he turned to me. "Georgia, can I ask you something?"

"Sure, Glenn."

"Can I kiss you?"

I sighed. "I thought you'd never ask."

That was to be our first and last kiss. At the final stop sign going out of town on the Lexington Road, the mushy world of fast-beating heart and flushed cheeks still enveloped me when a car pulled up behind us. As we accelerated, it followed closely. I still wouldn't have thought much of it had Glenn not kept glancing in the rear view mirror. Looking relieved, he slowed down to make it easier when the car went to pass. I saw two heads in the front seat and two in the back, and those in the back turned toward us.

"Crazy driver," he muttered. We both knew local officials were calling for speed limits after a local girl just home from college that summer overturned her car on a curve outside Augusta, doing over seventy miles per hour.

The other car accelerated around a curve and out of sight. We clasped hands again, smiling at each other. A few minutes later we rounded another bend in the road.

"Oh, God," Glenn breathed.

He was more religious than me, so I imagined he was praying, although I didn't know why until I saw that on a narrow portion of highway flanked closely by trees, that same touring sedan had pulled sideways across the road. I braced myself against the dash as Glenn stomped on the brakes. He didn't have a choice. The ditches and woods did not leave enough room to bypass the obstacle.

"Whatever happens, Georgia, stay in the car and lock the doors. If you have to leave me, you drive this car home to your father."

"Glenn, they're getting out. Oh, my God, they have hoods on."

He tried to put the car in reverse, but the men surrounded the Oldsmobile. The one nearest Glenn swung something, and glass shattered. As his gaping mask loomed in the jagged opening of the window and his arm shot out, my mind's eye saw the twelve candles extinguish.

CHAPTER THIRTEEN

The next day, everything conspired to delay Jennifer's talk with Stella. Jennifer knew she could have texted or called her, but she wanted to broach the subject in person. First, however, she needed to stop in the convenience store to pick up biscuits for everyone at the house. Amy and Horace were delivering the interior paint today, and it seemed like a nice thing to do for their trouble. Plus she hoped something hearty to eat might put a smile on Michael's face. But Jennifer found the cook behind a column of steam, flipping sausage patties depleted during the store's seven a.m. rush, and she must wait. Like. Forever. It took so long she told them she'd be back for her order after an errand, because she still had to return Rita's casserole dishes and carrier. She'd already put that off as long as she politely could.

Beauty shops held a certain fearful fascination for her, listing toward the fearful end. Kelly had spent plenty of time in them, but she'd cut her children's hair herself in their younger days. During college, Jennifer frequented those eight dollar quick cut type of places that did not go in for perms, dryer machines and eyebrow waxing. The biscuit delay could work in her favor. Rita did not open until at least eight, so she could return the items on the front step.

To her dismay, a shiny, late-model silver Mercedes occupied one of four otherwise empty spots in front of the tiny brick shop. When she mounted the steps, Rita spied her and waved her on in.

"Oh, good mornin', Jennifer, how are you?" The older woman greeted her from a work station as she vigorously shook a solution in a squeeze-top bottle.

"Fine, thank you. Just stopping in to return your dishes." Her nose tickling with the smell of chemicals, Jennifer peered around and placed her burden on a wooden counter sporting a vintage cash register. She noticed a young girl next to the counter, bent over markers and paper.

"Why, thank you. Did you enjoy the food?"

"Most definitely. It was probably the best breakfast I've had in ages."

"Well, meet the cook. This is my granddaughter, Montana."

"Hi, Montana. Your sweet rolls were delicious," Jennifer said.

The short twelve-year old responded with a shy but delighted smile. "Thank you." The clever bob cut of brown hair the color of Jennifer's still failed to counteract Montana's plain appearance. Immediate kinship flared in Jennifer's heart. "I have muffins today!"

"You do?" Jennifer noticed a large woven basket of plastic wrapped goodies perched on the stool behind the counter.

"Yes, fresh baked. I'm making a sign for them. They're going to be one dollar each."

"Oh, my. That sounds like a deal I can't pass up. What kinds do you have?"

A still-stubby finger pointed out the options. "Cinnamon streusel and banana nut."

"Montana keeps me stocked with a good selection daily," Rita said. "My customers love to take one or two home to have with their coffee."

"Well, would it disappoint them too much if I bought about six of those? I can just picture how happy that will make my boss."

"Your boss?"

"Yes, Michael Johnson who owns the Dunham House down the street is my boss right now. I'm fixing up the place for him, and he and his dad sure love to have something tasty with their coffee. I think it would be smart of me to keep them happy, don't you?"

Montana nodded. "Sure, pick some." Her excitement couldn't be disguised as she placed the basket on the counter in front of Jennifer. Rita smiled warmly from behind her pump-up chair.

"I'm surprised to see you here this early, Rita," Jennifer commented as she selected her pastries and set them aside.

"Oh, honey, there's some old ladies in this county who get up at five a.m. every single day of their lives and call me lazy if I'm not ready to go before eight. Mrs. Dawson is comin' in for her bi-annual perm today, and she's very particular. So I'm gettin' everything just so." Rita started sorting through a tray of curlers, color coded by size. It appeared Mrs. Dawson preferred tight curls.

"We get up early a lot at my house, too," Montana announced. "To milk the cows."

"You live on that big dairy farm?"

"Yep." The girl nodded her bob emphatically, then wrinkled her nose. "Isn't it stinky?"

Jennifer laughed. "Sometimes, though, I think I prefer that kind of stink to perm solution." She grinned as Rita gave the anticipated gasp of mock offense, then asked Montana, "So how much do I owe you? Is there tax? Do you have to ring me up on the machine?"

Montana giggled. "No, you just have to give me six dollars. Unless you need a receipt for your tax write-off."

"Oh, ho, ho, look who's quite the little business woman! Tax write-off, is it? What do you know about that?" Jennifer glanced at Rita, who smirked and nodded her head.

"I told you she was a smart one."

"A lot," Montana said, raising her rounded little nose. She reached behind the counter. Jennifer thought she was going to come out with a brown paper bag, but she placed a white donut box on the level surface and started arranging the muffins inside. "I've been reading up and watching 'Pastry Chef'. I want to win 'Pastry Chef Junior' and use the money to start my own bakery."

"Really, and where would that bakery be? New York City?"

"No, silly, right here!"

"Montana is a firm believer in strengthening local enterprise," her grandmother said.

"Well, I applaud you." Jennifer offered her hand for a shake. "A pleasure doing business with you." She started to reach for her box when the girl held up a hand.

"Wait, I'm not done. Visual presentation is half the experience."

In astonishment, Jennifer watched as Montana whisked a red polka dot ribbon from a jar swirling with other ribbons of all colors and designs, tied the box off, then stuck the cut stem of a white silk daisy into the knot. With a proud smile, she slid her creation forward.

"Oh, my goodness gracious. I am so glad I came in here today. Those men are going to fall over with joy when I walk in with this. I could just forget those greasy biscuits I ordered up at the convenience store if I wasn't afraid they'd get mad at me."

Montana squeaked out another self-conscious giggle at Jennifer's speech.

"Thank you, Jennifer." Rita walked her to the door, held it open and gave her a wink. "That was extra special kind of you." Then, following her out onto the porch, she added in a lower voice, "I do all I can to help the sweet child. She's not got a lot goin' for her except for her baking and her determination. Her mother, my son's wife, had to pull her out of school due to bullying this past year. It gives her something to do, makin' her pastries and helpin' out with cleaning and little chores at the shop."

Jennifer's opinion of Rita's good heart increased. She smiled. "I understand. Bullying has been around forever, you know."

"Honey, you just stop in any time, and I'll work you in. I'm not kidding, I'd love to get my hands on that thick, healthy hair of yours. You never style it, do you?"

Jennifer shook her head, trying not to be uncomfortable as Rita's red-nailed fingers purled through her tresses.

"Mmm, mmm, well, I can tell. Virgin hair. I can tell you, when I get through with you, you won't need muffins to make those men faint dead away. I've got another girl who comes in here part-time. She works after school in the rush. But don't you go to her. You come to me. Hear?"

Easing away to her car, Jennifer assured Rita she heard. She *would* be needing a cut soon, but she had the uneasy feeling that what Rita had in mind was much more life-altering than the quick re-tracing of previous trim lines she was comfortable with. Kelly's years of fakeness inside and out had turned Jennifer off of doing things just for appearance sake. Still, she had the sense Rita would never give up until she had taken her captive in her swivel chair.

Buzzing up to the convenience store, Jennifer retrieved and paid for her foil-wrapped sausage biscuits which were then stuffed into a plastic bag. At the house, Horace's new Dodge truck already nosed up to the side door when she pulled in, but the buckets in the bed testified of a recent arrival. She found everyone clustered in the kitchen.

"I hope y'all didn't eat yet," she announced. "I've got sausage biscuits and Montana Worley's cinnamon streusel and banana nut muffins!"

"Oh, my land, let me see those," Horace cried, wiggling his fingers over the fancy box Jennifer sat down on the counter.

James said, "Coffee's made for anyone who wants a cup."

Michael smiled at Jennifer from his place near the sink, then he reached up to get mugs down from the antique general store glass-paned cabinet the previous owners built into the kitchen. As everyone buzzed around them putting breakfast on paper plates, she felt sorry for him having to be sociable when she knew his mind dwelt on deeper matters. They'd talked for about an hour after he'd charged in last night, discussing Jennifer's library research and scrolling through photos he'd taken of furniture in the Lawrenceville storage unit. Most of it would not be usable for the house, reflecting the same era as Ettie Mae's possessions. A few reproductions would do, basic side tables and chairs to fill in gaps and save money, and a mid-1800s four-poster bed could be used in James' bedroom. He'd let her mull through the pictures while he sat beside her staring into space, mostly without comment. When he was like that, his lowered guard allowing her to glimpse some vulnerability, that insane urge to touch him stirred again, but she refrained. She didn't know where this sudden nurturing instinct came from, but she didn't like it. Didn't need it. It made her weak. She determined to keep things kind, yes, but professional. On safe ground.

Now, Stella gave her a quick hug. "Thank you for thinkin' of us this morning."

"Of course. I'm sure you probably already cooked Earl a huge breakfast, but ..."

"Aw, that man can eat any time of day."

"Well, *I'm* sure grateful. Amy and I were going to ride up to Waffle House after we stopped by here. Now we won't have to!" Horace exclaimed.

Amy swatted at him. "Horace!" She turned to nibble her muffin. "You say these were made by that little Montana Worley?"

"Yes. She's twelve now."

"Twelve? My, it's hard to imagine it. It seems like yesterday Rita did up my hair for prom."

Horace rolled his eyes.

"Not like you would remember. You weren't my date."

"Well, I do remember. I fell in love with you that night and determined I must have you, swishing around in your red sequined dress with that full skirt. And those red lips."

"And hair out past my shoulders," Amy laughed. "I think Rita teased it for an hour."

"If Earl wasn't your date, Amy, who was?" Jennifer asked. "That quarterback you mentioned before?"

"Right. Chad Fullerton. He was a *dream*." Amy now rolled her eyes. "You remember him, Stella."

"Sure do." Stella's tone hinted she might rather forget, but Amy didn't seem to notice.

"He went on to play for the University of Florida until he blew out his ACL. He started talkin' about comin' back home then, but I guess he never did. I just lost touch with him."

"No big loss," Horace muttered under his breath. He slurped from his coffee cup.

"Well, it wasn't anything personal, because I hear his parents did, too," Stella said, either not hearing or ignoring the real estate agent. "If you remember folks said for a while that something must have happened to him. His parents mounted a search with the police in Gainesville—Florida—cooperating. But nothing ever turned up."

James guessed, "Maybe he had an accident."

"Or became a beach bum," Horace suggested.

"Horace, that's not funny." Amy cut her husband a reproving eye.

"Was I being funny?"

"An injury like that for a sports star can prove devastating in more ways than one," Michael put in.

James nodded. "Yeah, remember that boy you swam with in college, Michael, the IM'er? Tore a rotator cuff right before nationals and never went back. I think he became an orthopedic surgeon."

Michael swam in college? Jennifer looked at him, but before she could press further, Michael said, "Hey, Horace, I'm ready to bring the paint in if you are. Let's get this show on the road."

"Sounds good to me."

"I'm done, too," Earl said.

James held up a finger and raised his coffee cup. "Got to finish cup number two first. You guys go on. I'll catch up with you later." He chuckled as they went out the door, dismissing his banter with shooing hands.

While Michael slipped on his shoes on the porch, Jennifer heard Horace ask if they'd taken care of the rattlesnake problem and Michael answer, "Yeah, at least for now. We haven't seen any more."

"Still gonna tear down the old outhouse?"

"Yeah, eventually, when we're set to replace the boards on the back of the apothecary. Jennifer's professor wants to excavate it this fall."

"Aw, what's she gonna find in an old outhouse? I'd be scared it's a snake pit, anyway."

Jennifer shuddered. He voiced her exact fear. Amy's slowness with her muffin rivaled that of James with his coffee. As the interior decorator carefully dabbed up every crumb with her gel-tipped fingernail and commented how the muffin improved on those served at Starbuck's, Jennifer asked Stella, "Can I speak to you a minute?"

"Sure. We can talk in the dining room while the men bring the paint in. Excuse us a minute, y'all." The others waved them on. Once they stood in front of the unusual stained glass window, Stella asked, "What is it?"

"Michael found a photograph among his grandmother's things that belonged to Gloria's mother when he went to the storage building yesterday. It was of a young black man in a World War I uniform." Jennifer paused. When Stella merely nodded, she continued, "His grandfather also told us on Tuesday that his wife, Gloria, admitted to having some African American blood before she died. When I went to the library yesterday, I found Hampton Dunham's will. It revealed that he'd left his house and property to a woman named Luella, and upon her death, to her youngest daughter, Georgia Pearl. Stella, now that photo I found in the shed here makes sense. That picture was of Hampton, Luella, and their children together. I don't know who the young man was in the picture that Michael found, but I imagine he is related some way. It wasn't the brother, Cecil, because someone wrote a name on the back. Glenn."

Stella remained silent over the sounds of footsteps and thumps in the main hallway. Then she asked quietly, "How's Michael takin' all this?"

"Upset."

"About his blood kin?"

"No, actually, that his grandmother didn't tell him. He's afraid he's going to look foolish to people here who know his history better than he does. Do *you* know, Stella? Can you help us?"

"Michael wants to know?"

"Yes. He asked me to speak with you."

Finally, Stella nodded. "Yes, I do know, Jennifer, and yes, I can help him. Give me a couple of days. I need to check with my mama. She have some information I don't, and I'd like for her to be there when we sit down together. We can aim for Saturday when we have plenty of time. Tell Mr. James to come, too."

CHAPTER FOURTEEN

ennifer again occupied the same chair at Stella's, only Truffle must have been shut up in a back room this time, no tea steeped, and the Belter sofa supported both Stella and her petite mother, Dorace. James and Michael perched on arm chairs that caused their larger frames to appear out of proportion, but that might have more to do with their internal state than their Victorian surroundings. Another addition to the room, a CD player with a tape deck, squatted on the coffee table. Having met Stella's mother, the men waited for Stella to speak, their fixed eyes measuring the composure on her face.

"So I asked Mama to come today because she remembers your great-grandmother, Michael, Georgia Pearl."

"You do?" Michael shifted to gaze in shock at the older woman. "But I thought Georgia Pearl moved to Atlanta when she was quite young and did not come back."

"She didn't," Dorace said, "until 1981."

"What happened in 1981?" James wanted to know. "Besides it being the year Michael was born."

"That was when my uncle Cecil died." Dorace's voice possessed a slow and calm Southern lilt, clear predecessor to her daughter's manner of speech.

"Cecil was one of the siblings of Georgia Pearl," Jennifer declared. "So that means ..."

All eyes sought Dorace.

"Georgia Pearl was one of my two aunts. My mother was Hazel Dunham, next-to youngest daughter of Dr. Hampton Dunham and his housekeeper, Luella."

Jennifer watched Michael's astonishment bloom as his attention swung to Stella. "But that means you're some sort of cousin! Why didn't you tell me?"

"A distant cousin, yes. I wanted to wait for the right time, Michael."

"Seriously? All those days painting in the house, eating lunch together, talking about your family, and it never occurred to you, 'Michael might want to know we're—um—*related*?'"

184

"Now don't you go getting feisty with me, young man. I watched for a good moment to tell you, I surely did, and it never came. You never asked about the family that remained in this area. Other things always occupied your mind, always the job to be done that day. This little lady here 'bout pestered me to death about it, but not you. I knew eventually something would come up that would lead you to start to wonder. I just thought it better to wait for that moment than to drop something like that on you out of the blue."

Michael made a visible effort to straighten his face, but Jennifer recognized his consternation. To cover his son's heated silence, James redirected. "Miss Dorace, you said you saw Georgia Pearl in 1981. Did you meet her then for the first time?"

"Yes, sir, that's right. I'd always heard tale of her, the youngest of the children who looked as white as Dr. Hamp, but I knew she'd chosen to cut her ties to everyone here. You see, Georgia Pearl's father died shortly after she went to Atlanta to nursing school, so her main reason to come home to visit was gone. And some things happened before she left that made her decide it was just easier to be white. I didn't understand that for a long time. Not until she came home for Uncle Cecil's funeral."

"I was only around ten," Stella inserted, "but I remember meeting her. My, what a grand old lady she was, even at seventy-five, but Mama didn't let me listen to the tape she made then until I was much older."

"Wait. Tape?" Michael cut a hand through his hair.

Dorace reached in her purse and pulled out a plastic bag with two cassettes in it. She fumbled with it, then held one of the tapes out to Stella. Jennifer noticed her hand shook slightly. "Uncle Cecil became very well-known as one of the early colored doctors in Athens. He had his own place there, a nice house for his family, so he didn't need Dr. Hamp's house. Everyone knew it would go to Georgia Pearl, in hopes that she would come back here for her later days. Then, just before Cecil's death, the great-grandson of his lifelong best friend, a medical student himself, decided to do a graduate paper on the challenges faced by early black doctors in Georgia. He interviewed Cecil before his death, and when he heard Cecil's little sister, a former WWII combat nurse, was coming up to Athens for the funeral, he asked to interview her as well. None of us expected her to agree. But she did. I think it was her way of tryin' to give us an explanation in her own words for why she ran away."

Michael popped out of the easy chair and paced the tiny area void of furniture and decorations. Jennifer's heart ached for him. "But my mother and grandmother had to have known about such a visit. Since I was born that year, they probably would have arranged transportation for Georgia Pearl by someone else in the family."

Dorace shook her head. "I don't think Georgia Pearl wanted to tell them, probably because they were busy and she was uncertain of how things would go. Those distractions, your birth, and the recent death of your great-grandfather—Carl Reed, the white doctor she'd met and married in Atlanta—were probably the very things that allowed her to slip away. Why not just hop a Greyhound bus over the weekend?" Dorace chuckled. "She was one feisty lady."

"Gloria always did say that," James agreed. "Sit down, Michael."

"Yes, I want you to hear the tape," Stella told them. "It will make so much more sense in her own words." She waited for Michael to take his seat again, then looked him in the eye. "Are you ready for this?"

He nodded.

"It's long, and her story is not an easy one. Before you heard it, I knew you needed to have a feel for this place and know a little bit about your ancestors. Is this something you're ready to accept into your history?" She asked him to assess, Jennifer realized, whether the racial tensions of the past century could unsettle him past the point of reconciliation.

"Just play the tape, Stella. I think I've been kept in the dark long enough."

Stella's slender finger mashed a button, and a young man's voice stated matter-of-factly: "I'm here with Georgia Pearl Reed of Atlanta, Georgia, daughter of Dr. Hampton Dunham of Hermon, Georgia, and youngest sister of the recently deceased Cecil Dunham, also interviewed for this project. Mrs. Reed, I know it's a hard time for you because you've not only just traveled to Athens for the funeral of your brother, but recently lost your husband as well. Thank you for talking with me."

"I'm happy to be of assistance if I can." The frail but clear voice drifted into the room, a presence from 1981, from 1920, like having

186

Georgia Pearl alive again and right there with them. It raised the hair on Jennifer's arms.

"As the daughter of a white doctor father and an African American mother, I understand you defied the odds to attend the Grady school for nurses in the 1920s and went on to become a combat nurse during WWII. Will you tell me how that all came about, from your growing up years here in Oglethorpe County on?"

Georgia Pearl gave a light chuckle. If she felt nervous, the emotion did not speed her drawl. She chose her words with care. "I was born into a small world with a big name. Georgia Pearl, my daddy called me ..."

Interrupted only infrequently by the interviewer when direction became necessary, Michael's great-grandmother went on to re-create the world Jennifer had visited through the newspaper microfilms in the library. As Georgia Pearl told of hiding under the counter in the apothecary while her father treated patients, her outings with Hampton to Athens, and attending church with her mother and school at Jeruel Academy, her great grandson clasped his hands between his knees. Squeeze and relax, squeeze and relax. Jennifer watched the knuckles turn white and red. Most of the time he stared at the rug. His eyes fixed on nothing, but burned with an awareness completely new to him. Having lost his mother and his grandmother early in his life, what did hearing the story of his great-grandmother do inside that intense brain of his?

Jennifer glanced at Stella, who gave her a tight, rather sad smile. She was watching Michael, too. Jennifer realized these women had had a lifetime to accept the heaviness of their inheritance, the sheer determination required to forge an upstanding life path in the predominately white past, but Stella pitied Michael the struggle of trying to fit this foreign piece of history into his own heritage.

When Stella flipped the tape, Georgia Pearl had just described meeting Glenn Swanson, the young African American soldier-turned-clerk from Athens. "Shall I go on?" she asked.

Michael answered in a tight voice, "Yes."

And they soared with Georgia in the skies over her home state and relived the joy of budding romance. Then the story darkened like the skies that day of the aeroplane ride. Georgia Pearl took them to the club and described how, on the ride home, the men who had been incensed that Glenn had parked in the white section of town followed them out of Athens. But it wasn't really about the parking lot. It was about her.

Jennifer's heart pounded as Michael's great-grandmother recreated the horrible moment the masked man smashed the window of Glenn's Oldsmobile, reached inside and opened the locked door. As Georgia Pearl screamed, he dragged Glenn out onto the road.

"Who do you think you are, steppin' out with a white woman?" had been the first question shouted.

As Michael's eyes met hers, Jennifer felt like she was intruding on a very personal moment that did not belong to her. The discomfort she read there, however, had nothing to do with her presence and everything to do with the unfolding story. Everyone sat in complete silence as Georgia Pearl's voice filled the parlor:

He couldn't answer because the man had him by the neck. The others gathered around him, talkin' about teaching him a lesson. They smacked his face, and he tried to swing a punch, but they all held him.

Despite my terror, I knew I had to speak up to try to save him, so I cried out, "I'm black! I'm black! My mother is black!"

It was the first time I'd publicly announced that truth, but they just laughed at me.

One of them said, "Sure you are, sweetheart. You'd say anything to save your swell here."

"Tie him up!" they yelled. And called him terrible names. They put a gag in his mouth. He tried to bite them, but they were too fast. One of them brought a rope from their car, and the others held Glenn while the man bound his feet and hands. He struggled for all he was worth, tearin' his fine suit, but there was no use against four.

I stayed in the car, but I thought I could still talk them out of whatever they were going to do. In my world, adults responded to reasoning. I cried out again they had made a mistake, I was not full white, but if they did this they would get in trouble. My father, a white doctor, would see to it.

"Maybe she needs a lesson, too, for havin' such poor judgement," the tallest man said. "How can we protect women from these savages if they don't know how to behave decently themselves?"

Glenn swung around to face me. His eyes were wild with fear, and I could see him trying to say, "Go!"

I saw before me three choices. I could stay and try to fight them, but if Glenn had been no match for these men, I certainly would not be. I could even try to run over them with the car, but most likely the ones I did not hit would then grab me and consign me to a terrible fate. Or I could leave him and try to go for help. In the split second the men debated, I jumped over to the driver's seat and grabbed the clutch. I had only driven a car a couple of times, with my father there to instruct me. Now I had to finish backin' it around in the road to go back toward Athens. When I tried to do that, our attackers leapt on the car. Arms and hands flailed in the window, grabbin' at me. I kept going in reverse until I felt the back tire dip into the ditch. Then I changed the gear and stomped the pedal. I was sobbin' and screamin'. The acceleration caused the men to fall off the car. I left him there, I left him with them.

In the wake of shame still audible in Georgia Pearl's voice, the interviewer spoke again. "Where did you go?"

"I was afraid they would follow me, that if I stopped at the first house I saw, they would catch up with me. I was a very spoiled young girl, and as much as I wanted to get help for Glenn, the urge to save yourself is often stronger. So closer to town I found a store still open. I ran in to tell them a man had been attacked on the Lexington Road. When they found out the man was black, they wouldn't go."

"They wouldn't go?"

"No, they didn't want to get involved. I had to take a different road all the way to Hermon, cryin' so hard the whole time I could hardly see. I couldn't stop thinkin' of what they might be doing to him. By the time I got home I was hysterical. Daddy had been waitin' on the front porch for me. I could hardly get out what had happened. He and Cecil both got their shot guns and went up toward town. I'll never forget waitin' for news while Mama tried to comfort me."

"What happened?"

Silence broadcasted for a minute. With a sinking sensation, Jennifer realized she already knew. She'd read the very account of it in the *Echo*. Then Georgia Pearl said, "Daddy and Cecil searched near where I had described. They finally found Glenn in a ditch halfway to Lexington, barely alive. They had drug ... excuse me ... dragged him ... behind their car for two or three miles. Daddy took him up to the new hospital on Harris Street in Athens that had just gotten an x-ray machine in the basement. He stayed there to tend him and sent Cecil home to tell me. Bones were broken all over Glenn's body and his skin scraped raw."

There was silence again on the recording. Jennifer fought the hotness of tears in her eyes. Michael and James both looked sick. "What kind of monsters would do something like that?" Michael burst out, talking over the interviewer's voice as he resumed.

"Did Glenn live, Mrs. Reed?"

"Yes, he did, although it was a miracle. He walked with a limp the rest of his life. But I never did see him again. I am ashamed to say I couldn't bring myself to. For weeks after the attack, fear paralyzed me. Sure the men would come get me, I didn't dare leave the house. The police came in to question me, and eventually they found the car they thought belonged to one of the men. But somehow they all had alibis. And of course the Athens police did not press the matter. Daddy used his connections to keep my name out of the paper, so the stories were written almost like Glenn was by himself when the incident happened. But I still couldn't go see him. I wasn't just afraid, either. I was ashamed. I had left him. I had not stopped at the nearest house, when if I had, it might have spared him so much pain."

"But you couldn't know that. And you were a young girl rightfully terrified."

"Yes, rightfully. And you're right, I'll never know. That's what haunted me. That happened to him because of me. I reasoned he was better off without me. I had thought I was safe in Athens and that my future would be there. Now I knew that wasn't true. That and the earlier lynchings were just the beginnings of what the Klan did in our area. Things became very bad in neighboring counties. They flogged a black minister for teachin' other poor blacks to read. They burned churches. They fired into homes on drive-bys. I just wanted to leave. When I got strong enough, Mama agreed for me to go to Atlanta to

Grady, to enter their program. Glenn was leavin', too. His father was sendin' him up to New York to be with an uncle there. So we never saw each other again."

"And you went to Atlanta."

"Yes, I went to Atlanta. I ate, breathed and slept nursing. I made the highest grades of anyone in my class, and shortly after I arrived they integrated the colored nursing school with the white nursing school. So when I met Carl Reed, a young white doctor working at Grady, I saw a chance for a clean slate. Our marriage made it easy to stop goin' home, to just become white. You see how bein' white was safer? And I had that option. Who wouldn't have taken it?"

"Did Carl Reed know of your background?"

"Yes, he did. I told him everything, but my preference to pass as a full white in Atlanta proved easier for everyone. His parents did not know, except to believe me estranged from my family. Carl met my father before he died, and Daddy gave his blessin' for our plan. He wanted me to have the best possible life, and with the memories I had at home, he understood that could not be in Athens."

"But your mother, Luella, lived until 1945, did she not? Did you never see her again?"

"I took Gloria to see her after she was born, but no, after that I did not go home again. It was too painful for me. I closed the door on that chapter of my life." The unspoken question hovered on the tape and in the parlor, until finally Georgia Pearl answered it, haltingly. "I know my decision must have caused my family much pain, too, although my father explained it to my mother, brother and sisters, and I wrote them all letters tellin' them I loved them but would not be comin' home again. That is a regret I have carried with me all my life. It's the price I paid for my freedom, like the slaves who had to sometimes leave their families in bondage behind them. But I am sorry that I hurt them in gettin' it. That is the reason I am doin' this interview, young man, to say that I am sorry for the selfishness of my choices in my youth, sorry that I took the easy road. It's like they say, the easy road is usually the wrong one."

Stella's finger snapped the button of the recorder down. "She was her father's daughter," she said softly.

For a long moment everyone sat as if frozen, then Jennifer asked, "Is that it?"

"The interview goes on to describe how Georgia Pearl volunteered for the Red Cross during WWII. She offered to tend the colored soldiers when others did not want to. I think that became part of her restitution. But that is something Michael can listen to later. Mama, if you'll give him the tape."

Dorace fumbled in her purse again and held up the other cassette. Michael rose and took it from her. "Thank you," he said. "I'll take very good care of this."

Dorace caught his hand and patted it just as she had Jennifer's in church. "I think the second half will make you proud of her."

A look of confusion crossed his face. "But don't you think poorly of her after what she did?"

"Honey, I think if we didn't have to live through that time, we shouldn't judge. We might have done the same thing in her shoes. Her life was a confusin' one, full of mixed signals about who she was and what she could accomplish. But you should be proud of the service she gave to her country."

"Maybe. But I'm not proud of the service she gave to her family." Michael's voice sounded tight, and his gaze cut to his father with a plea in it. "I'd like to go now."

"Sure, son." James stood up, and Jennifer followed his lead since she'd ridden over with them.

"Thank you for this," he said to Stella and Dorace.

Stella came over and opened her arms. "Can I hug you?" She only waited long enough for Michael to give the barest nod before wrapping him tightly in a big sisterly embrace. Low in his ear but loud enough for Jennifer to hear, she said, "Just take you some time to process this. I knew it would hit you hard. But it'll be OK. You have family here, and we love you."

Michael couldn't get out the door fast enough to hide the tears in his eyes.

CHAPTER FIFTEEN

ll the next week, Jennifer thought about Michael. She knew what it was like to feel shame about your family like Michael did about Georgia Pearl. Despite herself, she wished they were close enough that he would ask her to listen to the other recording with him, and help him through whatever he struggled with. Because he clearly struggled. She watched him leave for one of his runs Sunday morning, and he didn't come back for a couple of hours. He ran every morning of that next week, and he kept to himself, choosing tasks that prevented interaction like mowing and trimming the massive boxwoods.

One evening Jennifer walked over to Dunham house to water the plants just tucked by Gabe and Jamal under fresh pine straw when she heard part of a conversation between Michael and James on the back porch.

"God is trying to do something here, son, if you'll let Him," James said.

Michael replied, "It doesn't make up for all the other things He did."

About that time they noticed her approach to the water hose, said hello, and went in the house. When the door shut, she felt so alone. And angry at herself. Why had she thought for a second that they would include her? Her interest in the history surrounding the project should have nothing to do with the present state of their family and certainly did not entitle her to some sort of backstage pass.

But she couldn't stop wishing she knew all that was going on, and why Michael displayed hostility toward God, even more than toward his great-grandmother and grandmother. What had God done? That didn't sound like the "friend that never leaves" Jesus the pastor described at Stella's church. She had her own issues with God, but she'd never figured she belonged to Him like Michael apparently had. Actually, she'd never felt *worthy* of belonging. She could see where a person who thought they were under His protection and yet were dealt a tragic hand by life could feel betrayed.

Unlike Jennifer, Stella possessed the gift of knowing when to leave someone alone and when to press someone. Michael she left alone and Jennifer she pressed. Jennifer couldn't figure out her instincts. It was like she knew Jennifer would crack under a little positive pressure, whereas Michael would have exploded. As they smoothed on the beautiful diamond-pattern wallpaper Amy had dropped off for the dining room, Stella asked how she was doing.

"I'm good, spending all my spare time in the evenings this week finishing up my report for the National Register, now that I have a full enough picture of the family history. I plan to put it in the mail by Friday."

"I have something that may help you. Mama went home and went through her things after our meeting on Saturday. She had some old photographs that I've made copies of for Michael, and also copies for you of the ones that pertain to your report."

"Oh, Stella, did you really?"

"They're in a folder in the laundry room. I'll get them out when we all take a snack break. Let's finish this wall first," Stella suggested, lifting a strip of the beautiful red paper and waiting for Jennifer to help her pass it through the water-filled paint tray on the floor to activate the adhesive.

Earl and James relied on Stella's snack breaks, but Jennifer struggled to contain her eagerness. She sighed and moved to the top of the ladder, clutching the edges of the heavy, damp wallpaper.

As Stella came alongside her to help her position and smooth the paper, she asked, "What I meant was, how are you doing *inside*? How did you take listening to the tape?"

"Well, I appreciated getting the whole story at last, but I'm concerned that it upset Michael." She told Stella about the comment she had overheard on the porch and her subsequent thoughts.

The older woman considered a minute, then replied, "I figured Michael's not had an easy life. Lots of people blame God for bad things that happened in their past. Basically what they're asking is why God didn't prevent all suffering and evil in the world. But all that entered in the garden, you know, when Adam and Eve ate of the one fruit from the Tree of the Knowledge of Good and Evil God warned them not to."

Jennifer recalled brightly colored drawings in Sunday school books of naked humans covered by leaves, a shiny red apple and a snake on a tree. "You mean it was a test?"

"I mean there had to be a choice, don't you see? Because if there wasn't, we'd all be robots. God could have us all be good and do what we should, but where would the fellowship be in that? Would you want to be friends with someone who had to be your friend?"

Jennifer shook her head. She'd long ago decided she'd rather be alone than continue to let people use her, then leave her, or to pretend to be simple-minded just to maintain what really amounted to a shallow friendship. When early signs indicated that kind of using or pretending, she kicked in Social Plan B: strategically timed withdrawal. One saved a lot of face by being the one to disappear first.

"God created us to live lives that would bring Him glory and point others to Him, but also for fellowship with Him, Jennifer. He wanted Adam and Eve to avoid the fruit, not because they'd be like Him if they ate it, or they'd miss out on something good, but because He knew that once they experienced evil, it would break that fellowship. Their rebellion also opened the door for sin, death and sickness to enter the world. And for people to continue to make the wrong choices, which causes others to suffer."

Finishing up the final strip of paper, Jennifer remained silent.

Using the stiff bristles of a large, dry brush to work winkles out of the paper, Stella said quietly, "I believe Michael is not the only one who's had a difficult past. I figured after the sermon at our church you might have been thinkin' some things over, too."

Her eyes flicked up to Stella's fast, guarded, afraid Someone saw through her.

"It's OK, honey." Climbing down, Stella gently squeezed the end of her shoulder. "I could tell you found all that talk of godly mothers hard to stomach when you didn't have one. And maybe fathers, too."

"My father left us when I was nine. According to Mom, he took up with a waitress in a truck stop in Alabama. And my step-father ..."

When Jennifer didn't continue, Stella observed simply, "You didn't want him to come up for graduation, either."

She just shook her head.

Stella nodded in understanding. "Sometimes our earthly parents can really mess up our view of who God is."

"Yeah, what is He supposed to be? I keep hearing all these terms. Father, mother, brother, friend?"

"All of those, and most importantly, Savior. Did you ever get to go to church growin' up, Jennifer?"

"Yes, I know some basics. I know they told us in Sunday school that Jesus was the Son of God who died on the cross to pay for our sins."

"Yes, and in that moment, He broke the power of not only sin, but death, and suffering, and our enemy, the highest angel who had rebelled against Him, Lucifer … Satan."

Jennifer gave her a skeptical look. "You really believe in all that stuff? Devils and demons?"

"The Bible tells us that we have an enemy who goes about like a roaring lion, seeking whom he may devour. He's allowed power for a limited time, until the One who created *him* returns. When we live our lives for ourselves, for fleeting pleasures of this earth, and put our selfish selves on the throne, he pretty much leaves us alone. But he will do all he can to keep us from comin' into a relationship with God, and once we do, well, the battle's on for sure." Stella laughed heartily.

Jennifer didn't find that funny. She perched on a nearby stool. "That doesn't sound like a good reason to become a Christian, then, or whatever." She made a face. All those religious terms tasted foreign on her tongue.

But Stella appeared to understand her, her expression remaining unaltered. "Oh, but it is, because it's either God or Satan. We think we're in charge, Miss Jennifer, but we're not. We all have a sinful nature inside that takes us down crooked paths that may look real enticin' up front but really lead us to great pain. Only when we become a part of the family of God does God come to live inside us, and His Holy Spirit gives us the power over the enemy and over sin."

Jennifer shook her head. "All this talk of things we can't even see is making me crazy."

Stella whisked the brush down a seam in the corner. "I know it seems strange up front, but I can tell you from experience in my own life that the spiritual world is as real as you and I, the floor we're standin' on, and these walls around us. As real as the air we breathe, even though we can't see it. I promise you that the only real answers I've had to the hard questions of life have come through God. I can lend you some books that might make more sense of things, if you want. And we'd love to have you come to church again. This Saturday we're havin' a special singin' and a speaker—he'll keep it short, I promise—then a BBQ afterwards. You can meet some more of the family. I plan to invite Michael and James again as well. I thought it might be a good ... ice-breaker."

"Umm ... well ..."

"And perfect timing since you'll have finished up your report," Stella teased, her eyes sparkling. Stella's warm and genuine manner made it almost impossible to tell her "no." In the past few months, she'd proved more friend, sister and mother than Jennifer had experienced in a lifetime. If God was part of what made her like that, wasn't He worth learning more about?

Jennifer's phone shrilled, causing both women to jump. "Oh, my goodness," she declared, pulling it out of her pocket. "It's Barb."

Over the ringing, she felt pretty sure she heard Stella whisper, "Speak of the devil," but when she asked "what?" Stella just grumbled, "Is it just me, or is she the only one who gets reception inside this house?"

"I'm sorry, I need to take it. Hello?"

Barbara's voice purred in her ear. "Well, there you are. I've been wondering if Hermon swallowed you up and was never going to spit you out."

"I'm here. We've just been busy."

"I guess you didn't get the text where I mentioned the music fest downtown Athens this weekend." She had, but the vague, passing reference to the event had confused her, so she hadn't answered yet. Barbara proceeded to enlighten her. "I thought you might want to come up and meet me for drinks and fill me in."

By drinks Barbara referred to one of the many bars downtown. While Jennifer had occasionally gone to one or two, she wasn't much of a drinker. Any feeling of loss of control made her uneasy. She'd always gone in company, usually for special events like concerts or poetry readings, just to maintain connection with her artsy friends.

The idea of sitting at a table alone with her former professor struck her as both socially uncomfortable and strangely intimate. "Oh, um, I don't know. Once you get used to being in the country, it seems so far to town." She tried to make a joke out of it, but Barbara was having none of it.

"OK, now, you can't lose touch with the real world. If you're going to be stubborn about it, I could ride out to get you, and you could show me what you've done. I really want to see once all the rooms are painted. What are you working on now?"

Jennifer glanced up at Stella, whom she'd expected to leave when she'd answered the phone, but the woman remained, meticulously dabbing that scratchy brush against now-invisible wrinkles. "Stella and I were just hanging the wallpaper in the dining room."

"I bet it looks fantastic. So what do you say?"

She didn't understand Barb. Something about her insistence on staying part of the Dunham project and her apparent attempt to move from professor to friend felt awkward, off. Stella's eyes met Jennifer's. For a moment suspended in time, something in Jennifer told her this choice affected more than one Saturday. "Thank you so much … Barb, but I just made plans with Stella."

In a blinding flash of approval, Jennifer learned Stella's teeth were perfectly white and straight.

"OK, that's fine. I get it if you have plans. But just a tip for the future, it's always good PR to stay in touch with the people who can help you network. You never know what keeping those channels open can do for you. In fact, I might just be working on something now."

Barb's voice had turned teasing, but a hard, sharp edge brushed Jennifer's consciousness. Blinking at what she sensed, she recoiled. But other feelings struggled to the fore. Faintly guilty and eager to smooth over any offense toward the professor who had done so much for her, Jennifer couldn't resist the necessity of placation—or the dangling carrot. "Like what?"

"Well, there may be a magazine interview in the works."

"A magazine? What magazine?"

"I shouldn't say until it's confirmed, but I might have news soon."

News that she might not get unless she kept Barb in the loop. "OK, I do have plans Saturday, but by next week we should have all the rooms painted and papered. Stella will have the stenciling done, but you'd have to wait to see the mural. She hasn't started it yet, or the faux wood graining. Why don't you come out next week and tell me about it then?"

"Deal."

Stella got up and walked out with the paint tray full of glue-gooped water.

A few minutes later, Barbara mollified, Jennifer went to check on Stella. She found her in the kitchen, laying an assortment of photographs out on the counter while Earl munched a cookie and James pulled soft drink cans from the refrigerator. Yoda curled in his box, but he gave a stiff-legged stretch upon her entrance. As Jennifer walked over and picked up a 1960s picture of a man just past middle age sporting an afro and thick plastic glasses, nothing in Stella's demeanor suggested offense. She was not going to mention Barbara.

"Is this Cecil?"

"Mmm-hmm, that's Uncle Cecil. This here's Grandma Hazel. And this ..." Stella lifted a sepia print of a young woman in a sailor-style dress, dark hair bound at the nape of her slender neck ... "is Georgia Pearl. The photograph was taken when she graduated from Jeruel."

Jennifer held the picture while the men crowded around her. "She's so beautiful," she gasped. "This means she would only have been ..."

"About sixteen, just before the incident in 1920."

"My, she do look like Dr. Hamp," Earl declared.

As Jennifer stared into the girl's eyes, Georgia Pearl's youth and innocence struck her. What happened with Glenn stole that and catapulted a sheltered girl into the real world of cruelty and prejudice. *Just like what happened to you at age eleven.* The thought flashed across her mind like lightning, an awful lot like the voice that had spoken in the shed, and again when she'd rescued Yoda. Along with it, a powerful sense of grief and empathy engulfed her, almost like she stood outside herself. Some things changed a person forever, and some things, once lost, could not be regained. Jennifer blinked away sudden tears, confused and irritated by her emotional response. Any harsh judgment she'd held against Georgia Pearl evaporated as the door opened and

Michael came in. He'd been shoveling clay, dirt and brick away from the back of the apothecary, piling it in the woods, and he was a filthy, sweaty mess.

"What are you all looking at?"

Jennifer held the picture out to him. "Your great-grandmother."

Michael paused. Something in her face made him stop and look twice at her. Was her stupid chin wobbling? Then he swiped a rivulet of moisture from his temple against the T-shirt of his shoulder and moved around the counter to grab a Coke.

As the tab popped open, James said, "Son, look at the picture."

Jennifer offered it again. This time he took it and laid it on the counter in front of him. He studied it a minute and said, "Yep. She's pretty."

"She's pretty, an' you know who else she look like?" Earl asked.

"Who?" Stella replied.

Earl looked at Michael. "You."

Michael made a disbelieving blowing sound.

"Yes, it's true, she does," James agreed, moving around behind Michael. "Look at those thick-lashed eyes, the eyebrows, and the nose."

Jennifer waited for his reaction, believing that he would be softened by actually seeing Georgia Pearl like she had. Nothing. Closed. She didn't get it. Michael held the picture out to Stella and said politely, "Thank you for bringing these."

"That's your copy, honey. And here, this one is for Jennifer." As Stella made her distribution, she added smoothly, "You know, Earl and I sure would like you men to join us Saturday at Harmony Grove. We're havin' a big BBQ. Jennifer's coming." She said this last brightly, as if that would settle it.

"Sure would," Earl echoed.

"How much per plate?" Michael wanted to know.

"Oh, no charge, it's a church event, not a fund-raiser."

"BBQ. That's all." Michael's dead pan tone revealed that he knew a catch existed.

Stella smiled, more of a smirk. "Well, the pastor of Joyful will offer a short welcome."

Michael laughed. "A welcome."

"Michael, really, I know it's empty in here, but you can drop the echo," James joked.

"Yes, you know for our kind of church, family members travel from miles around to attend, even those who've moved out to Atlanta or Winder or way out in the country. That's true even on Sundays, but especially for special events. This here's more like a big family reunion. I was thinkin' it would give you a chance to meet that branch of the family, all at one time. And besides, you'd get the rare privilege of hearin' Earl sing in the men's choir."

"A choir and a message, sounds like a regular church service to me," Michael said in what was supposed to be a teasing tone.

"I didn't say message, now."

"Sometimes that man do get wound up, though, hon," Earl tried to warn her, but Stella shushed him with a quick elbow to the ribs.

"Well, I think it sounds good," James spoke up. "We could stop in for a bit, don't you think, Michael?"

"Maybe so."

"What time?"

"We're havin' it in the evening, so it's a little cooler," Earl said. "Starts at six p.m. Oh, look who's up." He gestured to the floor under the window facing the porch accessed through the sunroom. In a shaft of golden sunshine, Yoda's head poked over the top of his box, wise eyes blinking owlishly. They all laughed.

"Speaking of family, I've never seen a cat be so responsive so young," Stella observed. She told Jennifer and Earl, "You know, when James or Michael tell him to stay in his box or scold him, he listens. It's like he knows they rescued him, took him in, and they're the only family he's got."

"Yeah, and he runs to get away," James chuckled. "You can come on out," he said to the waiting Yoda.

Moments later, the kitten clawed his way over the edge and clamored over to bat at Jennifer's shoe string.

"See?" Stella laughed.

Jennifer shifted her foot around to amuse him, then bent to scoop him up, holding him near her chest. As soon as she did, Yoda crawled up to her neck and placed his tiny, cold nose on her skin, giving her a lick. She supported the lightweight body with a hand and chuckled.

"Better heat the milk," James announced.

"I think he missed Jennifer," Michael said. "You know, ever since he stayed with her, he meows a lot when she's not around. I'd say she's the new favorite."

The idea of being anyone's or for that matter *anything's* favorite was, in truth, a first, and that, coupled with the gentle approval she saw in Michael's gaze, made her blush. "Aw, I miss him, too."

"Maybe we should take turns letting him stay over at the double-wide," James suggested as he placed the saucepan on a burner, making the clicking sound that immediately turned Yoda's funny little head.

"Now there's a good idea," Stella agreed. "Who says he can't be a member of more than one family?"

The woodsy tang of meat smoking in two big black portable cookers hung heavy on the humid, early evening air, wafting, threading among hearty voices raised in praise and rhythmic hands clapping. The men's choir swayed and shouted during their upbeat, minor-key intro to the evening's festivities. They stood on a platform facing rows of wooden picnic and white plastic tables with folding chairs, all of this set up on Harmony Grove's back lawn. Most of the people also stood, but when the guest preacher, Rev. Dwight Culbert, stepped onto the platform, everyone took seats, including the choir. Even the women preparing the serving tables laden with slaw, beans, bread and banana pudding ceased their buzzing around.

The perfect June day, not a cloud in the sky, made Jennifer feel at peace. She didn't know why she liked being here so much. The warm welcome from Stella's extended family diffused the foreignness of the environment and made her feel almost like she, and not Michael, was the long-lost relative. Speaking of Michael, she looked around for him once more. She'd ridden with the Jameses, but Michael and James had not made their appearance yet. *If* they would. Most likely Michael would invent some excuse to not be ready on time, or even to miss the whole thing.

Rev. Culbert praised the good-looking crowd and pointed out that many among those gathered were related. "This is like a family reunion, yes?" he called. People started clapping. "Well, there's another family reunion we're going to one day, isn't there?"

"Yes!" the crowd affirmed.

"It will be one day in heaven, won't it? Because there is a bond that ties us tighter than even our blood relations, and that is the bond of Jesus. Once we ask Him to become our Lord and Savior, we become children of God. Look at the person seated on both sides of you and tell them, 'You are my sister in Christ. You are my brother in Christ.'"

Rev. Culbert waited while everyone complied. Jennifer studied her sandals until the moment passed, painfully aware the description did not apply to her.

"The Good Book tells us we are no longer treated like slaves in the household, no, not like slaves! He adopts us into His family. We become co-heirs with Christ. My friends, we have a rich inheritance. Now let me tell you the truth. The Lord Jesus said, 'In this life you will have suffering.' Things may be dark now. You may hear a diagnosis from the doctor you never thought you'd hear. You may suffer pain, physical or emotional. And one day, yes, all you brothers and sisters will be visited by the dim specter of death. He doesn't promise to exempt you from those things. But He does promise to walk with you through them, to give the light to guide you and to comfort you. And I'll tell you what else the Good Book says He'll do, and that is to turn what is intended as evil against you for good!"

"That's right!"

Jennifer glanced at Stella, who smiled encouragingly, her dangling red earrings swinging beside the coil of hair at the back of her slim neck.

"Whatever you have suffered, my brothers and sisters, is not to be considered more than a fleeting moment in the eternal scheme of God. Your future is glorious! For 'no eye has seen, no ear has heard, and no mind has imagined what God has prepared for those who love Him!'"

"Yes, Amen!"

Rev. Culbert spread both hands to quiet the enthusiastic response of his audience. Then he said, "We are here today to celebrate family. Each of us is part of that great family of God. Each of us is welcome at the table. God has no step-children. If you have been away, my friend, all you need do is tell Him you want to draw near, and He promises to draw near to us. So let us all draw near in fellowship and thanksgiving. I'd like to lead us in a prayer, and then our choir will come again as the table is prepared."

Jennifer bowed her head like everyone else, but she didn't hear the prayer. It felt like a huge spotlight illuminated her, making everyone aware that she *wasn't* a part of this family Reverend Culbert described. But he had said God had no stepchildren. That statement reverberated in her mind. What would it be like to have a father who didn't leave her or abuse her? A father who treated her like James treated Michael? She had watched them for some time now, and she was pretty sure they were a part of this family of God, even though Michael seemed like he might be one of those who had "been away" like the reverend said. Her whole life she had longed for such a family. Her whole life she'd felt exactly like that stepchild scrambling for crumbs, while others pulled up to a feast that did not include her, the little trailer trash girl with stringy hair. And now this man not only described such a family but said all she had to do to become a part of it was to "draw near." How exactly did one do that? And how could she be sure this God really existed and was who Rev. Culbert and Stella said He was? These people seemed convinced. They radiated a peace and a joy—and there was also that innate confidence Stella possessed—that she envied.

In that unusual way she had, Stella seemed to read her mind. As the people started forming lines and the choir returned, belting out an old gospel song, she came alongside Jennifer and said, "Remind me when we drive home that I've got those books in the car for you."

"OK."

Stella squeezed her arm. "You can ask me anything you ever want to, Jennifer."

"I know. Thank you."

"Now will you help Mama get her plate? I've got to go serve slaw."

"Of course." Jennifer turned to smile at the bright-eyed little lady who reached for her elbow as they crossed the lawn.

Minutes later, they gathered at a table with heaping plates and sweet iced tea. Jennifer didn't have a minute to feel awkward. All Stella's relatives wanted to know how the restoration was coming along. She understood their interest now. They also asked about her schooling, her background, her plans for the future. She hardly had a chance to return the questions and learn about them, much less shoo the flies off her delicious, barely tasted BBQ.

"Well, look who's here," Stella suddenly declared, with pride and joy thickening her voice. She turned to her brother. "Jake, come help me introduce Michael and James to everyone."

Jennifer looked up to see the father and son described strolling toward them, trying not to look uncomfortable with their tardy approach to the gathering, yet a silence descended as questioning gazes turned toward the white men. Then Stella enfolded Michael in one of her warm embraces while Jake, mirrored sunglasses and blinding grin flashing, pumped James' hand.

Stella drew her guests over to the nearest table and announced in a loud voice, "Everybody, this here's my cousin Michael Johnson! Well, it's true, y'all. His great-grandmother was Georgia Pearl, my granny's little sister. Y'all know he's restoring the Dunham House."

Jennifer watched with joy for Michael as the African American branch of his family enfolded him. This was the step he'd needed to take, a bridging of the gap created by Georgia Pearl. And maybe it would help reconcile him to whatever losses were in his own past. But if she admitted it, a tinge of something else colored her current emotions: the sickly green of envy.

CHAPTER SIXTEEN

The next week Barbara Shelley came to view the restoration progress on Dunham House. Knowing that the professor's critical eye registered every detail made Jennifer all the more relieved when only praise came forth. The only thing Barbara said upon viewing the swirl of gold-laced clouds that Stella had begun on the rear wall of the parlor was, "If there's any way she can finish this by the weekend of July 4th, she should."

"Oh, I doubt it will happen that fast. Why?"

"Because it's a critical piece of art that needs to be featured in the *Old Houses* article."

"*Old Houses!*" Jennifer squeaked. "Is that who wants to do the interview?"

Barbara smiled at her with a sort of proud ownership.

Jennifer jumped up and down. "That's a national magazine!"

"And will be great press for a budding young restorationist. No telling what could come out of it. Certainly something very strong to add to your resume, at the least." Barbara pressed her fingers together, as if preparing for a Namaste. "And I will be here to act as your professional mentor."

"What do you mean?" The springs in Jennifer's heels sagged. "You have to go to Savannah this summer to help head the field study."

Barbara pursed her lips. "A professor with more seniority than myself took a special interest in the project, and I am no longer needed. They have plenty of staff signed up."

"Oh. I'm sorry."

"It's all right. I've helped conduct the last five. To be honest, I'm looking forward to a little down time this summer, out of that wilting coastal heat. I'll still be teaching a summer course, but I also have some reading and writing to do." She brightened. "And I'll be here when the journalist from the magazine comes into Athens. His name is Bryan Holton. I'd like for you to plan to come into town for dinner. And by 'town,' I don't mean Pig and Shrimp, or whatever they have out here. I mean a nice dinner at a place like The Last Resort, which we will treat him to prior to a tour of the property the following day. He can only come the Friday and Saturday of the 4th weekend, so I know you'll accommodate that."

"Of course." Jennifer didn't say that she had a conflict. She'd had an idea about Montana Worley's baking which she'd shared with the girl's grandmother the week before, that Montana should rent a booth at Lexington's 4th of July Fest and bake up a storm. They'd gotten all excited about it, and Jennifer had promised to help that Saturday. She could still do the morning shift, couldn't she? She bit her lip. It was not like Barb gave her much choice. This article was more important than a twelve-year-old's muffins and sweet rolls, after all. She'd have to deal with the conflict closer to time. Now she asked, "If Stella can't get the mural done, couldn't we take a photo and send it to them later in the month? I mean, most magazines have several months' lead time, right?"

"Right. But of course Bryan Holton would be more impressed by seeing the mural in person. This could also lead to opportunities for Stella."

Jennifer nodded. "I'll tell her. She can put all her energies into the painting."

As they moved to another room, Barb appeared to link the delay of her tour with Stella, for she asked with a taint of suspicion, "What was your conflict this weekend, anyway? I mean, it's not like there's much going on around here."

"Oh, the local African American Baptist Church hosted a BBQ."

Barb stopped dead in her tracks. "A BBQ. Seriously? You chose that over the Music Fest?"

Jennifer knew she looked sheepish. "Well, yeah. I've gotten to be really good friends with the Jameses, and their church is very welcoming."

"You've gone with them?"

"Just once before."

"And you went back?" The condescending tone of Barbara's laughter caused Jennifer's defenses to rise. "There's something to be said for appreciating local culture, Jennifer, but you really don't have to go *that* native."

Jennifer felt her face turn bright red. "Dr. Shelley, I hardly think that would be considered politically correct," she pointed out, half-teasing but also half-shocked.

"Oh, simmer down. I didn't mean anything about their ethnicity. There's nothing wrong with that. It's just that in some of these country places, the religious practices aren't far removed from the 19th century."

"So it's not their race you object to, but their faith."

Barbara turned to stare at her from the door of Michael's bathroom. "Since when are you a defender of it?"

Jennifer shrugged. "I don't know. I just see a lot of joy and peace in their services. We could all learn something."

"Well, learn something then. It's fine to discover the highlights of each religion and piece together your own truth, but not to get sucked into some make-believe world. Just don't go backwards with your move out here, Jennifer. If I'm right, that's exactly what you originally feared." She waited, then when Jennifer said nothing, prompted, "Am I right?"

"Something like that," Jennifer mumbled.

"Conservative Christians shoot themselves in the foot with their brand of exclusivity. That kind of thinking only pigeon-holes you." Barbara turned her back on Jennifer, and the discussion. "By the way, you did a nice job taking out that stupid post in here and refinishing the attic access."

"Michael did it."

Barb glanced over her shoulder, an eyebrow tilted. "He did? Well, kudos to him."

At the end of the walk-through, Jennifer accompanied Barbara to the front porch, where they viewed a tall, muscular figure smoothing the ground behind the apothecary with a shovel. Michael waved at them. They waved back, then Barbara hugged Jennifer.

"I miss you," she said. "Did you know you were the brightest student I believe I've ever had?"

Jennifer shook her head.

"So you'll be patient when I keep butting my head in? I just want to make sure you're on the right track. You're a reflection on me, too, you know."

Jennifer hadn't thought of it that way, but it made sense. She'd be more patient. This job wouldn't last forever, and when it was over, Barb's recommendation would go a long way toward opening even more important doors for her. Although … her attitude toward Stella and Earl still rankled. Jennifer got the feeling that had she visited the temple of some other religion, Barb's praise would have matched that she'd given the work on the house.

Thoughts of Rev. Culbert's welcome message echoing in her mind as they had since Saturday, Jennifer went to get a bottled water out of the fridge. She also grabbed a stack of Pringles. Michael had looked like he could use a break.

When she approached, his smile confirmed it. "You're a god-send," he said, wiping his forehead on his arm and pulling off his thick leather work gloves. "Your professor gone?"

"Yep." Jennifer moved over to sit on a nearby stump, while Michael perched on a cut log. A logging truck whooshed by while he guzzled most of the water.

Finally he commented, "She's not the hands-off type, is she?"

Jennifer laughed. "No, not really. She just explained that what I do is a reflection of her mentoring." She went on to provide evidence of that relationship by sharing about the magazine article.

"Well, nice of her to tell us."

"Aren't you pleased?"

"Sure, it's fine if they come, if it will be good for you. But she should have contacted me and Dad about it, too."

Jennifer picked at a hang nail. "I guess she trusted me to do that."

Michael frowned and munched a chip. "Sometimes you shove the chicks out of the nest and stay out of the way while they fly."

"Oh, don't be too hard on her. She doesn't have children of her own, and my mother wasn't worth much, so I guess it works out."

He slanted a blue eye at her. "She's hardly the motherly type."

"You know what I mean. Speaking of family, I'm glad you came to the BBQ Saturday. It went well for you, didn't it?"

Michael nodded but didn't meet her eyes now. "Yes. It was a good day."

"Did you feel that going and meeting all of them helped mend the gap from your great-grandmother? Set things right in a sense?"

"Yeah. Something like that, maybe." The guards went up as Michael's rare teasing spirit fled. His reserve made her mad. Suddenly it occurred to her that what you didn't like in others often proved true about yourself. Did she come across this vague and irritating to other people? She decided to take a chance and say what she really thought for once, because it wasn't fair for him to squander what he'd been given.

"You don't know how lucky you are. Seems to me God's given you all kinds of blessings. I can only wish I had a dad like yours. And your grandpa, Donald, he's great. He obviously loves you to death. Not to mention all those aunts and cousins in Atlanta you go visit. And now, you get to be related to Stella and Earl, two of the best people I've ever met in the world. I know you lost your mother, and I'm sure you've had other losses, but really, look at all you have left."

At her outburst, Michael turned to study her. After a minute, he said, "You know, you're right."

She sat upright on the stump, hopeful. "So that's it? You'll stop being mad at God?"

"Who says I'm mad at God?"

Jennifer looked away, not wanting him to read in her face that she'd overheard that conversation with James on the porch. "You don't have to say," she muttered. "It just shows."

Following an uncomfortable silence, Michael swigged from his water bottle. "So you've heard of Job in the Bible, right?"

She nodded. "I've heard something about the patience of Job." She didn't want him to know she had no recollection at all of what had happened to the man, whether he be real or a fable.

He glanced at her. "Job was the most upright man of his time. According to the Bible, Satan came before God and said, 'He's only good and obedient because You bless and protect him. Drop the hedge around him, let me at him, and then we'll see if he doesn't curse You.'"

"So God said 'yes?'"

"Right. Within a very short amount of time, Job lost all his children, all his livestock, his health, everything but some supposed friends he would have been better off without and a nagging wife. Also better off without."

"I can't remember. Did he curse God?"

"He didn't. He actually said, 'the Lord gave, and the Lord has taken away; blessed be the name of the Lord.' What I've gone through has been more than you know, because like you, I don't like to talk about my stuff." He shot her a glance that dared her to dispute the statement. "Maybe it's not been as much as Job, which makes me ... even less righteous, because trust me, I'm not as good as he was. I'm not to the point where I can say what he did."

"How did your mother die, Michael?" She asked it barely above a whisper, hoping the words would be quiet enough to sneak past his defenses.

"Leiomyosarcoma."

"What?"

"A very rare and aggressive form of cancer."

She blinked, her mouth going dry as she imagined a boy having to watch a horrible disease erode the life from his mother. "How old were you?"

"I was seventeen. My whole senior year she battled it. She scheduled my campus visits on days when she would be strong enough to go. She filled out forms and applications with me. And she was there, cheering at all my high school swim meets, even though she sometimes had to wait for hours between my events. The day before high school state, she went in the hospital. She didn't get to see those four gold medals I earned, two individuals and two relays, but I earned them for her, because she told me to go do it even though she couldn't be there." Michael's voice got thick, and he swallowed, looking at the ground. "She died three weeks later, just before I turned eighteen."

Man, was she fighting that stupid urge to touch him again! Determined to resist, Jennifer mashed her arms down close to her sides. "That was a hard time to lose a parent. But it sounds like she was great, too."

"Yeah. She was."

Jennifer sighed. "Don't take this wrong, I would never wish a mother's death on anyone, but I'd rather have had a good mother who died early than a bad mother who ..." She let her words trail into the cricket-chirping heaviness of settling evening. Michael looked at her and nodded. Then she resumed, "That guest preacher at Harmony Grove on Saturday, he talked all about the family of God. And it made me feel sort of like I do about your family. Like I wish I was a part."

Michael pulled his shoulders back and focused on her. "You can be."

"But if God is cruel like you say, do I want to be? I've been reading these books Stella lent to me, and they say what Stella did, that God allows those bad things because people needed to have a choice. We had to be able to choose good or evil, or choosing God would be meaningless. I think sickness is like evil. It entered the world with sin. Right?"

He smiled like a parent giving approval to a small child. "Right. That's what the doctrine is. I just haven't been able to apply it where it counts quite yet."

"I'll probably have some trouble with that, too, but if God is all He says He is, it might be nice to have a good parent for a change."

"Look, Jennifer, if you're considering giving your life to God, I'm really not the person you should be talking to. Stella seems to have all the answers."

She said in a small voice, "Maybe I feel better talking to someone who doesn't have them all."

At that moment, Michael did something that shocked her. Rattled her so bad she stopped breathing. He reached out and took her hand. And the resulting feeling stole her breath even more, because instead of the usual self-protecting ramparts erecting, she felt safe, so safe that Jennifer breathed with new assurance, "You do know Him, don't you?"

"Yes. I do." Somehow the admission sounded sad, like it came from a past acquaintance instead of a vital current relationship. But that wasn't enough to discourage her. Michael would be with God like he had been with her, angry, defensive, guarded ... but he always came back around and did the right thing. She could trust him.

"What do I do?"

He blinked as if taken aback. Then he offered, "You can pray after me if you want."

Jennifer had never prayed aloud before. In fact, she hadn't really prayed at all since those elementary school days of Sunday school. Now she echoed the half-stranger to her right, telling God aloud that she wanted Him, not herself, in charge of her life, because He had her best in mind and had taken care of her sins when He gave His life for her on the cross. She only half-believed it, but she did want it, and when Michael prayed about becoming part of God's family, she was very clear on that. She didn't really expect anything to happen, but as she spoke of Jesus coming into her life, a warmth, peace and love like she had only dreamed of flooded the parched recesses of her heart.

"It's true!" she exclaimed when Michael finished. "It's really true! He does want me!"

"Of course He does. He created you." Michael released her hand, and Jennifer was further amazed to see tears standing in his eyes. "More than your parents, Jennifer, HE created you."

The idea of being designed, formed for a purpose, filled every crack in her spirit with meaning, pushing out the cold notion that she was a random act of nature, her race an accident of atoms. Without thinking, she did something totally out of character, wrapping her arms around Michael in a hug of thanks.

Michael's words stirred the hair at her ear, breath and life. "What you feel is the Holy Spirit, God's presence inside you."

She also felt something else: gratitude and a bond or kinship with the man sitting next to her that had not been there before. He seemed to sense it, too, for he looked away and stood up. But for the first time, his rejection didn't feel personal. It had to do not with her but with the secret heaviness he carried inside his heart. Jennifer caught at his hand because she knew something for certain, something she now had to say. "Michael. God does not want you to be sad."

A look of surprise passed over his features. Then he said quietly, "I know."

"If He can help me, He can help you."

Michael started to reply when a familiar voice called, "Yoo-hoo!"

Quickly untwining Michael's fingers, Jennifer saw Mary Ellen bustling over from the antique store, bearing two Cokes. Oh, no. By tomorrow morning all of Hermon and half of Oglethorpe County would suspect a little spring romance might be budding between Michael Johnson and Jennifer Rushmore.

"You two look like you need a Coke for that work break!" Mary Ellen cried, winking at Jennifer as she forced a frosty bottle into each of their politely outstretched hands. "You were talking so long I decided to come see what I was missing."

How long had she been spying? Had she seen the hug? Jennifer tried not to sound sheepish as she said, "Hi, Mary Ellen."

The three of them stood there looking at each other, the friendly newcomer smiling expectantly. When it became clear the conversation was not going to resume with her included, she burst out, "Jennifer, I've got the best little Meeks occasional table in from Madison, almost as good as a Belter at half the price! You've got to come over and see."

"Oh, OK, let's go then," Jennifer said.

She walked self-consciously, feeling Michael's eyes on her back, and she stayed in the store chit-chatting longer than necessary after approving of the table and the price to prolong her return stroll past him. Maybe if she lingered he'd finish his task and go in the house. But no, when Jennifer exited the antique store and snuck around the corner of the apothecary, he remained in view, although he was indeed gathering up his stuff. He hadn't seen her. Self-conscious of her earlier behavior, Jennifer tried to snatch back around the edge of the building.

"Jennifer!"

She sidled back into view, studiedly casual. "Um, yes?"

"I was thinking about what you said."

"What part?"

"You said you wanted to be a part of my family."

Had she really said that? Yes, she had. *Oh, freshly smoothed dirt, please open and swallow me.* "I meant in theory, of course. To be a part of a family *like* yours. I didn't mean to weird you out or anything."

Michael fell into step beside her. "You didn't. It made me realize something."

She let out a relieved breath. "What was that?"

"That maybe I've been so focused on what was lost, the torn places, the holes, that I could no longer see the picture remaining, the family tree that *is* there. I do have a lot to be thankful for. And this place, it's really starting to come together," Michael said as they walked toward the house side by side. The new red roof glowed in the soft evening light, the boards of the house glowing white, all framed in the fresh green of early summer.

"Yes," she agreed. "It is."

That night, Jennifer had the dream again. Only this time when the roof and walls were stripped away, the hurricane quieted. The sun emerged and bathed her in such a golden warmth she knew a presence hovered in the room with her even as she slept, a new, powerfully good and loving presence. She realized The Voice she'd heard unexpectedly three times now had belonged to The Presence. *OK, God*, she thought, *so you've got a lot of work to do. But now I'm eager to see what comes next.*

The Master Renovator held her safe in His hands.

DISCUSSION QUESTIONS

Chapters One and Two

1. What do you think Jennifer's dream means?
2. After a little research, discuss Georgia Pearl's relationship with her father and how he is setting her up to be "this century's Amanda America Dickson."
3. What attracts Jennifer to Hermon—and Michael—and what repels her? Why? How is James helpful in that initial meeting?
4. List the challenges within herself and from her past you pick up on Jennifer struggling to overcome.

Chapter Three

5. Why does Jennifer initially not want her professor to accompany her to Hermon?
6. What attraction does the abandoned plantation site pose for Jennifer?
7. As a parallel to the decay at the cabin, in what ways can too much weathering lead to rot in humans? Do you think some people are "past saving" if the deterioration has progressed too far? Paul, an apostle of Jesus who once persecuted the church in its earliest days, wrote in I Timothy 1:15, "Jesus came into the world to save sinners, of whom I am chief."
8. Which project and its history intrigues you most, and why, the house, the apothecary, or the log cabin?
9. Why does Jennifer decide Horace and Amy might be worth knowing? Why might her project-centered outlook need to evolve into a people-centered outlook?
10. What do you think the main reason for Horace's interest in the property is?

Chapters Four, Five, Six and Historical Section

11. What draws Jennifer to Stella and Earl?
12. How does the state of the storage shed reflect the state of Jennifer's heart? Has God ever spoken to you as He did to Jennifer?

13. Where did Jennifer's motivation come from to restore old houses? What deeper need inside her does her interest reflect? Discuss ways people turn to hobbies, jobs or other people to fill emptiness, and why they do this instead of believing God can fill their deepest needs.

14. Why does Michael want to get rid of the mantels in the front two rooms, and why does Jennifer insist he keep them? Discuss how what she says about the mantels could be applied to life in general. Can you predict how the mantels will serve as a type for something to come in Michael's life?

15. What things about Stella and her home surprise Jennifer, and what lesson does she take from that?

16. Why does Stella put off sharing details about Michael's family with Jennifer?

17. The 1918 voice of a teenage Georgia Pearl tells us she lived in a surprisingly volatile world. What things in this excerpt from history surprised you? How does change breed fear?

Chapters Seven, Eight and Nine

18. What do you think Barb and Michael think of each other? What about Stella and Barb? Why?

19. Why does Jennifer say she dreads her mother's visit for graduation?

20. How is Barbara both helpful and harmful to Jennifer on her visit to Hermon? What do you think of her advice to Jennifer to avoid romantic entanglements with Michael? How about to seek counseling and look inward for healing?

21. Why do you think Jennifer experiences shame as she receives her diploma? Has something from your own past caused you to fight similar feelings? What did you do to overcome that? The Bible speaks of the "godly sorrow" that brings us to repentance (2 Corinthians 7:10). This applies to sinful choices we have made, not bad things done to us we could not help. For those things, God promises to help us forgive others and to settle accounts with unrepentant perpetrators Himself (Romans 12:17-21). Once we settle things with God, He makes it clear that there is "no condemnation to those who are in Christ Jesus" (Romans 8:1) and that He is a shield about us and the one who lifts our heads (Psalm 3:3).

22. What are your thoughts about the way Barbara relates to the group at graduation?
23. What things about Jennifer does Kelly's rambling memories over dinner reveal?
24. Why do you think coming over to welcome Jennifer to her new home is difficult for Michael, yet he does so anyway?
25. What happens to cause Jennifer to withdraw again from Michael? Then what does she see that causes her to give him another chance?

Chapters Ten, Eleven, Twelve and Historical Section
26. There have now been two strange incidents on the Dunham property. Do you think they are coincidence, or is Jennifer too careless in brushing them off?
27. How can going past our normal boundaries like Jennifer does in attending church with Stella and Earl make us more open to an honest view inside ourselves? How can that provide an opportunity for God to work?
28. What makes Jennifer most uncomfortable at Harmony Grove?
29. What overall effect do you think the trip to Milledgeville has on Michael's and Jennifer's relationship?
30. How do the c. 1920 newspaper accounts Jennifer reads prove more helpful in some ways than the wills and history books?

Chapters Fourteen and Fifteen
31. What do you think of Georgia Pearl's choice to disconnect with her family in the 1920s in order to pass as white? Is there ever an instance when leaving behind one's heritage is the best choice?
32. Why is Michael's reaction to God creating confusion for Jennifer? Why is she not as upset at God about her own past?
33. How does Stella explain the way evil entered the world and why it is allowed to remain?
34. How has Jennifer learned to deal with false friends and potential hurt? Is her plan a healthy one?
35. Why does Stella say there is no middle road between God and Satan, good and evil? See Matthew 6:24.

36. What softens Jennifer toward Georgia Pearl? Why do you think Michael does not respond similarly?

37. Discuss how Yoda provides a spiritual type and how Stella's observation about belonging to more than one family applies to the broader story.

Chapter Sixteen

38. Why do you think prejudice towards faith would be acceptable in Barbara's world, whereas other types of prejudice would not?

39. According to Barbara's explanation, why does she keep inviting her out and "butting her head" into Jennifer's job? Why do you think she offers this explanation?

40. What two "words of wisdom" does Jennifer bring Michael in the final scene, and how do they help him open up to her and God?

41. Why does Jennifer say she wanted to talk to Michael instead of Stella about coming to God? What can this tell us about sharing our own faith?

42. Looking back on the story, Jennifer's dream before coming to Dunham House made her sense danger. Was it possible something did not want her to take the job, because God intended to use it for good? Do you think the threat she perceives is physical, spiritual, or both?

AFTERWORD

While the restoration process and buildings in The Restoration Trilogy are based on an actual project, and the Dunham doctors are based on an actual line of historic doctors, names and facts have been changed to suit the story line of *White, Widow* and *Witch*. You'll find the series cradled by the real county of Oglethorpe in Piedmont Georgia, with larger towns and topographical details unaltered ... but rest assured, no real characters from the series exist. That said, I wrote The Restoration Trilogy with the same goal in mind as The Georgia Gold Series: to weave an entertaining, fictional story among the sturdy framework of history, with its true-to-life people, places and events. I hope you enjoy it! And remember, real history is often the most shocking part of any story!

I would like to thank several local experts consulted by interview for The Restoration Trilogy, including: Jim Carter, 1800s architecture and interiors; Debbie Cosgrove, herbs and herbal medicine; Dr. Allen Vegotsky, historic medicine; and Bill Summerour, log cabins. Also, my thanks to the helpful staff of the Oglethorpe County Library. For readers interested in further study on the topics touched on in The Restoration Trilogy, I include a list of sources consulted. These are offered not in MLA format, but merely in the order I consulted them, through the completion of writing *White*. Many historical threads overlap and interweave in all three books of the series, but in bold are the sources most pertinent to *White*.

Sources:

The Travels of William Bartram: Naturalist Edition, University of Georgia Press, Athens, GA, 1998

Bartram: Travels and Other Writings, Literary Classics of the United States, Inc., New York, NY, 1996

The History of Oglethorpe County, Georgia, Florrie C. Smith, Wilkes Publishing Company, Inc., Washington, GA, 1970

Woman of Color, Daughter of Privilege: Amanda America Dickson 1849-1893, Kent Anderson Leslie, University of Georgia Press, Athens, GA, 1995

The Story of Oglethorpe County, Lena Smith Wise, 2ⁿᵈ Ed. by Historic Oglethorpe County, Inc., Lexington, GA, 1998

Scull Shoals: The Mill Village That Vanished in Old Georgia, Robert Skarda, Fevertree Press, Athens, GA, 2007

White Flood Red Retreat, Robert Skarda, Old Oconee Books, GA, 2012

Antebellum Athens and Clarke County, Georgia, Ernest Hynds, University of Georgia Press, Athens, GA, 1974/2009

College Life in the Old South, E. Merton Coulter, University of Georgia Press, Athens, GA, 1983

Confederate Athens, Kenneth Coleman, University of Georgia Press, Athens, GA, 1967/2009

Cotton Production and the Boll Weevil in Georgia: History, Cost of Control, and Benefits of Eradication, P.B. Haney, W.J. Lewis, and W.R. Lambert, The Georgia Agricultural Experiment Stations College of Agricultural and Environmental Sciences, The University of Georgia, Research Bulletin Number 428, March 2012

New Georgia Encyclopedia: History & Archaeology: Progressive Era to WWII, 1900-1945, online: World War I in Georgia / Athens / Oglethorpe County / Ku Klux Klan in the Twentieth Century ... and many other online resources

An Hour Before Daylight: Memories of a Rural Boyhood, Jimmy Carter, Simon & Schuster, New York, NY, 2001

Behind the Mask of Chivalry: The Making of the Second Ku Klux Klan, Nancy MacLean, Oxford University Press, New York, NY, 1994

Dr. Durham's Receipts: A 19ᵗʰ Century Physician's Use of Medicinal Herbs, Debbie Cosgrove and Ellen Whitaker, 2008

City of Maxeys Historic Interest Group Interview Report, Bereniece Jackson Wilson & Regina Jackson Wilker by Dennis and Faye Short, April 13, 2014

The Negroes of Athens, Georgia, Thomas Jackson Woofter, Phelps-Stokes Fellowship Studies, No. 1, Bulletin of the University of Georgia, Volume XIV Number 4, December, 1913

Send Us a Lady Physician: Women Doctors in America: 1835-1920, "Co-Laborers in the Work of the Lord: Nineteenth-Century Black Women Physicians," Darlene Clark Hine, W. M. Norton & Company, New York, NY, 1985

A Pioneer Church in the Oconee Territory: A Historical Synopsis of Antioch Christian Church, Billy Boyd Lavender, 2005

A Scythe of Fire: A Civil War Story of the Eighth Georgia Infantry Regiment, Warren Wilkinson and Steven Woodworth, HarperCollins, New York, NY, 2002

Resources of the Southern Fields and Forests, Medical, Economical, and Agricultural, Francis Peyre Porcher, Charleston, SC, 1863

ABOUT THE AUTHOR

DENISE WEIMER

Native Georgia author Denise Weimer holds a journalism degree with a minor in history from Asbury University. Her writing background prior to The Restoration Trilogy includes numerous regional magazine and newspaper articles, romantic novella *Redeeming Grace*, and the Georgia Gold Series (*Sautee Shadows, The Gray Divide, The Crimson Bloom* and *Bright as Gold*, Canterbury House Publishing), sweeping historical romance with a touch of mystery. *Bright as Gold* won the 2015 John Esten Cooke Fiction Award for outstanding Southern literature. Denise is a wife and the swim mom of two teenage daughters.

THE RESTORATION TRILOGY: BOOK TWO

Widow

Jennifer Rushmore has overseen the restoration of brooding bachelor Michael's ancestors' doctor's house long enough to work through their initial differences. They've begun applying the lessons of family and community learned from the past. Now the apothecary shop discloses a heart-breaking tale circa 1870 Georgia, shaking loose Jennifer's own carefully suppressed past. She fears that when Michael sees beyond her façade, her tentative steps toward trust and love may disintegrate into rubble. On her journey to forgiveness, Jennifer draws on her new faith and friendships, even as the mysterious accidents clouding her first preservation job escalate into imminent danger.